DEATH
IN THE
MAYFAIR HOTEL

BOOKS BY FLISS CHESTER

DEATH
IN THE
MAYFAIR HOTEL

FLISS CHESTER

bookouture

Published by Bookouture in 2024

An imprint of Storyfire Ltd.
Carmelite House
50 Victoria Embankment
London EC4Y 0DZ

www.bookouture.com

Storyfire Ltd's authorised representative in the EEA is Hachette Ireland
8 Castlecourt Centre
Castleknock Road
Castleknock
Dublin 15 D15 YF6A
Ireland

ISBN: 978-1-83525-255-0
eBook ISBN: 978-1-83525-254-3

'My candle burns at both ends;
It will not last the night;
But ah, my foes, and oh, my friends—
It gives a lovely light!'

'FIRST FIG' – EDNA ST VINCENT MILLAY, 1920

1

Sparkling sequins flashed and feathers floated to the ground as the dancers twirled and quickstepped across the ballroom of the Mayfair Hotel. It was Christmas Eve 1925, and the Honourable Cressida Fawcett, herself in an emerald-green silk evening dress, was doing the Charleston along with several of her London pals. Her matching green headband kept her shingled blonde bob from getting in her eyes, and her emerald and diamond earrings caught the light from the many glittering chandeliers that lit the dance floor with a blaze of crystal.

She laughed as she noticed her dear pug, Ruby, amble between the tables, the floor-length white tablecloths hiding her hunt for various titbits dropped from the forks and plates of high-society ladies and gentlemen as they tucked into the platters of cold meats, cheeses, jellies, marzipan fruits, mince pies and rich, white-iced fruit cake.

The Mayfair Hotel was famous for its Christmas Eve ball. For those in society still in London over the festive period, it was *the* place to be seen – and have the most fun. The band was always the most fashionable one of the moment, the dance floor heaved with the brightest of young things society had to offer and the champagne flowed until carriages were called at the strike of midnight.

Garlands of greenery and bunches of mistletoe adorned the elegant interior of the hotel, while silver candelabra laden with snow-white candles stood lit on every mantelpiece and sideboard. And the Mayfair Hotel's enormous Christmas tree was the talk of the town, with Christmas shoppers and London day trippers visiting the lobby of the grand hotel to see what the hotel decorators had come up with this year. With heavy snow forecast, it was no surprise that the hotel had stuck to a wintry theme, with icicles and silvered baubles exquisitely decorating the twenty-foot-high spruce.

Christmas Eve in the Fawcett household was usually a much less glamorous affair, though civilised enough, with the family enjoying small glasses of sherry with the vicar, Cressida's father retreating to his study to read (or attempt to wrap presents using newspaper and garden twine) and her mother filling her in on all the gossip from the small village of Mydenhurst. Although this was a perfectly pleasant way to spend the holiday, Cressida was delighted that this year she'd had an excuse to stay in London until Christmas Day itself.

And that 'excuse' was dancing alongside her, her chestnut-coloured bobbed hair swinging along to the band as she twirled and swing-kicked along with her partner. Lady Dorothy Chatterton, or Dotty as she was known, was glowing with happiness now that her beau, George Parish, was back from his archaeological dig in Egypt. His long-awaited return had finally come as he'd disembarked off the boat at Southampton docks just the night before, and the besotted pair had been reunited here at the Mayfair Hotel just as the Christmas Eve ball had begun at six o'clock.

George had arrived in the lobby – his suitcases still carrying traces of Egyptian sand upon them – laden with presents and souvenirs, so much so that Dotty had had to wait impatiently as he unloaded them all to a waiting porter before she could fling her arms around his neck. That George's boat – and this infamous annual ball – had landed on the same day had given Cressida and Dotty the ideal excuse to stay in town, and once they'd ascertained that a few others of their circle were in London on Christmas Eve too – mostly due to the inclement weather – tickets for the ball were purchased from the hotel and plans made to all drive home to respective country piles on Christmas morning.

Cressida was delighted that Dotty and George looked so happy. Ever since they'd met in Cornwall in the summer, the pair had been inseparable – or at least as inseparable as people living thousands of miles away from each other could be. Their letters had been frequent and impassioned, and Cressida hoped that tonight might be the moment that George finally proposed to her dear friend.

It hadn't escaped Cressida, throughout her ruminations on the subject, that she was enjoying this romance of Dotty's almost as much as Dotty was. And it worried her. Cressida prided herself on being as level-headed as a schoolmaster on speech day when it came to matters of the heart – but was she secretly a romantic soul too, after all?

If further proof were needed, Cressida only had to think back to when she had squeezed her friend's arm earlier in the evening as they'd paused in their merriment and taken glasses of champagne from a passing waiter. When she'd said, 'Oh Dot, do you think he'll kiss you under the mistletoe? Or wrap you up in furs and silks and propose to you in the fountain courtyard?' she'd realised she'd rather like that sort of thing for herself, too.

'Cressy,' Dotty had all but squealed back. 'Perhaps! He's given me this beautiful shawl, knitted from the softest camel down. It's simply the most beautiful thing I've ever seen.'

Cressida had grinned at her friend, despite disagreeing

wholeheartedly with her on the beauty of the plain dun-coloured camel-hair shawl (a shade, she decided that was more akin to setting plaster than fashionable evening wear), and they'd carried on dancing, meeting up with George, and Dotty's brother, Alfred, Lord Delafield, in the midst of the dance floor.

If Cressida was searching for the reason she might have developed a romantic soul after all, she need look no further than Dotty's older brother. As the eldest son he took on one of his father, the earl's, subsidiary titles, hence Lord Delafield. But he was just plain Alfred to Cressida – though, recently, she had been finding absolutely nothing about his handsome face, sportsman's physique and affable personality 'plain'.

She looked on as he spun their friend Victoria Beaumont around, her long blonde hair whipping him in the face each time, which only made her laugh more and spin again and again, like a whirling dervish with a glass of champagne in hand. Victoria was a married woman, but even so, Cressida was relieved when she moved on to dancing with a handsome tall man with slicked-back blonde hair. Victoria didn't seem to find this blonde chap half so diverting as she had Alfred, but Cressida didn't care – Alfred had given her a look with eyes that had positively twinkled with mischief. And that twinkle had had a direct correlation to the strength of Cressida's knees and her inability to Charleston properly for the next few songs.

Luckily for Cressida and her trembling limbs, the band, having played a few more hits, now came to a harmonious if boisterous stop at the end of a tune and the friends slumped and laughed, smacking their hands on their thighs and looking about for willing waiters in order to gulp down more champagne.

Cressida was tempted to take her shoes off to ease the pain across her toes, as one or two others of her friends had done, but she was far too pleased with her new patent leather, emerald-green Mary Janes, to risk tossing them to the side of the room.

Alfred was just gesturing to a wine waiter when Cressida

noticed George whisper something in Dotty's ear and guide her out of the ballroom. Dotty left willingly with him, their arms intertwined, and Cressida, excited at the prospect of what might happen, kept an eye on which direction they headed. She clicked her fingers for Ruby and the small dog left her sanctuary underneath a gilt-coloured dining chair and trotted over to her, dodging duchesses' handbags as she went. At the same moment Alfred returned bearing a bottle of champagne and four glasses.

An eyebrow raise and a nod of the head was all it took for Alfred to follow Cressida as she scooped up Ruby and weaved her way out of the ballroom. A gust of fresh, cold air hit her and goose-pimpled her bare arms as she approached the large, glazed doors that led from the hotel's ballroom to its stone terrace. They stood ajar, and as she let Ruby down from her arms, she accepted her silk shawl from Alfred.

A moment later, he had poured them both a glass a champagne.

'Fancied some air, old thing?' he asked just as Cressida raised her finger to her lips.

'I'm following Dot,' she whispered, then pointed to where two figures were standing next to the monumental, carved-stone fountain in the central courtyard.

Snowflakes fell around them, with the larger ones quickly settling on the frozen ground, while the more delicate ones danced around the lovers' heads and skittered over the stone cherubs and prancing horses of the impressively large fountain.

Cressida's heart was bursting with excitement. She didn't want Dot to spot her though, so she nudged Alfred and they both hid behind a large urn on the balustrade of the terrace. This was Dot's special moment, and she didn't want to be a distraction.

Ruby, on the other hand, had other ideas, and before Cressida could stop her, she was slipping and sliding down the wide stone steps that led from the terrace to the fountain courtyard.

'Rubes!' Cressida hissed, and pointed to her dog as Alfred stifled a laugh. She chuckled, and wondered if the pounding she could feel was only her heart, doing its own quickstep in Dotty's honour, or if she could sense Alfred's hammering away too. They both stood, barely able to take sips from their glasses of ice-cold champagne as they watched the handsome George Parish get down on one knee.

Cressida gripped her glass and found herself holding tightly onto Alfred's arm with her other hand. Was this really to be the moment when Dotty would finally say 'Yes!' to the man of her dreams? She could feel the warmth of Alfred's body close to hers, and while the music played and the sound of voices and trumpets wafted through the open glass doors, she waited with bated breath.

But it wasn't a 'yes' that emanated from Dotty.

It was a scream of such magnitude that even Ruby, who had been sniffing around the rear of the stone fountain, skedaddled out and slipped on an ice patch, skidding along until she bounced off a statuette of Venus next to the flower bed.

'Dotty!' Cressida exclaimed, and looked to Alfred, who had a similar expression of horror and confusion on his face.

Then Dotty screamed again, and Cressida saw her bury her head in George's shoulder. She had raised an arm and was pointing towards the ornate stonework of the fountain.

Cressida, with Alfred at her elbow, carefully made her way down the icy steps, then came to an abrupt halt as the same ghoulish sight confronted them.

There, face-up under the water, was a young woman, her blue silk dress cascading over the rim of the ice-cold stone bowl, its chilly waters churning despite the freezing temperature. Her hair was loose from its pearl-encrusted headband and was floating in tendrils. As Cressida got closer, still grasping Alfred for support, she could plainly see that the young woman in the fountain was dead.

And even more horrifying than that, Cressida recognised her straight away. She had been on the dance floor with them only minutes before.

It was their friend, the vivacious and fun-loving Victoria Beaumont.

2

Great, fat flakes of snow continued to fall in the courtyard. They drifted around in gusts of air and skittered on the iced flagstones. They swirled around and settled on the friends' heads, shoulders and arms as they themselves stood like the stone statues of Venus and Apollo in the courtyard garden; absolutely still and cold as marble. It was only Ruby, slipping on another icy patch on the flagstones, who seemed to have any life to her at all. A heavy, pug-shaped nudge against Cressida's leg roused her, and she turned to Alfred.

'Oh crêpes. Excuse my French, but get help. Quickly, Alfred.'

'I don't think there's much we can do for her...' Alfred started, but then nodded, turned on his heel and made his way as quickly as possible up the slippery steps to the terrace, and from there, the ballroom.

Cressida took a step towards the body. Alfred was right. There was nothing that could be done to save Victoria. Her lips were already a pale greyish hue that matched the ice-blue of her evening dress and the sheen of the pearls strung around her neck choker and on her headband.

'It's not... Victoria, is it?' Dotty's voice wavered as she asked. George's hand was gripping her shoulder tightly and Cressida noticed how deathly grey he looked, despite the unseasonal tan he had picked up from spending months at his archaeological dig. George, it seemed, was only used to seeing ancient corpses, mummified for centuries. Not one as recently departed as this.

But Dotty's hesitation had made Cressida doubt herself too, and she leaned over the fountain to double-check. Long strands of blonde hair floated on the water, surrounding the pretty face like a liquid halo of gold. A halo tarnished with the iron-red of blood near Victoria's left temple.

Of course she'd recognised the face, despite the colour of the lips and eerie blanching of the submerged skin. How could she not when she'd known her for so many years and had been dancing with her only moments ago?

Cressida stumbled back; she couldn't bear to look at the deathly pale version of her friend again.

As she recoiled, Dotty left the safety of George's arms and wrapped a comforting one of her own around her friend. 'Oh Cressy, is it her? Is it really? I couldn't bring myself to look properly, but the hair...'

'Yes... it's her. It's Victoria.' Cressida shuddered again and let Dotty wrap her up in a hug.

When she reluctantly pulled away, Dotty looked at her, her face full of concern. 'You look unwell, Cressy. Are you all right?'

'Not really, but I will be.' Cressida regretted the champagne and cocktails she'd been rather overindulging in and felt them turn sour in her stomach. 'Poor Victoria,' she whispered, remembering that, however she felt, it wasn't as bad as what had happened to their friend.

'I still think of her as one of us debutantes, but she's been the Countess of Worcester now for a few years. I'd so enjoyed seeing her again tonight,' Dotty all but whispered.

'She was always such fun.' Cressida looked back towards the dead body. She dared herself to take in more of the scene, knowing that now, before help arrived, or indeed before any other Christmas revellers out on the terrace noticed, was the only time she'd have to observe any clues.

As usual, Dotty seemed to read her mind. 'You're trying to see if anything's suspicious, aren't you, Cressy?' Dotty pulled away and accepted her new shawl again from George.

'Suspicious?' he asked, finally finding his voice. 'A terrible accident, don't you think?'

'Tipsy and tipped right over? Well, maybe. She did look quite unsteady on the dance floor.' Dotty shook her head, then paused. 'But perhaps it wasn't an accident, and if that's the case, maybe there is a clue here. Cressy has an amazing eye for details, you see. She can often spot the things the rest of us miss. It's what makes her so jolly good at decorating and finding colours and patterns that match.'

Dotty paused again, then, as if the enormity of what was in front of her had only just sunk in, she turned her whole face into George's shoulder and shook as he wrapped his arms around her.

Cressida looked back at the pair, and then up at the terrace, where Alfred had appeared with a man she assumed was the hotel manager in tow. Behind him, she could see the large ballroom curtains were being hurriedly drawn, no doubt to try to keep the scene in the courtyard as private as possible, for as long as possible.

She glanced over to the other side of the courtyard. The curtains, or in places, shutters, had already been closed there too. No one would be able to see Victoria's body.

Cressida turned back to the fountain.

Just a few more seconds... it was all she had before the scene in front of her was corrupted. And Dotty was right, she was good at spotting details. *An eye for design...* and as she'd proved too many times already, sadly, it meant she had an eye for a crime, too.

Was this a crime, though? What of George's suggestion, that the countess had been drunk and fallen into the fountain and died?

She looked again at poor Victoria's body, picking up a shivering Ruby, who had been patiently standing by the fountain. Cressida nuzzled her pup's soft, warm body to her chilled nose and cheeks while she thought. Victoria was a slim woman, who had clearly had a martini too many. And unlike Cressida and Dotty's glossy patent leather, Victoria's shoes were made of exquisite slubbed silk and the damp of the falling snow was staining them. Although she hadn't walked far in the settled flakes, it had been enough to ruin a perfectly good pair of shoes. Would an entirely sober person do that? Even the richest countess would baulk at ruining her best evening shoes, surely? And the snow... it was falling so heavily now that it was changing the scene around her by the moment.

Cressida wiped a snowflake off her eyelashes as she noticed something else. Something that was disappearing as each one of those flakes hit the ground. There were Victoria's footsteps towards the fountain, and she could see where her friend's silk-covered heels were now at awkward angles to the last place they stood.

But there was another set of footprints, too. A double set next to Victoria's, which led to – and away from – the fountain. Cressida clocked all of this before she felt a warm hand on her shoulder and the welcome presence once again of Alfred.

'The hotel manager is here, Cressy,' he said.

Cressida looked at the short, balding man in the smart navy blue tailcoat and gave him a nod as Alfred guided her away.

'Come on, old thing, let's get you in and warm.'

'He seems a sensible man,' Cressida acknowledged,

thinking of the privacy the curtains now afforded them, and Alfred agreed.

'Yes, he took it all in and acted immediately. Said he'd do what he could to stop this from getting out to the rest of the guests – last thing the hotel will want is a stampede out the door. He'll fetch that poor woman out of the fountain.' He glanced back, as did Cressida, and saw a team of hotel staff appear with blankets and a stretcher.

'Poor Victoria. And everyone acting like it's just an accident.' She dared one last look at Victoria, then shivered and pulled her shawl tighter around her as they headed up the steps to the ballroom, where the party-goers were blissfully unaware of the tragedy.

'Victoria, you say? Not the Countess of Worcester?' Alfred whispered, despite the trill from the trumpet and the many tapping feet on the dance floor.

'The very same. Fanshawe "as was", but Lady Beaumont now.'

'And don't think I didn't hear the second part too. You don't think this is an accident, do you?' Alfred said, though his voice was still hushed.

Cressida raised an eyebrow at him. 'No, I don't. I'm certain Victoria was murdered, here at the Mayfair Hotel. Right under our noses.'

3

'Murdered?' Alfred said, a frown crossing his forehead. Cressida was trying not to look at his handsome face too much in the current circumstances. She'd been having some very strong feelings about Alfred of late. He would, of course, be a very sensible choice, and a man no one in her family could object to her marrying – but marriage had never had the draw for her that it did for other young ladies. In fact, she hated the idea of becoming someone else's chattel, of being known simply by his surname, of perhaps giving up all the freedoms that women like Mrs Pankhurst had fought for before the war.

No, Cressida had her own wealth, thanks to her very generous Papa. She had her own independence, thanks to her pied-à-terre in Chelsea, and the thrill of being able to hit the open road whenever she chose, thanks to her darling little red motor car. Not to mention all the love she could need from her wonderful friends – and of course her pug, Ruby. Too many women she knew – bar a few exceptions – had lost their independence when they'd married, swapping sports cars for sedate sedans, and parties for parish council meetings. Not that growing up wasn't inevitable and might bring these things with them anyway, but the thought of having her independence stifled in any way had always been anathema to her.

But Alfred sparked something inside her and she couldn't stop thinking about him now. Marriage couldn't be on the cards; but over the years she'd known him, and more especially in this last year when he'd been most useful during a few of her unofficial investigations, she had to admit she had started to fall in love with him. His chestnut brown hair, and dark, chocolate brown eyes that crinkled at the edges as he smiled all helped too, but mostly it was his good-humoured nature and knack of being able to make her laugh and cheer her up during the most heinous of occasions that had enamoured him to her.

And the jolly amazing thing was, she was pretty sure he felt the same. A couple of months ago, they'd both been in Winchester, and although Alfred had got himself caught up in the most frightful scrape – charged with murder, no less – she had discovered as part of her investigation a rather romantic list of ideas he'd been planning for them both to enjoy in that beautiful part of the world. Pony trekking in the New Forest, driving down to the south coast...

Cressida sighed. It should all be so easy, yet Alfred's mother, Lady Chatterton, had barely let her dear son and heir out of her sight since he was exonerated. This meant Cressida hadn't seen much of him since those gloomy October days. So being with him now, his concern for her as she shivered, his help in getting the hotel manager involved, and not to mention how handsome he looked in his white tie and tails, caused her mind to start popping like caviar, just when she needed to keep it focused on who might have killed her friend.

Cressida had pondered all of this as the four chums were ushered through the ballroom by one of the hotel staff as stealthily as possible, and shown into a smartly decorated, if smaller, room, close to the terrace. It was panelled with dark, glossy wood, though its high ceiling and blazing chandeliers kept it looking bright and cosy. Candles set in holders decorated with holly leaves and bright-red berries stood on every surface, adding to the warm and festive feel of the room. Stubbs-style paintings of racehorses, along with framed prints of Hogarth cartoons from the eighteenth century, hung on the walls and a humidor for cigars was placed on one of the mahogany sideboards. The smell of the cedar wood from it mingled with the smoke from the fire that was glowing in the grate.

Cressida appreciated the warmth from the fire as shock had turned to shivers. She put Ruby down next to the hearth, sat down on one of the leather Chesterfield sofas and gathered her thoughts. Now was not the time to analyse her feelings for Alfred. Now was the time to investigate a murder.

'Cressy, did you say murdered?' Alfred repeated himself. He was perched on the arm the other end of the same sofa, and she looked across at him as she answered his questions.

'Yes, murdered. I noticed blood around the side of her head, the result of a nasty blow I should imagine.'

'That could have come as she fell into the fountain,' he countered, pulling a pipe out of his tailcoat pocket, and jamming the stem between his back teeth. He was dressed in a well-tailored and traditional black tailcoat with a starched white shirt and waistcoat and a white tie, but even so, whatever he was wearing, there always seemed to be a pocket for his pipe.

'Perhaps,' Cressida agreed, 'but there was something else I saw too. You see, I noticed a second set of footprints, next to Victoria's, on the way to the fountain.'

'Could they have been there already?' Alfred removed his pipe and waved it in the air to make his point. 'Made by another guest here tonight, admiring the fountain in the snow?'

'I don't think so,' Cressida replied. 'There wasn't *much* snow on the ground. It looked like it had only started settling a little before we followed Dot outside.'

Dotty, who had been looking from her brother to her friend

and back again as if she were watching a tennis match between them, stopped when she heard that.

'Oh, you were in the courtyard too, just as George was...' She sighed and looked demurely at her beau, who was sitting next to her on the other leather-upholstered Chesterfield sofa, and he smiled at her and shrugged as if to say, 'just our luck'.

'I couldn't help it, chum.' Cressida leaned over and squeezed her arm. 'I saw you two heading out of the ballroom and I just wanted to be there too. I'm so excited... well, I will be when...' It was her turn to tail off. Dotty deserved all the happiness in the world, and an *uninterrupted* marriage proposal to start it off. 'Anyway,' she continued, 'in that dusting of snow, there was one clear set of footprints that must have been Victoria's. They ended just where her body fell. Her silk shoes were damaged by the snow.'

'Unlike our leathers, snow would leave a nasty tide mark on silk,' agreed Dotty, looking at her own patent leather shoes and bending over to wipe away some melted damp spots from them, leaving them none the worse off for it.

'Exactly,' Cressida agreed. 'But there were other footprints too. They looked similar to Victoria's, pressed into the fresh, new snow to the same degree. But these prints went both ways – to the fountain, and back again.'

'You say both ways.' Alfred used his pipe to indicate the movement. 'To the fountain, but *from* where? I mean, did Victoria and her killer – if those really are the footsteps of a murderer – come from the terrace like we did? I didn't notice any other footprints in the snow and those stone steps were darned lethal in their own right, what with the ice on them.'

'Not as lethal as whatever hit Victoria over the head, Alfred.' Cressida frowned. 'And no, they didn't come from that direction, but the other side of the courtyard. Which is why we couldn't see them, or Victoria's body, when we were standing on the terrace.'

'And I only saw her when we were standing right in front of the fountain. I saw her through the gap in that prancing horse's legs.' Dotty shivered and George laid a protective hand on her knee, which she grasped before carrying on. 'So what is over there, on that side of the courtyard? Where do those footsteps lead to?' she asked.

As if on cue, Ruby snort-snuffled, as she was wont to do, and Cressida smiled at her pup.

'That's right, Ruby, the kitchens.'

'Ah,' Alfred, Dotty and George all said in unison.

'Ah indeed,' Cressida agreed. 'And before you all ask me how I know, just remember I've been to this hotel before and may have needed an escape route once or twice—'

'Oh, yes, that time Timmy Upwaltham was determined to dance with you despite his terrible halitosis.'

'Exactly. I remember glancing at the fountain as I ran down the corridor, dodging waiters in my haste...' Cressida shook her head as Dotty readjusted her glasses and posed a new question.

'Why would Victoria be coming from the direction of the kitchens? Not the party, like the rest of us? She'd been dancing with us only a little while before George asked me to join him outside.'

Cressida bit her lip. 'It's a good question, Dot. What was she doing near the kitchens? And who do those other footprints belong to?'

'The murderer, as discussed.' Alfred pointed his pipe stem into the air, then clenched it back between his teeth.

'Yes, Alfred.' Cressida looked at him. 'But who wanted Victoria dead? And why kill her in the middle of our Christmas Eve ball?'

4

'I'm afraid I'm a bit out of the loop,' George said, squeezing Dotty's hand again as he sat next to her. 'You all know the poor girl in the fountain?'

Cressida, with her shawl pulled around her emerald-green dress, her earrings and jewelled headband glinting in the soft glow of oil lamps, nodded. 'Victoria Beaumont was a friend of ours. Of course, we knew her as Victoria Fanshawe while we were all knocking about at school, but she became Victoria Beaumont, the Countess of Worcester, when she married.'

'She debbed at the same time, didn't she, Cressy?' Dotty said, referring to their debutante year, five years ago, when both the Honourable Cressida Fawcett and Lady Dorothy Chatterton were presented to the Court of St James and set loose by their mothers to find husbands. Dotty looked coyly up at George as she continued. 'We didn't do so well on the husband-finding bit – though now I'm rather pleased of it—'

'And we had a marvellous time at all the parties,' Cressida reminded her. 'I don't think failing to find a husband has ever been so fun.' She looked back at George. 'But Dotty's right, Victoria was a debutante the same year as us, as well as some of the other girls here tonight – Pansy and Rosie Wainwright, and Dora Smith-Wallington among them.'

'Ah, and here's coffee, thank heavens!' Dotty interjected with relief.

A young waiter had entered bearing a tray of cups and an elegant silver coffee pot. The sound of the party happening in the ballroom was much clearer with the door open and Cressida wondered if anyone else on that dance floor and hovering around the buffet had the faintest idea of what had happened in the courtyard.

She glanced over to the window, which looked over the street outside, and saw the heavy flakes falling faster than ever. The hotel manager had drawn the curtains in the ballroom and the cold would probably keep any of the guests from venturing out to the terrace. It was likely then that no one else here at the Mayfair Hotel would realise anything was amiss – until Victoria herself was missed.

As the noise of the party was muffled again by the door closing behind the retreating waiter, Dotty continued their discussion.

'But do you remember the tongue-lashing our mothers gave us when Victoria secured herself a match almost instantly, Cressy?' Dotty shuddered, then sipped her coffee. 'Dora and I were in the doghouse for weeks.'

'I think my mother gave up on me long before our deb year, Dot,' Cressida snorted, though she did risk a sideways glance to see how Alfred was reacting to their reminiscences and noticed that he was staring into the fire, seemingly a world away.

'It did cause a bit of a scandal though, at the time? Don't you remember, Cressy?' Dotty carried on. 'Victoria was barely twenty and Peter Beaumont almost sixty. Everyone said she was marrying him for his title. The Countess of Worcester. Quite grand really.'

'Or his money,' Cressida added. 'He has that massive pile in the Midlands, doesn't he – Beaumont Park?'

'Well, marrying for money, or titles, isn't exactly unheard of,' piped up Alfred, turning back to face them all, noticing the coffee for the first time and helping himself to a cup. 'Mother says it's the only two things I've got going for me.'

'Oh Alfred,' his sister admonished him.

Cressida however, looked more softly upon him. As far as she was concerned, Alfred had a lot more to offer a bride than mere money and estates. He had a great sense of humour, and those eyes that Cressida had to hold herself back from looking into too much lest she come over all funny. And he had a spark too. A spark she rather hoped they could both ignite at some point... She shook the thought away.

'I don't mean to gossip, or speak ill of the dead, but weren't there rumours almost straight away?' Cressida asked, bending over and picking up Ruby, who had started to chew the leather around the edge of the sofa end that Alfred was perching on. 'Sorry, Alfred, thought she was about to get your ankles.'

'One day I'll earn her regard.' He shook his head at the small dog. 'But it doesn't look like it's today.'

'Devilishly nosy of me,' George said, leaning forward in his chair. 'But what rumours?'

'The usual sort that accompany a marriage like that,' Dotty said matter-of-factly. 'Pretty young wife, much older husband. She in London quite a bit, for dressmakers and milliners, the theatre and whatnot, and him more curmudgeonly and preferring the country estate. It was said that she took lovers here in London and played the patient, country wife less and less, until...'

'Until what?' George asked.

Cressida took over. 'Until quite recently, when she stopped all that. We saw less of her here in town and apparently she and Peter started spending more time together.' She let Ruby settle on her lap, despite the claw marks in the delicate silk, and leaned back in the sofa, gently ruffling her small dog's ears. 'Tonight was the first time we've seen them together since the wedding, don't you think, Dot?'

'Yes, come to think of it. He never usually comes to London. What a beautiful wedding it was, though? That lovely abbey near Beaumont Park. All those lilies. So pretty.' Dotty suddenly blushed, remembering that George was right next to her.

Her brother saved her from her awkwardness. 'Speaking of rumours, Clayton Malone's here tonight too. Did you see him in the games room? White tux and big bow tie in that new American style.'

'Who's Clayton Malone?' George asked. 'Sorry, I'm more used to dealing with Cleopatras than Claytons. Been out on the digs too long and haven't caught up with all this gossip.'

'Don't apologise, George,' Dotty comforted him. 'From your letters, it sounds like Ancient Egypt was more awash with scandal and gossip than all of London society thrown together. I wouldn't be surprised if what we're jabbering over tonight isn't exactly the same sort of thing your hieroglyphs have been telling stories of for aeons.' She squeezed his knee.

A blush rose up George's cheeks and he cleared his throat.

'Well, there was some incest and a fair bit of murder, so...'

'Murder's one thing,' Dotty pulled a face at her beloved, 'incest is quite another! Yuk.'

'Sorry. No incest then. But you're right, Dotty darling, there were a lot of nefarious things going on by the banks of the Nile. And the Euphrates. And the Tigris. I just didn't expect it to all be happening here by the Thames too.'

Cressida felt so sorry for the poor man. Only a week or so ago, he was in Cairo, now a sea voyage and several trains later and here he was in the smoking room of a smart London hotel, trussed up in white tie and tails, expecting to be betrothed to his beloved but instead discussing a murder. Still, she was pleased that he was here and by Dotty's side, despite this not being the best welcome home for him. And that he wasn't making a beeline for the door and scarpering after that botched engagement attempt made him an even more admirable chap in Cressida's book. So she answered his question as best she could.

'George, you're doing marvellously well keeping up with all of this. It must seem so trivial to you, all our society hot air, when you're more used to academia.' George waved that away and she continued. 'Clayton Malone is the man who is rumoured to be, or to have been, Victoria's lover. Much younger than her husband and a bit of a player in California, I hear. He's American, you see, and trying to make it big in Los Angeles through producing movies and the like, though I'm afraid I don't know him that well. We used to see much more of Victoria before she embarked on her affair with him, didn't we, Dot?'

'Yes, she was always one for a party and I think that's where she met Clayton – at a party. But you're right, it's been a while since we've really seen her. She did have the most extraordinarily fun dos.'

'Yes, do you remember the one when Kitty Pole found that fox on the bed and thought it was her stole? Only for it to be very much alive,' Cressida recalled. 'The shock of it made her faint.'

'Wasn't that the party when the soprano from the Royal Opera House did that thing with the copy of *The Times* and the peacock feather?' Dotty squinted, recalling the memory. 'She hit the highest note—'

'Yes, exactly.' Cressida raised an eyebrow at her friend, then addressed them all. 'But let's not get distracted from the case in hand: Victoria.'

'Do you think either this Clayton chap, or the husband, might have done it, then? Statistically, they're the most likely,' George ventured.

This time, Alfred answered.

'Clayton perhaps, although I don't know the fellow. But I can't see Peter Beaumont killing his wife. He's friends with our parents, Dot. And yours, Cressy.' He pointed his pipe stem at both of them.

'Marrying someone old enough to be your father...' Dotty pulled a face. 'It does seem a bit sickening.'

'Alfred's right, though. Lord Beaumont, as curmudgeonly as we find him, is very well connected. We'll need to tread carefully. Subtly.' Cressida paused. 'But we owe it to Victoria to work out what happened to her. She was our friend, wasn't she, Dot? A young woman just like us. I hate to think of how cold and scared she must have been as she fell, or was pushed, into that fountain.' She shivered, then looked each one of them in the eye and made a vow. 'I know it's Christmas Eve and we're meant to be having a jolly time, but I simply can't think of anything else now. I'm going to find out what happened to her. And who did it.'

5

Cressida's impassioned speech was interrupted by the door to the smoking room opening and two familiar faces arriving.

'DCI Andrews! Sergeant Kirby!' Cressida exclaimed, jumping out of her seat and going over to greet the Scotland Yard policemen. She glanced at her watch. 'It's barely half an hour since we found the body. Gosh, you got here quickly. And I tell you what, you're a very welcome sight.'

'Good evening, Miss Fawcett,' Andrews replied, handing his overcoat to a waiting maid. The snow caught on it had melted, creating damp patches on the shoulders of the waxed fabric. Cressida glanced out of the window and saw how heavily the snow was falling now, as Andrews continued. 'Switchboard received a call from the hotel manager and we came as soon as we could. New Scotland Yard isn't far. And good evening to you too, Lady Dorothy, Lord Delafield – and Mr Parish, isn't it?' He nodded a friendly greeting to them all. 'And Ruby too, I see.' He nodded down to where Ruby was lying by the fire, on her back with her little legs swimming blissfully in the air, making the most of the warmth from the coals.

'Yes, the gang's all here. Merry Christmas and all that,

though it feels horrid saying that what with what's just happened.'

'Indeed.' There was a resignation to Andrews' sigh. He had come across the Hon Cressida Fawcett on many occasions – more often than not when she or her friends had just stumbled across a murder. But he'd known her for far longer than that. DCI Andrews had served in the Boer War with Cressida's father, Lt Cl Sir Sholto Fawcett. Indeed, each credited the other for saving his life and it had been Fawcett Senior who had eased Andrews' way into civilian life by recommending him to contacts within the Metropolitan Police and the newly insti-gated detective branch at the New Scotland Yard headquarters.

This connection with Cressida's family had earned her, from him, a certain fondness, and in turn, Cressida had grown up with a papa who had the utmost respect for the policeman who had saved his life all those years ago. But DCI Andrews was often left at his wits' end, pulling his lightly grizzled-with-grey hair out as he tried to protect Cressida from running head-long into some very dangerous investigations.

In that one word, 'indeed', along with the little sigh after-wards, Cressida knew what Andrews was trying to express. 'You don't want us helping you investigate, do you, Andrews?' she asked, putting her hands on her hips. 'Sticking our noble old noses into a Scotland Yard case?'

'I wouldn't have put it quite like that,' Andrews conceded. 'But, from that, I assume that you've already decided it's murder?'

'Of course. Victoria was with someone when she walked to the fountain, ruining her lovely silk shoes in the process, then she sustained some sort of head injury, either by being pushed into the fountain, or she fell in after she was hit. All the evidence – that bump to her head and the second set of foot-prints next to Victoria's own – points towards murder.'

Sergeant Kirby, in his smart, midnight-blue uniform and

gleaming buttons, was already scribbling Cressida's observa-
tions down in his notebook. His carrot-coloured hair was
peeking out from under his helmet, which Cressida was
relieved to see was back to its proper shape after she'd acciden-
tally-on-purpose tossed it into the path of a passing dray cart a
few months ago. She smiled at him, and was relieved when the
smile was returned. Then she turned her attention back to
Andrews.

'It has to be murder, Andrews, and I'm afraid I am determined to investigate. I was just telling the others here, we owe it
to Victoria. She's one of us.'

It was Dotty's turn to chip in now. 'Chief Inspector
Andrews, Sergeant Kirby,' she greeted them. 'Cressy's right.
Poor Victoria... it looked so grisly too. And she'd been such a
pretty deb, and a hoot at parties, and not a bad egg at all, despite
the extramarital, well... Anyway, the thing is, Cressy and I
would like to investigate it, but I think we may have stumbled
across our first hurdle.'

Cressida turned to her dear friend. It delighted her that
Dotty was so game to help her. There had been times when
Dotty hadn't been so keen on Cressida getting into scrapes, but
she really had got behind it all now. 'What do you mean, "hurdle", Dot?' She pointed at the policemen. 'Andrews had the
"powers that be" say it was all alright for us to help out last
time.' She looked at Andrews. 'And I assume that still stands?'

Andrews nodded, though it was with a certain resignation.

Dotty, however, carried on. 'Just that it's going to be nigh on
impossible this time, Cressy. Unlike back in the summer when
we were all – for want of a better word – trapped, up in Ayrton
Castle, or on the Scotland Express, or when the murderer in
Winchester had to be someone in the cathedral community...'
She raised her hands in despair, 'Here we are, Christmas Eve in
the middle of London. The murderer could be anywhere by
now. It's what, a few minutes past eight? And we think the

murder happened about half an hour or so ago? In that case, the murderer could be in New Cross or Clapham or on his way to the coast by now.'

Cressida crossed her arms. Dotty was right. There was a ballroom full of people, any one of whom could have snuck off during those few dances and done it, not to mention staff and other hotel residents. And any of them could have left the hotel in the time between when they had killed Victoria and now.

Andrews cleared his throat and Cressida looked up at him.

'Actually, Lady Dorothy, we've done a preliminary check of the building. The hotel manager, a Mr Reginald Butcher, said he locked all the auxiliary doors and made sure the fire exits were manned as soon as the body was found. No one, according to him, has left the building since then.'

'Is he absolutely sure?' Cressida perked up.

Andrews nodded, but he still frowned. 'There is a small window of time between the murder happening and you coming upon the body, but the manager seemed to think that no one left during that time. They've had doormen on all the public entrances, and the staff doors have been locked when not in use as there's been some problems with vagrants, what with it being Christmas and times being tough. We'll question all the staff to check, though, of course. But, to use Lady Dorothy's phrase, there is another hurdle...'

'Which is?' Cressida quizzed him.

'We can't keep everyone here indefinitely,' he replied with a slight shrug.

'It's Christmas after all,' Dotty agreed.

'Christmas I'm not so fussed about, Lady Dorothy,' he replied. 'I'm afraid a murder investigation trumps Christmas, but we do have a limit on how long we can hold a ballroom of people – nay, a hotel full of guests – against their will.'

'Carriages at midnight,' murmured Cressida.

'Excuse me, Miss Fawcett?' Andrews queried.

'Carriages at midnight,' she sighed. 'That's what the tickets for tonight said. So that's when those not staying at the hotel will expect, and want, to go home.' She looked again at her wristwatch, an elegant piece with a simple sapphire cabochon that she wore around her wrist whether she was in evening wear or not. 'So that gives us just under four hours to work out who killed the Countess of Worcester.'

'And find them if they're still here,' Dotty added.

Cressida, who had been holding her shawl tightly around her loosened her grasp and as she did so felt her own diamond and emerald necklace. She paused as she thought, then answered Dotty. 'You know what, I really do think they will be. Of course, Mr Butcher has done all he can to seal the entrances and exits now, but more than that, Victoria was still wearing her pearl choker and diamond earrings when we found her body, meaning it wasn't a murder for money or jewels, else those valuables would have been grabbed as she fell. If they had been missing, then it might have been a tragic theft gone wrong and the assailant might have snuck out of the hotel in double-quick time with his loot. But this feels more personal. An argument or an attack on her specifically. I think whoever did this to her is still here. And I think we need to start with who knew her best.'

'Find out who, apart from us, knew Victoria well enough to be at a Christmas ball with her,' agreed Dotty.

But Cressida took her thought one step further.

'Or knew her well enough – and hated her enough – to kill her.'

6

'I'd best go and speak to his lordship.' DCI Andrews put his notebook away in the top pocket of his tweed jacket and gestured for Sergeant Kirby to follow him. 'Kirby, can you conflab with Mr Butcher, the hotel manager, to check the alibis of the staff and ascertain that no one left via the service entrances? I think concocting a reason as to why policemen might suddenly be guarding the doors might help too – alleviate the worry and all that.'

'That's not a bad idea,' reasoned Cressida. 'Didn't you just say that this Mr Butcher chap had been complaining of vagrants? Maybe he can suggest to the guests that some low-level thievery has happened. Nothing for them to worry about, though. And tell him to keep those curtains shut in the ballroom and lock the doors to the terrace. I doubt anyone would venture out there now, it looks like Siberia out there, but it would be best if they didn't see the stretcher-bearers or anything like that.'

DCI Andrews nodded at Kirby, who in turn nodded to Cressida. Then the two policemen left.

'I think all that nodding means they were both on board,'

Cressida said a few moments later when the four friends were once again alone.

'Not a bad idea of yours to suggest the thieving thing,' Dotty praised Cressida. 'All the innocent party-goers tonight will buy it, and possibly be more observant, which could help us if we need to question them later, and it shouldn't rile the actual murderer. Not spook them, if you see what I mean?'

'Yes, I do, Dot. And I agree. The thing is, I've been thinking. As I said to Andrews just now, I'm sure this is murder rather than an accident, and it feels like a very personal murder to boot. As you said, Dotty, we must find out who here tonight knew Victoria. They must be the people with the strongest motive.'

'Well, we won't get very far on that particular mission sitting here all night.' Alfred stood up, slapping his hands on his thighs as he came up with a plan. 'And I for one am parched. All this talk of murder really leaves one dry as a tinderbox. There's a perfectly decent bar out there, full of the people who knew and loved – or, indeed, knew and loathed – Victoria. Who wants a drink along with their side order of investigation?'

'Rather,' George agreed. 'Arid as the desert over here, what with everything. Can't think I'll be much help on the investigating part, but I can help with the drinks.'

'We should be on the champagne by now,' sighed Dotty, then pulled a face and rubbed her forehead. 'More champagne in any case.'

'Your plan makes perfect sense, Alf. But no drinks for me, thanks,' Cressida answered, taking a sip of the steaming coffee cup in front of her. 'And yes, before you all ask, I am feeling quite well, and no, fairies have not whisked the real Cressida Fawcett away and replaced her with some martini-shirking changeling. But I think I need to keep a clear head – well, as clear as it can be after the amount we've already drunk – and we only have a few hours to solve this mystery.'

'The emphasis on "we" there I think?' Dotty narrowed her eyes at her, knowingly. 'I shouldn't imagine Andrews or Kirby will give up on the stroke of midnight.'

'No,' Cressida said sheepishly, 'but I shall need to be at Mydenhurst Manor in time for Christmas morning service tomorrow and I can't see Mr Butcher allowing the hotel guests – the ones who aren't staying here – to be barricaded in for too many minutes past midnight.'

'What a funny notion, to stay in a hotel over Christmas.' Dotty cocked her head.

'I suppose some people have to, but bar a few Americans and some real out-of-towners, I should imagine most of us here tonight are evening guests only.' Cressida slurped the coffee and then swore under her breath as she spilt some down her chin. 'Definitely no more champagne for me tonight,' she muttered, wiping it away, hoping Alfred hadn't noticed her unladylike mishap.

'Well, where to first?' Dotty asked, subtly passing her friend a clean napkin before getting up from her seat and brushing her skirts down. Her dress had crinkled in the snow, and she frowned at it, then shrugged.

Cressida looked over to where Alfred and George were standing by the door and then gently took Dotty by the elbow. 'I think you should stay with George, Dot.'

'But I—'

'I'll be fine, I promise. I'm going to start by talking to Lord Beaumont. Hopefully I can catch him just after Andrews breaks the news. And I'll be careful, just in case the middle-aged earl is murderous after all. I'll take Ruby with me. When she's not showing that expanding tummy of hers off to the fire-place, she's a useful pup.' Cressida raised an eyebrow and Dotty rolled her eyes.

'All right then, I suppose. But do be careful. As George said, statistically he's likely to be the murderer. You know, in nine out of ten – well, to be more exact, thirty-seven out of forty-five – of those detective books I've read, it is the husband who did it. If not, it's the wife. Or butler actually, quite a few were the butler.'

'I'll be fine, Dotty,' Cressida said with the confidence a few glasses of fizz gave, and a little mirth to her voice. She loved how Dotty inhaled – and often regurgitated – books. That it was now pulp detective fiction that was her new favourite genre both amused and impressed Cressida. But it did put some rather thrilling notions of what might happen into Dotty's head and Cressida was sure tonight would be much less dramatic than those books would have you believe. Though, bearing in mind she herself had been shot at, clubbed over the head and aimed for with a plummeting alabaster bust of a Chatterton ancestor, perhaps she couldn't be so sure. She reassured Dotty in any case. 'Andrews and Kirby are only a shout away, as are you all. And I think you should spend some time with George. He's come all this way to see you from deepest, darkest Mesopotamia, or some such. He's obviously keener than the hottest mustard. Oh Dot...' Cressida reached out for her friend. 'I'm so sorry that your proposal was interrupted—'

'He got as far as kneeling, Cressy,' Dotty whispered, her voice full of pent-up excitement. 'And I know he was saying something, and I'm sure it was super romantic, but then I saw the body, and I feel terribly bad as I screamed so loudly and—'

'You mustn't feel bad for screaming, Dot. Or not listening to him in the circumstances. I'm sure George understands. And if he doesn't, he's not the chap we thought he was. But go and be with him now. He's travelled miles, and possibly aeons, to be with you.' Cressida pulled her friend into a hug and then adjusted her new camel-down shawl around her and smoothed down her glossy conker-coloured bobbed hair until it was once again perfectly bouncy. Looking her in the eye, she said, 'But I do have a mission for you.'

'Oh yes?' Dotty said with a twinkle. 'Do you fancy another martini after all?'

'Oof, no. But just as Alfred suggested – while you're at the bar, or back in the ballroom, and you're dancing and whispering sweet nothings into George's ear—'

'Oh Cressy, behave.' Dotty poked her in the ribs. 'And Alfred will be with us too, eurgh.'

Cressida chuckled. 'Well, *instead* of whispering sweet nothings to George, then, look around to see who else is here. Anyone who we know was a friend – or foe – of Victoria. We barely said hello to anyone earlier as we headed straight for the dance floor, but I did clock some familiar faces. I thought I saw Cordelia Stirling for one.'

'Sir Richard's daughter? From Ayrton Castle?'

'Yes – and no doubt still with an eye for Alfred.' Cressida scrunched her face in a frown. 'And Dora Smith-Wallington – visiting her rich London relatives, no doubt. The Wainwrights if you can peel them away from any eligible men on the dance floor. Anyway, see what you can gather from who's there and what they're saying.' Cressida stifled a hiccough but maintained a serious expression.

'Right-oh. A mission. Well, count it accepted.' And with that, Dotty saluted her friend and then joined George and Alfred by the door to the smoking room.

Cressida waved them off, then walked over to the fireplace, where Ruby was reclining.

'Come on, you. No time for relaxing. We have a murder to solve.'

7

With one last look out of the window at the snow, which was falling heavily, covering the tops of the railings outside the hotel and dusting the roofs of the motor cars parked on the street, Cressida left the quiet of the smoking room. She was relieved to see that the Christmas ball was carrying on just as it had been. There were still couples and groups of friends on the dance floor and the band were belting out classics. Older guests drank hot mulled wine from punch bowls and sat around the tables, which heaved with winter delicacies. A waiter carried a tray of empty champagne bottles away from the tables and a rather handsome man with a pencil moustache and slicked-back hair caught a young lady in his arms and swept her into a dip under the mistletoe. Did any of them know that one of their cohort had just been killed?

One of them did, of course, and the thought hit her with a familiar shiver.

But as far as everyone else was concerned, the party was still in a swinging mood.

Cressida slipped between the tables and chairs, pausing at the buffet table briefly to snaffle a cocktail sausage for Ruby and a small caviar blini, or three, for herself. Fortified, she scanned the crowd looking for the Earl of Worcester, Victoria's bereaved widower.

Suddenly, an older woman in a dress that was the height of fashion about ten years previously, but was still of excellent quality and cut, bustled up and accosted her.

'Cressida Fawcett, thank heavens I've found you.' The woman paused for breath, her bosom heaving in the crushed velvet of her dress. She fanned herself with the hand that wasn't clutching a large fabric bag and puffed out her cheeks.

Cressida recognised her as Mrs Ottoline Spencer. She was a widow, Cressida remembered, and a friend of her mother's, and indeed Dotty's mother, Lady Chatterton, neither of whom were here, thank heavens. In fact, Ottoline Spencer was one of the oldest ladies in the room – in her late fifties, Cressida thought, an age where unless one lived in London permanently, one would usually be back at one's country estate for the festivities. Her own parents and the Chattertons certainly were and had made it quite clear to Cressida and Dotty that it was most irregular and highly modern of them to be staying in London right up until Christmas morning. Cressida briefly wondered what Mrs Spencer was doing here, but was more worried that she looked as if she were about to pass out.

'Hello, Mrs Spencer,' Cressida greeted her. 'Are you quite all right? Would you like a seat?' Cressida reached out to guide Ottoline to a chair, but she seemed to recover herself.

'Cressida dear, I'm glad you remember me.'

'I do. I saw you at the garden show at Chelsea this summer, with Mama,' Cressida recalled and Ottoline Spencer looked relieved.

'Yes, yes. Quite the floribunda we saw this year. Though that sculpture of the nymph with the suggestive fruit basket was quite... Well, enough of that. I'm so glad you're here.'

'I'd love to chat, but I'm afraid I'm rather busy at the

moment Mrs Spencer, I—' Cressida looked over the older woman's shoulder, still scanning the crowd for the Earl of Worcester.

'Do call me Ottoline. And you have to help me. You see, someone I know has just been murdered.'

Cressida's eyes snapped back to the older woman. 'Victoria Beaumont?' she asked, suddenly very interested.

'Yes, yes, that's right.' Ottoline confirmed but looked askance at Cressida. 'How did you know?'

'I was there when her body was discovered,' Cressida answered. Then, with a note of suspicion, asked, 'You?'

'Young Victoria is my dear friend Peter's wife. I was there just a few moments ago when the policemen told him.' She threaded her arm through one of Cressida's, the one that wasn't holding a patient Ruby, and started to lead Cressida through the ballroom. Ottoline lowered her voice as she continued. 'Poor Peter, he was flabbergasted. And the police asked such searching questions. I think Peter's in shock. At least that's what the policeman said, I heard him telling his underling, and they've left him to grieve for a bit, no doubt to revisit later to continue the barrage of questions. It's all so ghastly, Cressida.' Ottoline shuddered at the thought.

'So he couldn't tell them anything?' Cressida asked, but Ottoline either hadn't heard or decided to ignore her.

'I hear you have an eye for these things. Murders, that is. And finding out who did it?'

'Well, yes... I suppose.' Cressida didn't know how she felt about her fame spreading like this. She'd always rather thought she might become more well known for her lovely interior decorating schemes, knowing how to position a cushion 'just so' and how far into a room to place a Persian carpet... but then, as Dotty had reminded her earlier, her eye for design meant she had an eye for a crime. And as Dotty had also just reminded her, it was more often than not the husband who was the killer.

Cressida leaned down so that she could speak more quietly to Ottoline. 'Do you know where the earl is? I would like to speak to him.' She quickly thought of a reason. 'Pass on my condolences before the world and its wife finds out about... well, his wife.'

'Yes, yes. That's where I'm taking you. To see him now, of course. It's all rather horrid. He's terribly upset. We do so need your help.'

'Oh, I see.' Cressida shook her squiffy head. She really had to sharpen up if she were to live up to these expectations. 'Thank you, Ottoline, and yes, poor Lord Beaumont, I should imagine he's distraught,' Cressida said, wondering why Andrews had spent so little time questioning the most prominent suspect. Lord Beaumont must indeed be in shock and too catatonic to speak. Whether that would be from hearing about his wife's death or coming to terms perhaps with what he'd done himself...

Cressida took a breath. She mustn't assume anything yet. Still, she was glad that she'd found a way to get to the earl. Ottoline Spencer had a firm grasp of her arm and was leading her through the throng of party-goers, straight to the deceased's husband; the very person statistics told her must be the prime suspect. The Earl of Worcester himself.

8

Ottoline Spencer led Cressida through the crowded ballroom, allowing Cressida just enough time to quickly wave at Dotty, who gave her a thumbs up from the other side of the room. Then she mimed using a pair of binoculars and writing in a notepad. Cressida smiled and waved again, before she found herself being escorted by Ottoline's birdlike hand at her elbow into a lobby type of room, with a fabulous white-veneered grand piano in it and several suites of Rococo-style upholstered chairs and settees.

The piano room, or lobby, connected the ballroom to another corridor and from there other rooms and a side entrance to the hotel, no doubt now manned by a burly policeman. The lobby space was pleasingly well proportioned, Cressida thought, being square in shape, and on the walls, where there weren't doors with fancy architraves, there were floor-to-ceiling gilt-edged mirrors, each one framed in the curled and flouncy Rococo style that dominated the hotel.

The pianist was tinkling the ivories, and doing a remark-ably good job at having his notes heard over the more ener-getic band in the ballroom. His music was more on the traditional side, and his festive spirit was amplified by the large bunch of mistletoe that hung just next to his piano and the large hamper of Christmas crackers that was positioned next to his stool. Cressida spotted their navy blue velvet ribbons and matching dark blue logo of the Mayfair Hotel before Ottoline steered her towards a portly man in his sixties who was sitting on an elegant upholstered settee, his legs splayed and a handkerchief being swept from side to side over his brow.

The older man was in traditional evening wear, a tailcoat and white waistcoat, with a small white bow tie under his starched collar that looked rather tight on his podgy neck. His once blonde hair was now greying and what was left of it was swept over his bald pate in the most unsubtle way. Cressida couldn't help but draw the comparison between him and Alfred; both wearing the same evening wear, yet Alfred so much more handsome. And young. And, more importantly, definitely not a murderer, whereas Lord Beaumont...

'Peter!' Ottoline called shrilly to the man, who looked up at her, a lit cigar in one hand and a small tumbler of what looked like whisky next to him. 'Peter, this is Cressida Fawcett. Sholto and Rosamund's daughter from Sussex.'

Peter Beaumont, Earl of Worcester, looked up at them, and Cressida was slightly taken aback by the sight of him. She wondered if Ottoline had been entirely correct. He didn't look terribly upset. In fact, he looked thoroughly nonplussed. Yet, in his favour on the murder stakes, he also did not look like someone simply enjoying a Christmas party.

Cressida stuck out the hand that wasn't carrying Ruby, and although he took it and shook it, he took his time moving his cigar from one hand to the other before he did.

'Sussex, yes. But latterly of Chelsea. How do you do, my lord,' Cressida greeted him, and took a seat on one of the delicately moulded and upholstered armchairs opposite him.

Lord Beaumont assessed her, while patting the seat next to him for Ottoline to sit on. She obeyed like a well-trained dog.

With no instant reply from him, Cressida continued. 'I'm so very sorry about Victoria. She was a friend of mine. I remember your wedding well, in fact. Shorty Dunstable got a bit carried away with the summer punch, if I remember and... Well, now's not the time. It's simply hideous what's happened to her.'

Lord Beaumont, who had been sucking on his cigar, exhaled a cloud of smoke before nodding. 'Yes, yes. Poor little thing. Terrible, terrible.'

'I hear DCI Andrews of Scotland Yard has already spoken to you. He's an awfully good detective. I'm sure he'll find out who did this to her.' *As will I*, Cressida added the thought on silently at the end.

'Cressida here has a frightfully good eye for working out what's going on.' Ottoline settled herself in next to Lord Beaumont, though she looked tense, with her arms wrapped around her extraordinarily large evening bag.

'Fawcett, eh?' Lord Beaumont eyed Cressida again. 'Weren't you due to come and look at the drapes in the drawing room next month? Or was that Colefax?'

Cressida looked at Ottoline, who had been caught unawares by this news. 'Yes, that's right. Victoria was in touch only a few weeks ago and asked me to come to Beaumont Park in the new year. I was rather looking forward to it and having a jolly good catch-up with her,' Cressida paused, thinking of her friend. Then remembered to add, 'and you, of course, Lord Beaumont.'

'Dare say, dare say,' he muttered and pulled on his cigar again.

Cressida thought back to both Dotty's and Alfred's assertion that it was so often the husband in murder cases like this. She had to find out if he had an alibi.

'Lord Beaumont, when did you and Victoria arrive tonight? I assume it was together?'

'Peter and I arrived together,' Ottoline answered for him, then gestured towards some of the other guests who were listening to the pianist from other chair and settee suites. 'We were here early so we could bagsy these seats in a quieter part of the hotel, and Victoria met us, having been in the West End at some appointment, then with some girlfriends. Us oldies take a little more time to powder our noses.' She simpered a sort of laugh, then recovered herself. She folded her fabric bag onto her lap and Cressida noticed that although rather large, it was made from a very fine silk, which complemented her outfit.

'So Victoria met you here? What time?'

'About six o'clock, don't you think, Peter?' Ottoline nudged him.

'Hm? Yes, yes, about six.' He shifted his legs and made himself more comfortable on the sofa, which creaked a little under his weight.

'And you were all together for most of the evening, before Victoria was... well, before she left to...' Cressida was struggling to find the words. Ghastly visions of her old friend in the fountain kept coming back to her. She was relieved that Victoria's husband and friend Ottoline hadn't had to see her like that.

'Oh, you're asking where we were when she was killed,' Ottoline said quite matter-of-factly. 'I see. Yes, of course. Tell me, when was the murder committed?'

'We think it was just before seven thirty. Perhaps ten or so minutes before then. Victoria was dancing with me and Dotty and some of our friends, then she moved on to some other pals and...' Cressida gathered her thoughts. Remembering exactly when she last saw Victoria was important. '... And I lost sight of her. Then it was a good ten minutes or so, I believe, until I followed Dotty outside and we found her.'

'You were with her? Just before she died?' Ottoline frowned. 'Did you see anything?'

'No, no I didn't.' Cressida felt like it was her who was on the spot now. She really hadn't noticed much, but then she hadn't been paying attention to Victoria, not while she was on the receiving end of an Alfred eye twinkle. Though there had been that blonde man she'd seen her dancing with... Cressida clocked the thought, then brought the conversation back to their alibi. 'So, yes, just before half past seven.'

'Ah, well, if it was then, the simple answer was that we were here, weren't we, Peter? Listening to the pianist. He was playing the carols that they must have been singing at King's College Cambridge at about the same time. The service in the college chapel starts soon after half past six, and, of course, we don't know the exact timings of the service in Cambridge, but the fellow on the piano was playing the same carols. They're always the same, nine lessons and carols, though, of course, we weren't getting the lessons here—'

'And I lost my pocket watch and you found it under the chair over there, Otty, didn't you?' Lord Beaumont said, inter-rupting Ottoline. 'And remarked that it was twenty past seven.'

'Oh yes, that's right.' Ottoline looked thoughtful, but Cres-sida wondered if she saw her eyes flicker up to meet her own for just the smallest moment. Ottoline, however, retained her sombre expression and continued. 'You must fix that chain it's on, Peter. You're lucky I found it this time.' She turned back to Cressida and shared an indulgent roll of the eyes. 'So, you see, we were here at the time of the murder and, of course, completely ignorant of it until the hotel manager and that policeman came to tell us the terrible news.'

'That must have been devastating for you both,' Cressida sympathised, though she glanced at Lord Beaumont to assess his reaction.

He merely grunted and muttered something about youth today.

Cressida frowned, but it was Ottoline who carried on the conversation.

'We were – *are* – devastated. Of course. And to think, we'd barely seen Victoria this evening. It doesn't seem fair that our last words were made in such haste.'

This piqued Cressida's interest. 'So after you'd all met up in the hotel reception, you didn't see much of her?'

'Oh, she barely paused for five minutes with us old fogeys, she headed straight to the ballroom. I know the dance floor is such a draw for you younger folk.' She drew a breath as Cressida made a mental note to ask Dotty if she could remember the exact times they were Charlestonning while Ottoline continued, speaking loudly and clearly. 'We hoped she'd come back and join us later in the evening, didn't we, Peter?' Then she lowered her voice again. 'Though, of course, there was that incident...'

Cressida frowned. 'What incident?'

Ottoline was staring into the middle distance and muttered, 'I do hope it didn't have anything to do with her... her mother would be most upset... but they looked very angry with each other—'

'Ottoline.' Cressida leaned forward and gently shook the older woman. 'What did you see? What incident?'

Ottoline paused, then focused her eyes on Cressida again.

'I saw Victoria having an argument. A very nasty argument.'

9

A fog of cigar smoke from Lord Beaumont's Montecristo enveloped them, and Cressida wafted it away with one hand as she let a fidgeting Ruby down from her lap. The small dog scuttled off towards the piano, but Cressida could only concentrate on Ottoline and this new lead.

'Who was she arguing with? And how nasty are we talking?' She leaned in.

'If Victoria were here, of course, I wouldn't be gossiping like this, but it does seem relevant now she's dead.' Ottoline reached into her voluminous handbag and pulled out a large white cotton handkerchief. As Ottoline dabbed the corners of her eyes with it, Cressida could make out an embroidered monogram on one of the corners.

PB.

Peter Beaumont?

Cressida pulled her eyes away, not wanting to be caught staring at it, and pressed Ottoline again. 'Please, do go on if you can. This might be very important. Who was she arguing with? And what made it look so nasty?'

Ottoline sighed and collected herself. 'It was Dora Smith-

Wallington, I believe. A friend of hers. And not someone I'd have thought she be cross with. They'd been together before the party tonight.'

'One of the West End girlfriends?'

'Yes, quite. But from our seats here, we can see right into the ballroom and I saw them, fingers pointing at each other's faces, scowls writ across brows. It was horrible, quite horrible.' Ottoline shuddered at the memory.

Cressida sat back and watched as Ruby scratched at the hamper of crackers by the piano stool, the pianist oblivious. She wondered if Ottoline's version of nasty was what others might merely deem 'unladylike'. A few cross words between friends, though not nice, was not necessarily a motive for murder. Plus, Dora Smith-Wallington, known to them all as Dodo, just didn't seem the sort. She looked back at Ottoline, who was still dabbing her eyes with Lord Beaumont's handkerchief.

'Jolly bad show this whole thing,' Lord Beaumont mumbled, with the same level of emotion he might express if his horse had come in second at the Derby.

Cressida narrowed her eyes. He was overweight, to be sure, but he definitely had the strength to deal a deadly blow to a lady. But if Ottoline was to be believed, they both had a very convenient alibi for the time of the murder. Each other.

Before Cressida could come to any more conclusions, Ottoline stood up and beckoned her to follow her over to the piano. Once there, and gracious smiles had been made to the pianist who was trundling through, rather aptly, 'In The Bleak Midwinter', Ottoline turned to Cressida once again.

'Poor Peter, he really is quite overwhelmed. I can tell.'

Cressida, though begging to differ, simply nodded as Ottoline carried on, wringing the monogrammed handkerchief in her hands as she leaned against the glossy white veneer of the piano.

'I wanted to ask you about something you said earlier. You

said you were invited to stay at Beaumont Park in the new year, is that right?'

'Yes.' Cressida felt on firmer ground. 'Victoria telephoned one morning – as I said, a couple of weeks ago, in fact – and once she'd mentioned several times how absolutely wonderful it was that I was on the telephone exchange and had my own receiver in my very own apartment and we talked about how terribly nice it is to have one's own pied-à-terre, though frightfully expensive too, she asked for my help with renovating one of the bedrooms at Beaumont Park. After a bit of toing and froing with our diaries we settled on March.'

'Hmm, I see.' Ottoline clutched her bag to her chest. 'A bedroom, you say? It's just I don't think Victoria would have still been mistress of the house come March.'

Cressida looked surprised. 'What do you mean?'

'Only that I think Victoria and Peter might not have stayed together much after Christmas. D-I-V-O—'

'*Divorce*,' whispered Cressida, before Ottoline could spell out the whole word. 'Why?'

'He'd found out about the A-F-F—'

'An affair?' Her mind went straight to what she and Dotty had been discussing back in the smoking room. It was an open secret after all. But one that Lord Beaumont had finally grown tired of ignoring?

'Yes, that American chap. Malone.'

'Clayton Malone,' Cressida said almost to herself, but Ottoline nodded fervently.

'That's him. An Italian-American, linked to all sorts of mafiosi, I'm sure. Could it have been a lovers' tiff? Him that walloped her and left her to die in the fountain?'

'It's a possibility,' agreed Cressida, thinking back to the footsteps she'd seen alongside those of Victoria's as the snow had settled around the fountain. And, of course, the strength needed to hit and drown her poor friend.

'Oh dear.' Ottoline was dabbing her eyes again. 'Poor Victoria. I know this might sound a touch over-emotional, but she was like a daughter to me, you know? I've never been blessed with children, unlike your dear mother with you, and Honoria Chatterton with her three. But when Victoria came to Beaumont Park, which is just so close to my own modest estate, well, she was a breath of fresh air. Such fun to be around. Always laughing. And so pretty. I was quite enamoured. Possibly more than Peter. So please,' she gripped Cressida's arm. 'Please do find out who killed her.'

Cressida nodded. 'I will, Ottoline, don't you worry. Thank you for all the information and I'm sorry I had to ask those questions of you and Lord Beaumont.'

Ottoline waved her hand. 'Think nothing of it. I knew you'd be the girl for the job. More discreet than that galumphing policeman in his hobnailed boots. He'll be poking his nose into everything and asking questions of people wholly unrelated, I'm sure, and leaving nothing but gossip in his wake. I hear you have his ear? Make sure you find out who did this and don't let him ruin all of our reputations with a long, drawn-out investigation.'

Cressida didn't think Andrews would like this character sketch of him, or any other officer of the law, and she wasn't sure if Ottoline was perhaps more worried about her and Lord Beaumont's reputations and quiet country life rather than really finding out who killed Victoria, but she had to admit that Ottoline had a point. The police could be intrusive and blunt. She, though not as skilled at the art of interrogation and often too hot-headed to plan ahead, could at least flit between lords and ladies and use her charm as best she could to detect the undetected.

With a quick embrace and a look at her watch, Cressida left Ottoline to look after the supposedly grieving Lord Beaumont. Dora Smith-Wallington and Clayton Malone had to be on her list to question. However nasty the disagreement was between

Dora and Victoria, it was at the very least an altercation, moments before one of them was killed. And if Clayton Malone and Victoria had been having an affair, there could be a myriad of reasons he might have wanted her dead.

Still, something bothered her about Lord Beaumont and Ottoline. Yes, they had an alibi, but despite Ottoline's protestations that he was grieving, Lord Beaumont just didn't look that upset. And her use of his monogrammed handkerchief... Despite her tears, was she actually pleased that the young, beautiful wife was now out of the way?

Cressida decided she could rule no one out yet. And she knew now who she had to concentrate on. The lover, the husband, the rival and the friend.

10

Cressida left Ottoline and Lord Beaumont, taking Ruby in one arm, much to the appreciation of the pianist, who no longer had to contend with the sound of clawing and gnawing around his piano stool. She had a host of unanswered questions rattling around her head.

'If only I hadn't drunk quite so much champagne before we found poor Victoria,' she confided in Ruby. 'I need a mind fizzing with ideas, not so much actual fizz.'

She moved through the ballroom, noticing that most of the guests either didn't know or didn't care about the death – nay, *murder* – that had occurred only a few feet from them just over an hour ago.

She spied Dotty, along with George and Alfred, sitting at a table in deep conversation. A woman with a feathered head-dress blocked her view and then, when she moved, Cressida gasped as she saw Cordelia Stirling sitting rather close to Alfred, her chin resting on one hand, her long eyelashes flutter-ing. She'd met Cordelia in the summer and had realised that her mother, Lady Stirling, had been eyeing up Alfred as a possible match.

My Alfred, she thought to herself, narrowing her eyes as she glared across the dance floor at the interloper among her friends. Then she sighed as she looked up at the elaborate Rococo clock above the stage where the band was still playing. It was almost twenty minutes to nine o'clock. On Christmas Eve, no less, and it wouldn't be long before all these party-goers would want to head back in time to ensure their stockings were hung upon their own mantelpieces.

DCI Andrews had said he could manage to keep everyone here until midnight, meaning she only had just over three hours to solve this mystery. Alfred – and Cordelia – would have to wait.

Cressida moved along the side of the room, once more skirting behind the large buffet table, this time taking a chicken skewer for Ruby and a decorated prawn for herself from the luxuriantly decadent table spread.

'Can't think on an empty stomach, Rubes,' Cressida said once she'd nabbed a further slice of cake from the very end of the table, admiring the floral display of berried holly and ivy tumbling from a marble urn as she did so. She remembered Alfred saying that Clayton Malone, Victoria's rumoured lover, was in the billiard room and she couldn't help but think what an excellent, if rather hard-to-conceal, murder weapon a billiard cue would be. Or indeed – much easier to conceal – one of the small but heavy, round red balls from the table itself.

Cressida could feel the hairs prickling up her arms. Horrid.

If he had wielded either cue or ball – or simply given Victoria a hard push – would Clayton confess? There was only one way of finding out.

Brushing the last few cake crumbs from her slice of Christmas cake off the top of Ruby's head, Cressida headed in the direction of the games room.

. . .

There was no sign of Clayton alongside the large green-baize-topped billiard table. Instead, as she pushed the door open, expecting to make out a handsome American in a white tux amid the fog of cigar and cigarette smoke, she found DCI Andrews and Sergeant Kirby, their heads together deep in conversation.

'Ah, what ho, Andrews,' Cressida said, attempting to keep the disappointment from her voice. 'Am I interrupting?'

DCI Andrews shot her a look that she chose not to interpret as 'when are you not?' Then he said, 'We've been taking some statements, Miss Fawcett. This room is relatively soundproof and far enough away from the general melee to be suitable for the conversations.'

'Gosh, well done. And I haven't been slacking either, of course. Shall we trade notes?' Cressida put Ruby down, who headed under the green baize table on the trail of some morsel or other.

Andrews sighed. After Dotty's uncle, Sir Kingsley Mountjoy, who was rather high up in the police force, had intervened back in October, the beleaguered detective had run out of reasons to bar Cressida from his investigations. Mountjoy had even insisted that DCI Andrews' immediate boss, the Metropolitan Police Commissioner, allow Cressida to help – or at least not forbid her from doing so – hence the detective chief inspector couldn't even use that as an excuse. Mountjoy had had his reasons, of course; there was his family connection to the Chattertons, but it was mostly because, despite her being an aristocratic amateur, Cressida had excellent form in sniffing out murderers with her noble old nose. But Andrews still needed to keep his investigations formal and make sure his evidence was permissible in court; two trump cards he carried with him in case her rather unorthodox methods interfered with his own. He had to admit, though, her insights were often quite useful, however frustrating that might be.

'Who have you been speaking to, Miss Fawcett?' Andrews got straight to the point.

'Me first, I see. Well, if you must know, the big cheese himself. Lord Beaumont, the Earl of Worcester. Though his friend Ottoline Spencer did most of the talking. She's a great pal of my parents, and Dotty's ma and pa too, and, believe it or not, has heard about my prowess in the detecting game and asked if I'd help find out what happened to Victoria. Of course I was going to already, but it did make me feel like a proper paid-up gumshoe. Like those chaps in Dotty's books.' Cressida shook her blonde shingled hair a little and touched her emerald silk head-band, checking it was still in place. A gumshoe, yes, but a very well-dressed one.

'Your reputation is preceding you, Miss Fawcett,' Andrews chuckled. 'You better watch out or those society invitations will dry up. Nice folk'll wonder if a body will turn up as soon as you ring the doorbell.'

'Oh.' Cressida stopped playing with her headband. 'I hadn't thought of it like that. That would be a shame. Oh well, hopefully we will get this one wrapped up before too many people in that ballroom notice anything is wrong, else we'll have an upper-class stampede on our hands. Anyway, as I'm sure Lord B and Mrs Spencer told you, they have a rather convenient alibi. But Mrs S did suggest that Victoria's lover might have reason to harm her, and she mentioned a nasty argument between Victoria and one of our other friends, which I'll look into. Otherwise, there wasn't much else to be gleaned. What have you found out, Andrews? I told you about the footprints in the snow, which your chaps could never have known about if I hadn't spotted them at the time, so tit for tat.' She placed her hands on her hips and looked expectantly at the detective, who gave another sigh before he replied.

'We've spoken to the staff positioned nearest the doors and

ascertained that no one left the building between six thirty and when we arrived, so we're sure we have a secure scene.'

'And a murderer still in our midst. That's good... I think.' Cressida rolled her eyes at her own contradiction, then carried on. 'Any more on how Victoria might have got that blow to the head? Ottoline said a lovers' tiff might have had her falling into the fountain and hurting herself that way. I admit, it's a possibility. Perhaps I was a little hasty to declare it a murder.'

'Well, Mrs Spencer may be correct, but so might you. We found a smashed champagne bottle, you see. By the fountain.'

'Oh, I missed that.' Cressida frowned. 'It's unlike me not to be able to spot a champagne bottle at fifty paces, let alone one right next to the body.'

'Don't be too hard on yourself, Miss Fawcett. It was hidden under the body. Well, under her ladyship's legs, which were hanging over the edge. We only found it when Lady Beaumont was moved,' Andrews assured her and Cressida nodded, feeling better for not missing such an obvious clue. 'We *can* say for certain that it was used in the attack.'

'Murdered by champagne? How frightful! To be so betrayed by such a friend. Ghastly.' Cressida thought longingly of all the fun evenings she'd had drinking glass after glass of the sparkling stuff instead of solving murders and muttered another quiet 'ghastly' before continuing. 'You're right though, one could suffer quite the blow from a bottle of fizz. The glass is extra strong to contain the pressure of the bubbles, or so old Boffy Boffington told me after one of the lectures he made me sit through at some Royal Society for something or other.' Cressida paused, pressed her palm against her brow and gathered her thoughts. She really was prattling on, as she always did after a glass or three. She focused again on the case. 'How do you know it was the weapon, though? And not just discarded on the ground by someone earlier in the evening? You said it was found under her legs? So perhaps she tripped over it and sort of pirouetted into the fountain, falling backwards and hitting her head.'

'Well, your own theory about the footsteps would make that unlikely,' Andrews scratched his beard. 'And, what's more, there was blood on it.'

'On the champagne bottle?' Cressida pulled a face.

'Indeed. And the size, shape and weight of the bottle matches the wound to the late countess's head. It was also broken, perhaps with the force of the attack. The neck sheered straight off. No sign of that, though, which is rather odd.'

'Well, that is interesting. And, as you say, paired with the second set of footprints, lovers' tiff or not, we can rule out an accident that didn't involve another person,' Cressida clarified to herself as much as anyone.

'Precisely. We're working on the theory that the countess was hit over the head, stunned or killed outright, and then she fell or was pushed into the fountain. The bottle dropped as she did, possibly rolling under her, with the neck still left in the murderer's hand. If she were still alive when she went into the water, she drowned before she could come round. It was definitely murder.'

Cressida had suspected all of this, but to have it confirmed by Andrews caused her to shiver. Still, she persevered. 'And will the pathologist confirm the cause of death soon; drowning or the blow to the head?'

'Ah, that's where we have a slight problem, Miss Fawcett.' Andrews hooked his thumbs into his waistcoat pockets and rocked back on his heels.

'What is it, Andrews?' Cressida was concerned. They had barely any time as it was. Of course, the police would continue investigating over Christmas, but she couldn't be part of that. Not once she was in Sussex with her parents for the rest of the festivities. And even from Andrews' point of view, it would be best to tie it all up tonight. She frowned as she looked at

Andrews. 'If spanners are to be thrown in the works like currants into a figgy pudding, it's going to make the next three hours a devil lot harder.'

'Not so much spanners as an entire toolbox, I'm afraid. The first one' – he moved along the length of the billiard table to where the large sash window of the room overlooked the street outside, before pulling the curtain back to show the thick, swirling flakes settling on the rooftops, road and railings – 'is that the snow has got worse. Dr Campbell, the pathologist, left this morning for his country house. He won't be able to get back into London now, even if he wanted to, which I should imagine he wouldn't.'

'A spanner indeed. You hinted at another one though, Andrews?'

'Well, same goes for the mortuary staff as it's Christmas Eve. Christmas Day being the biggest spanner of the lot. No one wants to work over Christmas, Miss Fawcett.'

'I see. Christmas is the proverbial glacé cherry on top of all the spanners, if you'll excuse the mixed metaphors. I suppose one can't blame those mortuary chaps. But murderers do not seem to respect the bounds of Christian holidays, Andrews, and, as you said earlier, murder trumps Christmas.'

'Does the current atmospheric condition, vis-à-vis, the snow, mean that our esteemed guests cannot exit the hotel either, sir?' Kirby piped up in his usual verbose manner from his position by the billiard table, notebook in hand and pencil poised.

Cressida shook her head and answered for the detective inspector. 'No such luck, I shouldn't think, Kirby. You see, I should imagine your mortuary staff chaps probably have to come in from the suburbs, hence the reason they can't get into central town?'

'That's correct, yes,' said Andrews, a note of admiration in his voice.

'Yet those of us here tonight who aren't staying in the hotel will only have a few streets – perhaps a cab ride – back to our London homes. I can see the sweepers out there now, look,' Cressida pointed to a well-wrapped-up man out on the street with a wide broom. 'We'll be fine going back to Kensington and Chelsea, but anyone wanting to come in from Penge or Hounslow would struggle.' She paused, then asked another question. 'Tell me then, where did Victoria's body go? And who will let us know the official cause of death and all that?' Cressida felt a warm nuzzle against her ankle and was glad that at least one vital member of the team was still on duty.

'The late Lady Beaumont is still here in the hotel. We had the staff take her down to the cellar, where at least it's cool and she'll be undisturbed.'

A shiver crept over Cressida's shoulders. To think that Victoria Beaumont was lying down in the cold, damp cellar of this grand hotel as the Christmas Eve ball raged on above her.

She would have hated missing this party, Cressida thought to herself. And her resolve was strengthened further. Her own reputation be damned. She might never be invited anywhere by anyone again, but she would find whoever did this to Victoria.

And she'd do it before carriages at midnight.

11

Cressida left the billiard room and the two policemen to continue checking through their statements. Her meeting with Andrews had been most illuminating. Victoria had been struck over the head with a champagne bottle. The thought of it horrified Cressida, but it intensified her determination to find out who could have done such a thing to her fun-loving friend. Champagne *was* meant to be fun, after all...

'Cressy,' came a voice behind her with a tap on the shoulder.

'What ho, Dot.' Cressida reached out for her friend, who gave Ruby, now back in Cressida's arms, a tickle. 'How's the party going? Have you found out anything about Victoria?'

'Rather. You remember Cordelia Stirling, don't you?' Dotty asked innocently enough.

Cressida thought back to the summer and shuddered. 'I do, yes. I saw her talking to you all. Was Alfred paying her much... Oh never mind.' Cressida shrugged and put Ruby down. She was getting heavier and heavier these days.

'Oh, Cressy. You mustn't mind about that. I have a feeling my dear brother only has eyes for you, and in any case, Cordelia is quite taken with an artist called Marcus Von Drausch. She was telling us all about his paintings. Big bowls of fruit and rather suggestive... well, he's quite avant-garde.'

'I recognise the name, and not just from the art world.' Cressida's brow furrowed. 'I'm trying to recall when I might have heard or seen it.'

'Good luck with that. I read so much that I can never place where I've seen a name. I once spent a whole weekend trying to work out which book Mitzy Horner was a character in, then I remembered I'd read about her in that week's edition of *The Bystander* as she'd won a small fortune at the Leaconfield point-to-point. Anyway, Cordelia also said that she and Victoria had been thrown together rather, despite Victoria being a bit older.'

'Thrown together? How?' Cressida asked, an eyebrow raised as the focus once again was back on that evening's grisly murder.

'Oh, you know, tea parties and the like. Something about an inheritance, though I don't know how Cordelia Stirling from Scotland and Victoria Beaumont, née Fanshawe, from Berkshire, could share an inheritance.' Dotty shrugged. 'They're not related, as far as I know. Anyway, she confirmed that Victoria and Clayton *had* been a thing. But then she said something about it being over, though I'm afraid the band played a particularly loud bit, and I couldn't hear what she said.'

'Gosh, you've done excellent work—'

'*Stirling* work you might say,' grinned Dotty, adjusting her glasses on the bridge of her nose.

Cressida rolled her eyes. But Dotty was right; she had once more proved herself to be invaluable. 'I'm going to try to hunt down Clayton now. He wasn't in the billiard room. Andrews had cleared it for his own use. Any thoughts?'

'Oh yes, Alfred just saw him. Heading for the cloakroom.'

'The cloakroom?' Cressida jolted to attention. 'Oh dear. If he's thinking of leaving and is then stopped by a burly doorman, we might have trouble before the metaphorical – and literal – revolving hotel door has stopped turning.'

'Oh, good point.' Dotty looked flummoxed.

'Find Ruby, will you,' said Cressida, taking control. 'I think she's headed for the cake table again. If she has either the fruit or the chocolate, she'll be ill for days, poor pup. In fact, try to stop her eating altogether. I know it's Christmas, but she's getting more rotund by the day. Then meet me in the lobby, which is hopefully where I will find Clayton. I've got to catch him before he decides to leave. Ottoline Spencer thought he might have something to do with it all.'

'Just because he is – or at least *was* – Victoria's lover?' Dotty queried. 'A *crime passionelle*, as they say. We'd have a devil proving if it was the case, with only his word to go on now.' Dotty shrugged.

'I don't know, Dot. It made sense when she was telling me about it, and I can't shake the memory of Victoria dancing with that blonde man, just before she was killed. I need to work out who he is too. They looked... oh I don't know – close isn't the right word, but definitely not just acquaintances.'

'I remember seeing him too. I'll ask around, see what I can find out,' Dotty reassured Cressida. 'And noted, apropos the cake table. First mission, find Ruby.'

'Thank you, Dot. I'm off to quiz Clayton, let's hope he hasn't tried to leave already. If he is the killer, the last thing we need is him alerted to the fact the police are surrounding the hotel. I've got to get to him before he works out for himself that everyone here – very much him included – is a suspect!'

Cressida, picking up her evening bag from the table she'd left it on earlier, slipped out of the ballroom and followed the high-ceilinged and ornately decorated corridors back to the cloakroom in the lobby.

The hotel lobby was as magnificent as the rest of the hotel, more so even, as it was the first and the last image people had as they came and went. It was decorated with a vastly tall Christmas tree in the middle, regaled with silver ribboned bows, candles, long glass icicles and glittered baubles. It looked magnificent and Cressida remembered the scene of Dotty and George's romantic reunion in front of it just a few hours earlier. That was back when the evening had held such promise, before everything had gone so horribly wrong. She sighed sadly.

But then, as she moved around the opulently decorated tree, she recognised Clayton Malone. He was tapping a cigarette out of a silver case, his overcoat over one arm as if he was waiting for a cab to whisk him away. Still, he wasn't running, or arguing with the police constable who was standing the other side of the revolving doors.

'Mr Malone!' she called out to him.

The man in the white tuxedo looked up, the unlit cigarette in his mouth, a hand holding a lighter hovering just in front of it. He looked at Cressida while flicking the lighter and taking a deep inhale on the cigarette, then slipped the lighter and cigarette case back into his pocket, all the while maintaining eye contact. Finally, he removed the cigarette from his lips and nodded.

'That's me, little lady. Can I ask who wants to know?'

Cressida approached him, straightening her dress and brushing off the dog hair that had caught on the green silk. She smiled at him, despite never having been referred to as a 'little lady' in her life before. She had to admit, the way he said it, with those smouldering dark brown eyes just lingering over her, she really didn't mind. She reminded herself not to get distracted, however, and turned her mind back to the reason she needed to speak to him. Victoria. She had never met this man before, or indeed been introduced, which made things all rather more awkward. And she knew DCI Andrews would be aghast if he realised she was careering straight into interviewing a suspect with no idea of what to say or how to say it. Still, she was a hothead at the best of times, so she merely fixed Clayton with what she hoped was a tantalising look of her own, smiled and stuck out her hand.

'Cressida Fawcett. Hon. How do you do?'

Clayton took her hand in his, but instead of shaking it, he brought it up to his lips for the briefest of moments. Still holding her hand, he looked her up and down and Cressida, despite steeling herself, felt a blush rising in her cheeks. No wonder Victoria had been tempted to stray from her marriage vows if this handsome man was on the cards. His hair was dark, almost black, and slicked back in a stylish way, while his well-muscled body filled every inch of his fashionable white tuxedo. His eyes were laced with the longest lashes she'd ever seen on a man and his skin was tanned – a far cry from the portly, pale and balding aristocrat who Victoria had been married to. Suffice to say, Cressida could see the attraction. As she continued talking to the handsome American she gave a silent prayer of thanks for her finishing school education and ability to maintain a straight and disinterested face, which, admittedly, was learned the summer *after* finishing school, while in Monte Carlo. Her winnings at the poker tables had in part paid for her Bugatti.

'I'm a friend of Victoria Beaumont. I believe you knew her?' She noticed Clayton Malone's face change from cocky and self-assured, flirtatious even, to worried.

'Victoria Beaumont? *Knew* her? What do you mean?' He took another deep inhale of his cigarette, but the slightest tremble to his hand meant that this time it didn't seem so suave.

Cressida paused and took a breath. This was never easy, especially not when the victim was so well known to her. 'I'm afraid I have some terrible news. She's dead, Mr Malone. She's been killed.'

'Victoria's dead?' Clayton looked genuinely shocked. He wheeled around on one heel and smacked his forehead with his hand, which made ash fall from his cigarette and cascade down the front of his tux. 'Dead you say?' He recovered himself enough to ask again.

At that moment, a gust of ice-cold air blew through the lobby, tinkling the ornaments on the large Christmas tree. Both Cressida and Clayton turned to look and saw a policeman struggling to lock shut the large revolving door at the entrance to the hotel as a squall of snowflakes rushed through it. Cressida looked from there to Clayton's face as he paused a little longer, frowning at the scene. And more especially at the policeman.

Thinking she should distract him from raising questions about the boys in blue at the door, she caught his attention again. 'Yes, I'm sorry. Do you mind if I talk to you about her?' Cressida gestured for them to sit down on one of the upholstered button-back benches the other side of the Christmas tree. Clayton pulled his gaze back from the now-locked door and Cressida noticed a bead of sweat drip slowly down the very edge of his face. He quickly wiped it away, then followed her around the large Christmas tree to the seats. This change in his demeanour, and the bead of sweat as a chill wind blew, didn't go unnoticed.

Once they were seated, she asked him again about Victoria. 'So, I'm right in assuming that she meant something to you? Can I be gauche and suggest that it was more than friendship?'

Clayton Malone looked at Cressida and then shocked her by taking both of her hands in his. She would have thought it was a come-on, but he looked so devastated. 'Yes, it was much more than friendship. Especially your English friendships,' he huffed, then collected his thoughts again. 'We met here in London and at first we tried very hard to maintain a "friendship", and it helped that I had to go back to Los Angeles for a while. But I came back to London to oversee the installation of the electric billboards at the Pavilion and ran into Victoria again. That time, we could do nothing in the face of our... our attachment. I cancelled my production plans in the States and took a suite at the Carlton so that we could see as much of each other as possible.' A smile had crept across his face, but it fell away again as he said, 'Poor Victoria. Dead. Dead?'

'Yes. And more than that. Murdered.' Cressida extracted her hands from his, noticing as she did the smallest, yet brightest, daub of red on one of his cuffs. It was unmistakably blood. She hoped he hadn't seen her eye flicker to it, readjusted her headband and flicked some of her shingled bob out of her eyes to distract him. 'Clayton, I'm truly sorry for your loss. I had no inkling that you and Victoria were so... well, attached.' A thought occurred to her. 'You must have known her better than any of us. Do you know who might have had reason to kill her?'

'Murdered?' Clayton whispered, his eyes searching Cressida's. 'Why? What would Victoria have done to anyone?' It wasn't the answer Cressida was hoping for.

'I don't know, Mr Malone. Clayton. I was rather hoping you might be able to tell me. I know her husband, the Earl of Worcester is here, but—'

'Peter's here? Tonight? I... I had no idea.' Clayton's gaze moved away from Cressida and he looked over her shoulder to the lobby, his eyes darting across the room, scanning the almost empty room fervently.

'What is it, Clayton?' Cressida couldn't help but think that Clayton, large and muscled as he was, looked more worried than even a man with a guilty conscience about having an affair with another man's wife should look.

'If Peter's here then...' He patted the overcoat that was still draped over one of his arms. He shook his head. 'No, no... but could he? He wouldn't, but if he read...?'

'Clayton,' Cressida said sharply. 'What are you talking about?'

Clayton met her gaze. 'An inconvenience, an embarrassment perhaps – but that was before I knew Victoria was dead.'

'I still don't understand. Has Lord Beaumont read something of yours? Something embarrassing?'

'Some things that belonged to Victoria. Some things that might give him a motive.'

'A motive? Do you think Lord Beaumont might have killed his wife?'

Clayton fixed his eyes on her and Cressida could see a dampness around the lashes on his lower lid. 'Perhaps. You see, moments before you introduced yourself to me, I discovered something.'

'What?' Cressida leaned in, and almost took Clayton's hand as she could see the tremble in it again. Whatever had happened, he was properly shaken by it now.

He looked at her and shook his head, biting his lip and then picking a bit of stray tobacco from the corner of his mouth. 'They're gone,' he whispered. 'They're gone.'

12

'They? Who are you talking about?' Cressida pushed, frustrated at the lack of sense that Clayton was making. And with the clock ticking down to midnight, this confusion was more than just frustrating; it was crucial he got to the point.

'Not a who, but a what.' Clayton dashed his cigarette out in one of the ashtrays by the banquette seating and grasped his overcoat with both hands. He lifted it up in front of him and then checked every pocket thoroughly again. He yelped and pulled his hand away suddenly and Cressida noticed yet more blood appear on his otherwise pristine white sleeve. However keen she was to find out about whatever it was that he had been talking about, she couldn't ignore his bloodied sleeve any longer.

'Clayton, what is that?'

'Ouch is what it is.' He sucked on a bleeding finger, and using his other hand gingerly pulled the offending sharp object from his pocket. It was bottle-green glass, with a hole the size of a cork in it. Cressida gasped as she realised what it was.

'That's a broken neck from a champagne bottle.' She watched as he carefully placed it down on the leather uphol-stery between them. No wonder it had cut him, the glass was sliced and looked sharp as a knife, yet it was also jagged in places and, of course, covered in blood. She looked up at him just as he too pulled his eyes away from the horrible piece of old bottle. 'Why was it in your pocket?'

'I... I don't know,' he stammered. 'I felt something in there as I was handed the coat by the attendant...' He pointed to the broken glass and then, with the tremble still in his hands, pulled the silver cigarette case out of his tuxedo pocket, took out another cigarette and lit it. Once he'd inhaled, Cressida continued.

'The blood on your cuff, was it from that broken glass?'

'I guess.' He answered, more confidently this time: 'You just saw me get attacked by it.'

Cressida narrowed her eyes and took him in. Charming, to be sure, an actor as well as a producer, perhaps, but was he a liar? 'Clayton, you and I both know you had blood on your cuff before you came across that ghastly thing just now.'

His shoulders sagged. 'You're right, I did. I'm sorry. But I don't know where it came from, truly. I'd been looking through my pockets, so maybe I briefly touched it before?'

Cressida straightened herself, pulling her height up through her spine, and she fixed him with her gaze. She had to carefully observe how he would react to her next question. 'Clayton Malone, did you kill Victoria Beaumont? Did you smash her over the head with that champagne bottle?'

'No, I would never... I did not kill her.' His reply was emphatic. Then he looked up and met Cressida's eye. 'Why would I? What possible reason would I have?'

'You admit you were in a relationship, but I heard it was over. Perhaps it was for Victoria, but not for you...' Cressida trailed off as Clayton started shaking his head.

'I didn't, I promise. I did not kill Victoria Beaumont.'

'Tell me then, with what might be her blood very literally

on your cuff and perhaps metaphorically on your hands, what proves that you didn't kill her?'

'Her letters.' Clayton turned to face Cressida. 'Victoria's letters to me. I was going to return them to her tonight. Hence the coat.' He raised his arm that was still host to the folded coat.

'Letters? From Victoria to you?' Cressida thought for a moment, then gasped. 'Oh, love letters!'

Clayton sighed. 'That's right. And you're right in saying that Victoria and I had enjoyed a very, well, fruitful, relationship. Until recently, that is.' He rubbed his palms down his thighs as if wiping the sweat from them. Then he turned to look at Cressida and once more fixed her eyes with his own. 'I called it off, you know? We had to end it. And I hadn't seen her for a month or so. She'd gone back up to Worcestershire and that house of her husband's. But I wanted to do the honourable thing and return the letters she'd sent to me over the course of our relationship.'

Cressida nodded. She understood this. It was one of those unsaid rules at the end of a romance, be it clandestine or innocent, to return any love letters sent once the dalliance was called off. Love letters in the wrong hands could be incriminating, especially to a woman. Clayton's insistence on returning Victoria's to her showed him to be a man of honour – if you could call a man who had affairs with married women honourable at all. She appraised him again as he was sitting there, his coat next to him, a lost look on his face.

'I think I understand now,' Cressida continued. 'You think the letters were stolen from you tonight and they might have contained something that could have given someone a motive. Something in them might have got Victoria killed?'

'That's just it. I can't remember what was in them exactly. But some of the things she said to me...' He looked uncomfortable as he trailed off.

'Such as?' Cressida was desperately trying to build up an

image in her mind of both Victoria and Clayton's, and Victoria and Lord Beaumont's relationships. 'Was there anything in there about Peter, her husband?'

Clayton took a deep breath and then exhaled. 'Yes, yes there would be. She was always complaining about him. Fat oaf, grumpy curmudgeon, boring old fart... theirs wasn't a happy marriage.'

'No, I suppose not, not if she felt like that.' Cressida suddenly felt incredibly sorry for Victoria. Not just because she'd been murdered, but her friend had been living the very life that she so feared. She'd married for money and security, social position and no doubt to please her family who'd brokered the whole affair in the very first few weeks of her debutante season, much to the chagrin of other mothers vying for the same privileges for their daughters, yet Victoria must have despised every minute of it. 'So you think she might have got herself into hot water if Lord B had found out about your letters?'

Clayton shrugged. 'I guess so. He didn't know about the affair. I broke it off before he could find out—'

'Are you sure?' Cressida remembered Ottoline's insistence that Victoria was heading for divorce, as Lord Beaumont knew all about her extramarital adventures.

'Pretty sure, yeah. Victoria and I ran in very different circles to her husband. He was never in London and unless someone had written to him... But I don't think anyone we would have seen while we were together would do that.'

Cressida shrugged. 'It's not the most watertight of assumptions – in fact, it's as leaky as a bottomless bucket. I've heard that Lord Beaumont did know – as did his friend, Mrs Spencer.'

Clayton shrugged. 'In that case, there's your answer to who might have wanted her dead. Maybe those letters rubbed salt in the wound. Look, I felt bad for her, and Victoria was one hell of a girl, you know? Fun. And I loved her. But she couldn't be with me, not while she was married to him. It broke my heart, but I needed someone I could take to the theatre, a partner, someone free and single I could be photographed with, you know? I had to call it off with her before Buster Keaton's latest film premiered. It's one of mine, you see, and it hit big at home State-side last month. Of course I'd have loved Victoria by my side, but I was worried her husband might find out if we carried on as we had been. There'd been some close calls with the tabloid press in restaurants and the like.'

'So you ended your affair before Buster Keaton's latest film came out. Was that *Go West*? That premiered...'

'November. In Los Angeles. But I was coming here for the publicity tour, so we'd arranged to meet tonight, one last time. Exchange letters, and say our last goodbye. I didn't know Peter would be here tonight. If he found my letters on her, or the ones from her to me that have been taken, well, it's motive, isn't it?'

Cressida bit her lip. Clayton was right. It would be motive. A jealous husband who had discovered proof of his wife's affair. Victoria's letters, stolen from this man's coat pocket, could have pushed the usually complacent lord over the edge.

But how would he have known the letters were there?

And were they just evidence of the affair, or did they reveal something else?

13

Cressida had an idea. Carefully wrapping the broken bottle neck in Clayton's handkerchief, she put it into her bag for safe-keeping – and then got up, and with a wave of her hand gestured for Clayton to stay where he was. She walked quickly across the lobby, past the magnificent Christmas tree with its sparkling glass ornaments, to the cloakroom. Like many hotels, restaurants and nightclubs, the cloakroom was accessed by the guests via a hatch-like opening, with the attendant positioned behind a counter, able to close down the hatch at the end of the night.

'Merry Christmas, miss,' the young lad who was behind the hatch greeted Cressida. He was dressed in the hotel livery: a smart midnight-blue waistcoat underneath a full tailcoat. The hotel logo was embroidered in gold on his lapel and adorning it was a corsage of sprigged holly and a Christmas rose. If he'd been on the door, he'd have a top hat too, but, instead, his short, fair hair was slicked back neatly. He passed the palm of his hand over it as he carried on talking to Cressida. 'Do you have your ticket, miss? If so, I'll fetch your coat, though I have to warn you – and nothing to be alarmed about, I hear – but the police have asked for no one to leave yet, miss.'

Cressida nodded, she knew this was the plan; but she was concerned that if too many party-goers decided to get their coats before midnight, and the ruse of telling them it was because of a bit of light thievery and the odd rogue vagrant didn't hold, then they might have trouble brewing.

'I don't have a ticket. Not on me anyway,' Cressida lied, knowing full well that her ticket was safely stored in her emerald-green-silk handbag, which was now tucked under her arm, broken bottle neck within. But she didn't want her coat, she just wanted an excuse to talk to this young man. And, luckily, he was happy to explain the situation to her.

'I'm afraid I can't release a coat without a ticket, miss, that's hotel policy.' He looked genuinely distressed about it. 'You'll have to come back after the holidays, miss, or at the very end of the evening, and describe it to Mr Butcher, the manager, who can then use his judgement.' The word 'judgement' was pronounced with the same solemnity as if Mr Butcher was King Solomon himself.

'I understand.' Cressida smiled at him. 'I suppose so many of the coats are worth a lot of money and contain valuable items – wallets and the like.' She leaned on the counter, hoping it made her look tipsy, rather than inquisitive. And, to be fair, having sunk most of a bottle of champagne before the discovery of the body, she *was* a little tipsy.

'All coats are left at the owner's own risk, miss.' The cloakroom assistant frowned.

'Yes, of course. But you're here all the time, aren't you? Guarding them?'

'Yes, miss, of course.' He paused and looked at his fingernails. Then he mumbled, 'Unless the hatch is closed, miss, when I'm called away and the like.'

'Calls of nature,' Cressida volunteered and the cloakroom attendant blushed.

'Something like that, miss. And after most of the guests have arrived, I can close the hatch if I'm needed elsewhere.'

'And when you do, is there any way into the cloakroom?' Cressida leaned a little further on the counter. There had to have been a way for somebody to get into Clayton's coat pocket, if she were to believe his story about someone else planting the champagne bottle neck there.

'Well no, miss, not technically. The door at the back should be locked, but we don't always. Seeing as it's a nice crowd here usually. And Mr Butcher said the staff doors were locked because of the vagrants and what-have-yous, so I tend to just pull it to.'

'I see. So have you closed the hatch and left the kiosk tonight?'

The young lad's blush turned a deeper shade of pink and he scuffed a shoe against the underside of the counter. 'Well, now you mention it, yes. We had such a rush from six o'clock and we were quite full. I had to ask Mr Butcher if there were more hangers, but as he was dealing with the sad events, I had quite a time finding him. So yes, I suppose it was about seven o'clock, or soon after, that I closed the hatch.'

'What time did you get back here and open up again?'

He thought about this, silently adding up minutes with his lips moving. Finally he said, 'about ten minutes before eight o'clock, miss.'

Cressida worked out that that gave about forty or fifty minutes around the time of the murder. Time enough for the killer to rifle through pockets in any case.

'And you saw no one hanging around here when you got back?' She tried to narrow timings down further. If this young lad had actually seen anyone leaving the kiosk then that would help hugely. Her hopes were dashed though.

'I'm sorry, miss, no I didn't. Had to open the door by myself, though my arms were full of coat hangers.'

Cressida could quite imagine it and nodded in acceptance of his answer. 'Thank you... I'm sorry, I didn't catch your name?'

'Stanley, miss.'

'Thank you, Stanley. You've been a great help. And more so perhaps if you now close this hatch for a little while longer. The police are here and the last thing we want is guests at the ball deciding they want to leave early while they investigate. Just in case they were a witness to something important. Can you do that for me, Stanley? Close the hatch?'

'Of course, miss, if that's what Mr Butcher and the police want me to do. Oh, and miss?'

'Yes?' Cressida, who had pulled away from the kiosk, turned back to answer him.

'Did you want your coat, miss?'

'No, Stanley. Not right now. I've got a murderer to catch first.'

She walked away from the cloakroom, piecing together what she'd found out from Stanley. So someone *could* have got into that cloakroom, gone through Clayton's coat pockets and planted the champagne bottle neck, and more importantly, while there, have found Victoria's letters. Letters that, by the sound of it, contained some pretty juicy information.

14

'Miss Fawcett!' the American voice called after her. Cressida had quite forgotten the forlorn ex-lover of poor Victoria who she'd left sitting on a banquette in the lobby. 'Wait!'

'Oh, Clayton. Apologies.' Cressida turned around to see him striding towards her, adjusting the cuffs of his tuxedo as he did. A few of the lit candles on the Christmas tree flickered as he went past them. When he was next to her, she continued. 'I was just quizzing the cloakroom boy. Hoped he might have seen someone enter and go through all the coats. I must admit, saying it out loud like that, it does seem strange for someone to risk being caught searching coats for letters when they couldn't have known they were on your person tonight. Or, indeed, not on your person, but in your pocket. You really should have kept such personal things under better protection, Clayton,' she admonished him.

'There were a lot of them,' he explained, looking exasperated. Then he smoothed down the front of his tuxedo. 'And not much room in this cut for a bulge of letters.'

'A bulge, you say,' Cressida gulped, trying not to look at the taut fabric around Clayton's biceps. 'I see.' She took a deep inhale and was about to take her leave of the American when he caught her by the arm and looked her square in the eye.

'Miss Fawcett,' his voice was softer, conspiratorial even. 'There's another reason I think Peter Beaumont might have had something to do with Victoria's death.'

Cressida looked at where his hand was touching the bare skin of her elbow just above her satin evening glove, and he removed it. A shiver passed across her shoulders as he did so and he offered her his coat. She shook her head, but gripped her elbows as she crossed her arms. 'What is it, what makes you so sure Lord B's our man?'

'Look, I didn't think of this before. You rather blew me away with the news about Victoria and it shocked me. But waiting over there just now, a few minutes alone to think about her, well, I remembered something from the letters. Among the pillow talk.'

Cressida looked wide-eyed at Clayton and nodded in encouragement for him to continue.

'Victoria was bored at Beaumont Park. I flatter myself that she liked coming to London to see me, but she had other reasons for leaving the countryside.'

'Bored? Well, we all get a little bored of country walks and whist drives. Why would he kill her for being bored? It's hardly a motive.'

'Bored was only part of it.' Clayton looked to the ceiling for inspiration. 'Let's say she was nervous too.'

'Nervous? Why?' Cressida felt a shiver again and longed to be back in the warmth of the ballroom, but what Clayton had to say was of the utmost interest.

'When she was bored, she started exploring the library, at first for something vaguely interesting to read, but there was nothing more recent than Dickens in there. And you know Vix, she hated the classics...' His mirth turned to sadness as the realisation of Victoria's death sank in. He lit another cigarette and

Cressida let him have this space. After a deep drag on it, he continued. 'So, looking for something more salacious to read, she slipped into Lord B's study one day. And, by jingo, did she find something more interesting than Dickens.'

'What? What did she find?' Cressida kept her arms crossed but leaned in closer, intrigued.

'Papers, er, coroners' reports, post-mortems and the like. All relating to the death of the previous Countess of Worcester.'

'Lord Beaumont's first wife?'

'Yes. And she got it into her head that she hadn't died naturally. If you see what I'm driving at.'

Cressida was as frozen to the spot as a fondant snowman on a frosted cake. 'I do, yes,' she managed to answer as Clayton moved an inch or two closer. 'You're saying that in those letters Victoria wrote to you, she accused her husband of murdering his first wife.'

Clayton nodded. 'That's right. And more than that. Other goings-on had been unsettling her. Visits from a certain friend of the family—'

'Ottoline,' murmured Cressida, but Clayton shrugged and carried on.

'Finding out about the first Lady Beaumont only made things worse and she felt nervous staying for long periods at Beaumont Park. It worried me when I ended it and although we could never be together long term, at least seeing me gave her a reason to come up with an excuse as to why she needed to leave Beaumont Park every so often.'

Cressida nodded, then jumped as she felt something scratch against the inch or two of bare arm between her long satin evening gloves and her dress's sleeve.

'Only me,' Dotty said as Cressida realised the scratch had come from the shoulder epaulette of Dotty's beaded dress.

'Oh, Dotty,' she raised a hand to her chest. 'You surprised me.'

'Cressy, I found Ruby. Saved her from the cake table. And Sir Walter Cardew's feet – he really is the worst dancer.' Dotty handed over Ruby to her friend and then looked expectantly up at Clayton. Cressida took the hint.

'Clayton Malone, Lady Dotty Chatterton; Dot, this is Clayton Malone.' She raised an eyebrow and Clayton gave Dotty a small bow.

'Look here, this has been a bad, bad evening,' he said. 'I take it we can't leave the hotel for now.' Cressida nodded in affirmation. 'But I need a drink. Excuse me, ladies. If you need me, I'll be in the Belgrave Bar.'

'One last thing, Clayton.' It was Cressida's turn to clutch his arm as he turned to leave. 'I hate to ask you this, but where were you between seven o'clock and seven thirty this evening?'

Clayton straightened his jacket and fiddled with his cuffs before fixing Cressida with a look. 'You think I did it? After all I've told you?'

Cressida shrugged. 'I don't know, Clayton. Please just answer the question.'

Clayton looked at his feet. 'I saw Victoria earlier this evening. Six, or soon after. Half past perhaps. We agreed to meet again out here, at about quarter to nine. That's why I was getting my coat. So I could give her the letters.'

'And at seven or thereabouts?' Cressida pressed.

'We kept our distance, hard though that was. I went to shoot some pool in the billiard room, but I was by myself.'

'Alfred saw you in there,' Dotty said, then she narrowed her gaze and added, 'but only briefly. Not all the time.'

'I was there. I promise. I had to keep out of Victoria's way. Not because her husband was here – I didn't know he was – but because it was hard for me.' He looked down at the ground again. 'So, you see, I don't have an alibi, as they say, for her time of death, but I didn't do it. And I do now need that drink.'

Cressida and Dotty bade him goodbye and then, after a long

exhale with an exaggerated cheek puff, Cressida told her friend everything she had learned.

'So, I think I have to go and see Lord B again, Dot. If there's even a possibility that he had anything to do with his first wife's death, and if that was mentioned in those letters of Victoria's, it places him rather in the frame.'

'I thought she died of the dropsy?' Dotty remarked. 'The first Countess of Worcester. Or was that the Countess of Leicester? One of them definitely had it.'

Cressida frowned. She was pleased of Ruby's warmth against the thin fabric of her evening dress and she could feel her small dog's heart pumping away thirteen to the dozen. She looked at Dotty, who was admiring the tree, her neck strained up as she took in the sparkling star at the very top of it. 'Where are Alfred and George?'

'The Belgrave Bar. Perhaps they'll get more out of Clayton if he joins them there,' Dotty said matter-of-factly. 'And Lord Beaumont is still in the piano lobby. Shall we go and see him? It's all sounding rather rum, this letter business. Whether he killed the first countess or not, those missing letters might give him motive.'

'Yes, exactly. Lead on, Dot. Let's go and see him. Clayton may have just spun me a story worthy of Hollywood itself, but I understand his need for a drink. There's nothing I'd like more right now than the stiffest of gins—'

'Or a cheeky eggnog,' mused Dotty.

'Quite. Wine, mulled or otherwise... simply delicious. But I have to keep a clear head. It's twenty minutes past nine already. The evening is slipping away with us. And with it, any chance of finding out who killed Victoria Beaumont.'

15

As the two young ladies traded confidences, the candles on the Christmas tree flickered, their light twinkling off the baubles and glass icicles on every bough. Even the architraves above each doorway were festooned with garlands of fir branches, each one studded with baubles and Christmas roses. It was towards one of these doors that the two young women now headed.

'So, you see, it's not the easiest of mysteries to unravel,' Cressida sighed.

'And by midnight, too,' added Dot, though she then paled as she uttered the next few words. 'Or perhaps, worse, before the killer strikes again?'

They both stopped in their tracks at the thought.

'You mean it might not have been that Victoria was the target? Crêpes indeed.' Cressida squeezed Dotty's arm tightly, shifting Ruby in her arms as she did so. 'You're right, Dot. Until we know why Victoria was murdered, we don't know what the killer might be thinking.'

'I hope there's not some maniac on the loose hunting down society heiresses.'

'The chance would be slim. But it's not one I want to take. We have to find out who killed Victoria, and why.' She looked at her watch again and huffed out an exasperated breath. 'And look at the time. We've just lost another couple of minutes. And barely two and a half hours left to solve this case, Dot.'

'Well, you've spoken to Lord B and Clayton, and I agree, there's some interesting snippets from both of them. I still can't believe that bit about Lord B's first wife. Or that Clayton had that nasty bottle neck in his pocket. That's rather fishy. As is Mrs Spencer's rather well-timed – if you'll excuse the pun – discovery of Lord B's watch.'

'Yes, though it does give them an unshakeable alibi.'

'Hmm,' agreed Dotty, though she frowned as she did so.

The two of them passed through the ballroom once again, this time with Ruby held tightly to Cressida's chest, lest she squirm away and go in hunt of any morsels under the tables. Then Dotty pulled on Cressida's arm and as Cressida looked at her, she motioned with her eyebrows and a slight incline of her head towards a group of men standing at the edge of the ballroom.

'What is it, Dot? Are you quite well?' Cressida looked concerned as Dotty jerked her head again, with such force this time that her velvet headband became dislodged.

'Oh, darn it. Not even doing the shimmy made that happen,' she said, pushing the velvet ribbon straighter onto her head. She adjusted her glasses. 'What I was trying to say, though I've managed to be as subtle as a reindeer on a roof, is that's him, over there.' This time, she pointed to the same group of young men. One of them was leaning against the wall, a martini glass in hand, but the liquid within was bright green and Cressida found herself pulling a face at the thought of drinking it. One of the other men had his back to him, but he was bald on top, the bright lights dancing off his shiny pate. But the other man, *him*, she recognised. He was blonde, and although he leaned against the dado rail, she could see that he was tall. Definitely the right height to match the man who'd she'd seen dancing with Victoria earlier in the night.

'Aha,' she whispered to Dot. 'Bravo, Dot, you found our mystery man. Anything on him? Would jolly old Saint Nick have him on his nice or naughty list?'

'I'm not sure,' Dotty squinted through her thick glasses. 'But strap in, as I have the gen on him. He's a doctor. But not your average general practice sort of chap.'

'Harley Street?' Cressida asked, referring to the smart road just north of Oxford Street where many consultants and doctors had their surgeries.

'Well, yes. But more than that, he's a...' Dotty blushed and lowered her voice, 'a gynaecologist.'

'Oh, I see.' Cressida stared over to where the handsome young doctor was still leaning louchely against the wall with his friends. A group of giggling ladies walked past him and he stopped and greeted them, kissing at least one of their hands before they passed through the garlanded door next to him to the piano lobby.

'Fancy a potted history of gynaecology, Cressida?' Dotty asked hopefully. 'Strangely enough, I was reading about Sir William Blair-Bell recently and it led me down quite the rabbit hole, if you'll excuse the term.'

'Go on then, but make it snappy, Dot. Tick-tock and all that.' Cressida tapped her watch.

'Fine, well, that chap over there is a Dr Hart. I believe he's a Harley Street consultant who deals exclusively with the obstetrics side of gynaecology.'

'Babies and whatnot,' Cressida chipped in.

'Exactly. Of course, historically that whole thing was dealt with by midwives and before that, by wise women and village healers, until some twisted-minded fellow came up with the idea of forceps—'

'Makes one blanch at the thought.' Cressida shivered.

'Quite. Well, once "machinery" was involved, it became a man's game, and now we have men like Sir William Blair-Bell and Dr Hart over there who want to start a whole new college dedicated to obstetrics and gynaecology. Apparently it is causing quite the uproar in medical circles. The Royal Society of Physicians are dead against it and the same goes for the surgeons, they're up in arms too.'

'How do you know all of this, Dotty?' Cressida, who had been so transfixed by Dotty's brief history lesson, had all but forgotten how pressing time was.

Dotty fiddled with her handbag clasp and cleared her throat. 'Well, actually it was Cousin Lulu who said that if I thought George was going to propose, I should prepare myself—'

'Quite right, nails clean ready for the ring, a little speech prepared rather than a spontaneously screeched yes—'

'No, Cressy, not that sort of preparation. *Marriage* preparation.' Dotty wiggled her eyebrows.

'Oh.' Cressida caught on. 'I see. The higher bookshelves. So that's why you started reading about Sir William—'

'Well, I started reading a very informative text called *The Karmic Sugar* or something, but then I decided it was all in all too graphic and sought out a more academic tome. Sir William Blair-Bell has penned plenty of essays, and long story not that short, that's one of his protégés. Dr Hart of Harley Street.'

'Gosh, you really did complete your mission, Dotty. And picked up some very interesting facts along the way.'

'Yes, did you know a leg can bend—'

'Not now, Dot.' Cressida raised her eyebrows at her friend, who nodded, saying 'quite, quite, yes, of course,' and then she looked over to Dr Hart. 'The question, of course, is why would Victoria know him quite so well?'

'They were just dancing, don't you think?' Dotty said, but Cressida shook her head.

'No. I was rather attentively looking, what with her having just danced with Alfred, and I'm sure I noticed a frisson between them.'

'A frisson?'

'Yes, a tension. Victoria went from laughing and being playful with Alfred, to quite intensely glaring at Dr Hart. It wasn't that she didn't know him as well as she knows Alf, quite the opposite. It was almost as if she knew him better, but maybe not for the best, if you know what I mean.' Cressida bit her lip as she sought out the memories.

As she did so, Dr Hart shook the hand of one of the men he was talking to, then slapped him on the back as they walked across the ballroom and out of one of the doors that led to a corridor towards the billiard room. Cressida sighed. Her chance to quiz him might have just disappeared, but she would speak to him. She had to. He was one of the last people to have inter-acted with Victoria, and clearly something had passed between them. Something significant enough to cause the normally bright and beaming young woman to frown most intensely.

Might he know who wanted Victoria dead?

Or might he – for some as-yet-unknown reason – be the one who did it?

Gravitating towards where Dr Hart had been standing, Cressida and Dotty found themselves next to the door to the piano lobby. Cressida peered through and saw Lord Beaumont, the Earl of Worcester, still sitting there, large and leg-splayed, on an elegant Rococo-style upholstered sofa.

Cressida worried for the poor piece of furniture's spindly legs, not to mention the earl's waistcoat that looked strained at best. Ottoline Spencer was perched next to him, and, like a mother bird, attempting to feed him pieces of Christmas cake, which he occasionally accepted and sometimes batted away.

Ottoline was the first to notice Cressida and Dotty as they approached and put down the small side plate of cake and waved at them. 'Have you discovered anything yet, Cressida? Any reason as to why poor Victoria was' – she lowered her voice, though there was no way the earl couldn't hear her – 'murdered.'

'Nothing concrete yet,' admitted Cressida. 'But there is something I'd like to talk to Lord Beaumont about—'

'Mrs Spencer, do you remember me?' Dotty leaned across Cressida and reached out a hand to the older woman. 'Dorothy Chatterton. Lady Honoria's daughter.'

'Oh, yes, yes...' Ottoline briefly clasped Dotty's hand and then picked up the cake plate again and turned to Dotty, ready for a gossip. Cressida raised the quickest of eyebrows at her friend in thanks for allowing her two minutes to speak to the – twice – widowed man alone.

'Lord Beaumont. I'm so very sorry for your loss again. I really am trying to find out who would kill Victoria, and why. Do you have any inkling?'

'Kill Victoria?' He looked as if Cressida was bringing up the subject for the first time. 'No clue. Not one. Nice young thing she was. Got along very well in the end. Loved her well enough, you know, and her me, I think. Always reminded me of this lovely Labrador I had as a child. Bouncy. She died too of course. Terrible really, terrible.' He knocked some crumbs off his waistcoat that had become lodged on the horizontal shelf of his stomach.

Cressida couldn't help but think that, to Lord Beaumont, his pretty young wife dying was more of an inconvenience than a truly tragic event. But then, he still wasn't exactly coming across as a killer. She took her opportunity while Dotty regaled Ottoline about all the comings and goings at Chatterton Court, her family's rather grand mansion, to quiz the earl further.

'It must bring back awful memories for you too. You see, I heard your previous wife died, and I am sorry to hear that, too.'

'Yes, rum luck I have with wives, it seems.' The earl wiped his forehead with his handkerchief again and Cressida noted the monogram, PB, on it.

'Very rum luck, if that's what it comes down to, yes.' Cressida, who was now perched on one of the elegant armchairs next to the groaning, delicate sofa, pushed a little further. 'If you don't mind me asking, how did the first Lady Beaumont die?'

'Hmm, Caroline? Nice young thing. Never strong though. Couldn't hold the reins well enough, fell off her horse.'

A form of dropsy then, Cressida thought to herself, if dropping off one's horse counted. She had to admit she preferred the leather seat in her little red Bugatti to the saddled kind, but still, a riding accident couldn't really count as murder, could it?

Cressida could see Dotty flailing for conversation, so hurried up with her final question to the earl.

'Was it Victoria's idea to come to town for the festive season?'

'Indeed it was her idea. I couldn't think of anything worse. All these people and these tight clothes. What's wrong with suet pudding, a bit of wassailing and an old-fashioned quiet Christmas? But good old Otty said she'd come along too, make it more palatable for an old boy like me. Terrible gout, you know, can hardly stand, let alone dance. Isn't that right, Otty?'

It was all that was needed to wrest Ottoline from Dotty's conversation about detective fiction and all the novels she'd been reading recently and she leaned over Lord Beaumont and spoke to Cressida.

'Yes, horrible for you, but Victoria did insist. Said you should see that doctor about your gout and see some of society before you get too stuck in your ways. And I agree, bless her. Beaumont Park is beautiful, of course, but we have so little local society, you see. Mostly farmers nearby, except yours truly and the Bingley-Corbetts. I can quite see why Victoria wanted to come to town for her appointments and to see some friends. Oh, that it's come to this though,' she shook her head and seemed in need of a handkerchief again.

Cressida slumped a little in her chair. She looked over at Lord Beaumont. *A fine match*, was all the mothers could say when Victoria had accepted his proposal. Mrs Smith-Wallington had even retired to her bed for a week in a fit of pique that her own daughter had been overlooked. Yet Lord Beaumont seemed not at all fazed that his wife was dead. Of course, the upper-classes – of his generation at any rate – barely ever showed any emotion.

I should imagine he's the type to shed more of a tear over an injured spaniel or a bad Test cricket score than any relationship or loved one, Cressida thought. But, as Ottoline said, 'that it's come to this' – Victoria dead. The second Countess of Worcester to end up so in just a few years, it seemed.

But as Cressida looked over the corporeal figure of the earl once more, she noticed the fine watch chain strung through his waistcoat, attached once again to the gold watch in the pocket. Lord Beaumont and Ottoline had an alibi for the time of the murder; each other. And even if she didn't believe their alibi, the pair, him especially, looked the furthest from murderous than one could imagine. She didn't know much about gout, but had heard that it was very painful. No wonder Lord Beaumont hadn't moved from that sofa for most of the night.

There wasn't much more Cressida could glean from the stuffy old lord, and Ottoline only seemed useful for local tittle-tattle or melodrama. She had to go to the next stop on her Christmas list of suspects: Dora Smith-Wallington. Hadn't Ottoline mentioned that she'd seen her arguing with Victoria – and it all getting quite nasty – shortly before she was murdered?

'Lord Beaumont, Ottoline, will you excuse us?' Cressida

pulled Dotty away from where she'd just taken a piece of Christmas cake from Ottoline's proffered plate.

'What is it, Cressy?' Dotty asked, brushing some cake crumbs from her lap as she stood up.

'Ottoline mentioned that Dora Smith-Wallington and Victoria had a nasty argument. I think she might have meant unladylike rather than truly nasty—'

'I can't imagine Dodo getting "nasty". She has an amazing self-possession to her. Quite a talent when it comes to grinning and bearing it. She won festival queen three years in a row at the Lower Minchampton Fruit and Produce Show, which is lovely, of course, but she had to ride the tractor-pulled float, which she did with enormous dignity and grace, bearing in mind the amount of straw and live sheep she had on there.'

'And a rather magnificent headdress, I seem to remember too. Made her look like the Archbishop of Canterbury, but you're right, she bore it very well.' Cressida and Dotty were lost for a moment in reminiscences, before Cressida snapped back into action. 'Anyway, Dot, no time for this dawdling. Nasty or not, Dodo argued with Victoria in the very last moments of her life.'

Dotty looked appalled. 'You make it sound as if Dodo could have done it – killed her, I mean.'

Cressida shrugged, though she felt a shiver cross her shoulders as she replied, 'Well, what if she did?'

16

Cressida looked at her watch. Thirty-five minutes past nine. The evening was getting away with her, and not in the way she had imagined. She'd envisaged lots of dancing, plenty of mince pies and some wonderfully festive cocktails, but instead they'd got a very puzzling murder case. She slipped an arm through one of Dotty's, letting Ruby trot alongside them as they left the piano bar and headed back into the ballroom.

'Thank you for keeping Ottoline busy while I quizzed Lord B.' Cressida squeezed Dotty's arm. 'What did you find to talk about?'

'Oh, this and that. I mentioned what we got up to Winchester in the autumn and she seemed very interested. Said it was why she'd asked you to investigate tonight. So I told her we'd *both* found the detection very rewarding, if a little grisly at times. Then we started talking about those detective novels I like. She's a fan of them too. Better than magazines, she said, for when you want something entertaining. We agreed to swap a few copies via Mama when they next see each other. Oh look, there's George!' Dotty waved at where Alfred and George were standing by the buffet table and received an enthusiastic wave

back from George. Seeing Alfred quickly shove three melba
toasts smothered in pâté into his mouth so that he could wave
too made Cressida smile.

'What ho, chaps,' Alfred said, once he'd swallowed, though
really he said it to Cressida as Dotty had been swept up into
George's arms in a giggle and lowered to a dance-floor dip in
time with the music.

Cressida grinned at her friend and then looked back at
Alfred. A crumb of toast with a blob of pâté on it was stuck to
his lapel and she gently flicked it off and straightened the front
of his tailcoat. 'There you go, Alfred, all sorted. Handsome as
ever,' Cressida said as an unmistakable blush rose on Alfred's
cheeks and there was a straightening of his shoulders and
expanding of his chest.

Cressida sighed to herself. She had imagined perhaps one or
two other things happening among the mince pie eating and
cocktail drinking, things that a bunch of mistletoe and two
willing pairs of lips might have helped with. She ushered the
thoughts out of her mind. She had no time now to dally around
daydreaming. She had to find out who killed Victoria, and fast.

'We've been to see Lord Beaumont and Clayton Malone,'
she said, filling in Alfred. 'And while Ottoline Spencer thought
it might have been Clayton, and he had a pretty damning piece
of evidence on him, *he* gave some very convincing reasons as to
why it could be Lord Beaumont. Oh, and Dotty found out all
sorts of interesting things about a doctor who I saw Victoria
dancing with just before she was killed, but, so far, I can't see he
had much of a motive. So we're back at square one. And I
thought you two were in the Belgrave Bar? We rather hoped
you might be getting even more out of Clayton. He headed
there just after we spoke to him.'

'Must have just missed him. We had a stiff drink and a man-
to-brother sort of chat.' Alfred raised his eyes. 'Reminded him
that more often than not, in these sorts of things, it's the

husband who's the murderer. Or at least so say Dot's detective fiction books. She's acquired a vast amount, you know, and left them lying around the house and as I've been hanging around the old place a bit and not fancying the Trollopes in the library, well, they've been as easy a read as anything. I must say I enjoyed that Freeman Wills Crofts chap with that devilishly good book *The Cask*. And Mrs Christie, she's churning them out faster than Dot can lay her hands on them!'

Cressida chuckled. Back in October, Dotty's knowledge of how detectives worked, having read and loved several 'whodunnits', had been rather important in clinching the case. That Alfred was now inhaling them too was a surprise, but a welcome one. Still, she thought the implication that George would ever do anything of the sort, rather harsh.

'I hope you didn't scare your soon-to-be-brother-in-law off? Poor Dot would never forgive you! And I wouldn't blame George if he slipped you a cursed amulet or something for your trouble.' She stood with her arms on her hips, but both of them were smiling through their mock outrage.

'You can rest assured, Cressy, I did no scaring off. Though I've learned from her run-in with that dratted Bartleby chap not to just take a fellow at face value. I'm afraid I might have drilled him a bit more than necessary, but we've come out of it friends and I'm sure she's made the right choice this time.' Alfred pulled his pipe out of his pocket and clenched it between his teeth in a form of QED.

'Good. Though, to be fair, anyone who doesn't take pot-shots at pugs from a bathroom window would be a better bet for darling Dot. Basil really was a nasty piece of work.' Cressida could think of other things to call him, but it was, after all, Christmas and she decided that limited goodwill should be shown to all men, even Basil Bartleby.

'On that we agree – I mean the Basil bit. Though I'm not averse to the odd pot-shot out the bathroom window.' Alfred raised an eyebrow while holding the bowl of his pipe as he spoke. 'Squirrels only though.'

Cressida shook her head. 'Fine. Well, at least I know you wouldn't take a pot-shot at me, or worse, Ruby. I'm still sure Basil did. And on purpose too.' She crossed her arms and looked peeved, then, with a glance at the clock above the band, who were still playing enthusiastically to a dancing crowd, she brought the subject back to the murder. 'And speaking of murderous fiancés – or in this case husbands – I think you're wrong, Alfred. Lord B has an alibi, as does Ottoline. And although I don't think I've witnessed anyone less bothered by the death of a dear spouse, I also don't think he could muster the energy – or defy his gout enough – to actually whack someone over the head with a champagne bottle.'

'I don't know, Cressy,' Alfred said, though his back teeth were clamped down on his pipe. 'If reading Dot's books has taught us anything...' He took his pipe out of his mouth and with a certain mirth added, 'Well, it's always the person you least suspect.'

Cressida rolled her eyes and batted away Alfred's suggestion.

Dotty, who had extracted herself from George's arms and the dance floor, caught the end of this and put in her two pennies' worth. 'Speaking of least suspecting someone, don't forget the letters that Clayton told you about. If Lord B had found those, he'd have motive indeed.'

'Yes, but the alibi, Dot... he and Ottoline were in the piano bar when Victoria was murdered.'

'I'm afraid he's number one suspect,' Alfred said, cutting a large slice of terrine for himself. 'Just had a word with Andrews, who's now off to speak to the kitchen staff. Said the jealous husband motive is usually the strongest, especially when there's history with previous wives dying in suspicious circumstances too.'

'She fell off her horse, Alfred. I don't think there's anything too suspicious about that.'

'But who was with her, eh?' Alfred bit down on his terrine.

'I don't know. Do you?' Cressida waited for him to swallow.

'No, but it's the sort of question detectives ask, isn't it?' Suddenly, a little barrel-shaped dog lunged at Alfred's ankle, biting down hard on his trouser leg. 'Ow-oooh.' Alfred jumped back, but Ruby attacked again. 'Cressy, what's up with her?' Alfred looked pained, more at the fact that Cressida's precious hound was obviously not a fan of his, than any actual hurt.

Cressida laughed and stooped down to pick her up. After a quick admonishment, she explained. 'Well, it could be that she took offence to you suggesting that her mistress wasn't a very good detective...' Alfred opened and closed his mouth, but Cressida continued, 'But more likely she saw that lovely chunk of terrine that fell from your slice of toast and landed on your shoe!' She pointed at the ground and Alfred kicked his ankle around. A large chunk of pork flew off his shiny patent dress shoe. Ruby's blinking eyes followed its trajectory with a keen intensity.

'Ah, I see...' Alfred looked up at Cressida, abashed. 'Sorry, Ruby. I did think we were friends. But leg-attacking pugs aside, what did you mean earlier by damning evidence on that Clayton chap?'

'I was with him when he checked his coat pockets looking for a set of love letters written by Victoria to him. But they were gone, and, instead, lurking in one of his pockets was the top from the champagne bottle that was used to kill Victoria.'

'By jingo.' Alfred took a step back. 'Were you quite safe with him, Cressy? And what did he say about it?'

'Just that he'd never seen it before and had no idea how it got into his coat. Despite the fact I saw some blood on his cuff before he seemingly found the bottle neck for the first time.

Said it was likely he'd not realised he'd touched it when he'd first checked his pockets before I'd arrived.'

'And do you believe him?' Alfred scratched his chin, then jammed his pipe back into his jaw. Cressida knew he did this when he was about to think about something. Well, this was something to think on indeed.

'Yes, in a way I do. He could have been leading me up the garden path, but he looked genuinely upset that Victoria was dead, murdered even... unlike... hmm.' Cressida held her temples with her fingers as she thought. 'Oh, it's like a dozen fraying threads and I can't work out which one I should pull. Or not. Something doesn't quite add up and I can't quite grasp it.'

'Keep pulling that thread, old girl, you'll get there,' assured Alfred, and Cressida smiled at him.

'Anyway, Alfred, none of this is getting us anywhere. I hope Andrews is having more luck with the kitchen staff. Meanwhile, I must find Dora Smith-Wallington. Have you seen her?'

'Old Dodo? Yes, she's over there. Why?'

'Well, because she might know why Victoria was killed. They had an argument, it seems. She might even be the killer herself.' Cressida picked up Ruby, who was still licking her lips from the tasty bit of terrine.

'Dodo? Festival queen at the Lower Minchampton Flower Festival no fewer than three times. What on earth could she have been arguing with Victoria about? A rivalry over the daisy crown?'

Cressida raised an eyebrow at Alfred, but he kept talking.

'Don't get me wrong, Dodo is nice enough. I think old mater has even suggested she could be a good match for—'

'Not for you?' Cressida said, then slapped her hand over her mouth as Alfred looked quizzically at her.

'No, not for me. For John,' Alfred replied and Cressida could feel her shoulders relaxing at the mention of the youngest of the Chatterton siblings, Alfred and Dotty's brother John.

Alfred continued, 'But you know John, more intent on getting letters after his name, which is a laudable calling, of course, than finding a wife. He said something about not needing that sort of distraction and wasn't Dodo pining for someone else anyway and headed back to Cambridge.'

'Well, I better put my best thinking cap on, channel some of John's focus, and go and see her. And find out if this argument of theirs was over something more deadly than a daisy crown.'

17

Dora, who was sitting primly at one of the tables in the ballroom, as the dancing and music carried on closer to the stage, had never given anyone reason to suspect she wasn't as pure of heart as she appeared. And it wasn't just that she had the grace to ride on the tractor float at the local flower festival, she was just the sort of person you could trust not to bludgeon another young lady to death. At school, Dora had been the reliable one, the one who would keep watch on the other girls' clothes as they skinny-dipped in the pond, or played lookout for a games mistress while the others discovered the illicit treat of smoking French cigarettes behind the tennis pavilion. She'd also been inconsolable when her pet guinea pig had been found dead in a drainpipe outside the girls' dormitory, with no one ever owning up as to how the poor creature had made it all the way there from the pet shed.

Cressida spied her, recognising her mousey brown hair that was elegantly, if simply, swept up into a chignon. She wore a navy blue beaded dress with a matching hairband that had a stunning peacock feather sticking out of it.

'What ho, Dodo,' Cressida said, sitting herself down next to her. She let Ruby scamper off, fairly confident it was back in the direction of the buffet table.

'Oh, hello, Cressy, how are you? Thought I saw you tearing up the dance floor earlier. Time for a break?' Dora asked and Cressida wondered if she even knew of Victoria's death.

'Yes, knees aren't what they were,' laughed Cressida, then she frowned. Sadly, what she had to discuss was no laughing matter. 'Dodo, did you hear about Victoria?'

'Beaumont or Dudley-Ryder?'

'Beaumont. Though what Victoria Dudley-Ryder did at the Criterion last week was quite something.'

'I gather the chef was not impressed,' agreed Dora. 'And I hear the duck press is now off the menu.'

'Quite. Anyway, did you hear about Victoria Beaumont – Fanshawe as was?'

Dora cocked her head on one side and looked at Cressida. 'What do you mean?' she replied. 'What have you heard?'

'Well, that she's dead, Dodo.' Cressida couldn't skirt around the matter any longer.

'Dead?' Dora looked as shocked as Clayton had been. 'Dead? But I...' Her hand had raised to her neckline and she clasped her very nice rope of pearls. She looked white as milk and Cressida could detect a tremble in her pearl-clutching fist, while her other hand scrunched the skirt of her evening dress. The blue silk under the beading crumpled in her fist.

'You had an argument with her earlier, I hear,' Cressida said softly. She didn't want it to come across as accusatory.

'Hmm, oh, yes I did. I feel terrible about it now. I mean, I felt terrible about it at the time too, you know me, never one to say boo to the proverbial goose, but, gosh, now that she's dead. Oh dear.' Dora shook her head, but stopped gripping her dress and pearls. 'Oh dear, oh dear.'

'What is it, Dodo?' Cressida pushed a little more.

'Nothing really, I just feel simply rotten that the last words we exchanged were in anger. Not like me at all, is it?' She reached into her handbag. 'Do you mind if I smoke? I really shouldn't, it's my one vice.'

'Not at all.' Cressida paused while Dora pulled out a silver cigarette case from her handbag, which was navy blue silk with elaborate beading to match her dress and fastened with an exquisite marquisette clasp. She took out a pre-rolled cigarette and placed it into a long, silver cigarette holder, then lit it from one of the candles on the table. Once she'd inhaled, and elegantly brought the cigarette and its holder to rest, Cressida spoke again. 'I thought it was odd when I heard,' Cressida agreed. 'What caused it? Had she said something to rile you?'

'Well yes, of course. One doesn't fly into a fury for no reason.' The way she said it was more matter-of-fact rather than sarcastic and Cressida had to agree; one didn't.

'So what was the reason?' Cressida asked again.

Dora blushed. 'Oh, I feel terrible about it, of course. All seems so trivial now. But it did seem awfully important at the time. And what with her already married and me still on the shelf, well, I suppose that struck a nerve.'

'What did she say?' Cressida leaned in, cupping a hand around her ear to combat the noise from the band, who had just struck up another dance tune.

Dora winced a little against the brass instrumental too, but sweetly shrugged and then fetched her evening bag once again from the chair next to her. She opened it and pulled out a dance card. The little folded-over card had a tassel running through it with a tiny pencil attached.

Cressida smiled in recognition. She'd picked one up from the lobby too as she'd shown her ticket and entered the ballroom – everyone had, even though they had become rather outmoded in the years since the Great War had ended. The point of them was to secure a partner for a dance or two throughout the night, but with most of the room doing variations of the Charleston and other jazz-led dances, the whole thing had become rather redundant.

'Right at the start of the evening, before the more modern music started, the orchestra was playing the classics – a Viennese waltz and a foxtrot,' said Dora. 'For the oldies, you know, but I still enjoy them too. There's nothing more romantic than gliding around the dance floor with a wonderful dancer – it's all I dream of. And, as you know, I'm very much still available for that sort of thing. My dance card is literally and metaphorically empty.' She showed Cressida the unwritten-on card to emphasise the matter, before taking another long inhale on her cigarette through its stiletto-long holder. 'So, I asked that nice American chap – Clayton, isn't it? I asked him if he'd like a dance, and Victoria was suddenly on me like a rash, telling me to get my own chap and leave hers well alone.'

Cressida furrowed her brow. 'But Victoria and Clayton had parted company. As lovers, that is. A few months ago.'

'Well, that's what I thought!' Dora brought her hand back to her chest, splaying her fingers across the beads. Cressida noticed that a line or two of the fine beading was missing, though it was hard to see as there were so many. 'You know me, I'd never muscle in on another girl's chap. But I'd heard about them parting ways, as you do, and I'd seen them having a tête-a-tête.'

'Where? Here?' Cressida asked, further intrigued.

'Yes, I was perched on a chair just over there, minding my own business, and they happened to bump into each other right in front of me. Completely ignored me, of course, but the awkward thing was that if I'd have stood up, they'd no doubt notice me and think I'd then been eavesdropping, which I wasn't. I couldn't hear what they were saying, of course, but they certainly did not look like a pair of star-crossed lovers.'

'I see...' Cressida nodded.

'So I took from that, as one would, that their affair was over.

And I thought he might like to get to know an unmarried woman for once. Did you know I was festival queen again this year? You'd think someone would have spotted me on that float and made advances. Anyway, once Victoria had biffed off, I did stand up and say "what ho" to Clayton, and he did look awfully interested, actually. We'd just got onto me telling him about the Lower Minchampton Flower Festival when Victoria stormed back over to the both of us, for some reason showed Clayton the inside of her handbag, and then Clayton skulked off, which put me right off him, and she had a real humdinger at me.'

'Sorry, Dodo, how awkward for you. And with her now dead, not a nice way to leave things at all.'

'Men are so rarely worth it, are they, Cressy?' Though her eyes narrowed as she surveyed the dance floor, Dora's question was purely rhetorical and Cressida joined her in gazing into the middle distance of the ballroom for a moment or two. In many ways, she was right. Was having a man by your side worth losing not just your independence, but also a friend?

Luckily for Cressida, apart from Cordelia Stirling, who didn't really count as a chum, as far as she knew, Alfred wasn't involved with anyone else. She momentarily let herself hope that it was because she was the only one he had eyes for, but then gulped the feelings back down. She really had to concentrate on Victoria's murder tonight. Alfred she could think about until the proverbial cows came home, over Christmas. She turned back to Dora.

'Did you see where Victoria went after your argument?'

'She went straight over there,' Dora pointed to the bar. 'And drank a whole martini down in one. I was quite impressed. I haven't seen anyone do that since the time you managed it at Corky Shortcliffe's coming-out party. That time you did that thing with the silver nutcrackers. Humphrey Blofeld's eyes watered for weeks—'

'Oh yes, I remember.' Cressida cut her short with a raise of the eyebrow. 'So Victoria drank a very strong cocktail and then what?'

'Then she stormed off in the direction of the powder room, I think.'

'And you stayed here?' Cressida was edging towards the alibi.

'Yes. I was a bit shocked, to be honest. Having been shouted at for doing absolutely nothing wrong. So after she'd gone, I asked the waiter for a large sherry, and then went to join those chaps over there.' Dora pointed at a set of well-dressed and amiable-looking gentlemen and ladies at another table. 'That's my cousin Simon and his friends. I don't want to crash them too much; they've got their own gang from Cambridge and I'm not such a blue-stocking, but they were a nice distraction while I was bit upset. Plus, my feet were hurting.' She reached a hand down to rub her heel and slip on and off what looked like quite ordinary court shoes, then she carried on. 'I've just come back over here to look all available again. As nice as Simon is, it's frowned upon to marry one's own cousin these days.' She gave a nervous sort of laugh, which Cressida took to mean that perhaps she'd maybe thought of doing just that.

It was clear Dora didn't have much of a motive, and if Cressida wanted to go and quiz Dora's cousin Simon, he would no doubt confirm that she had a whole lot of alibi. Still, she'd given Cressida a good idea of Victoria's movements after she'd seen her dancing with the doctor and she'd been good for one other very important piece of hitherto missing information.

Victoria had had a handbag. Why she had opened it in front of Clayton, Cressida didn't know, and it seemed Dora had no idea either. Perhaps she was proving to Clayton that she had his letters inside and the exchange could take place as soon as he retrieved hers?

Still, the fact that really stood out to Cressida was this: even though Victoria had the bag when she was here in the ballroom, arguing with both Clayton and Dora, by the time she was murdered by the fountain, it was gone. Cressida may not have spotted the concealed champagne bottle, but there's no way she wouldn't have noticed a pretty evening bag. It hadn't been by the fountain when Victoria was killed. But it was somewhere in the hotel, and perhaps it contained some answers.

18

A crescendo of a trumpet solo and a loud cheer from the crowd on the dance floor as confetti fountains exploded caught Cressida's attention. Her eye was drawn again to the clock on the wall above the stage, and through the fluttering pieces of silver and gold paper, she noted the time with a shiver. It was almost ten o'clock. That meant only two hours before most of the guests left the hotel. There wasn't a minute to waste.

Cressida said cheerio to Dora, leaving the seat next to her for a nice young man to hop into, and headed towards the buffet table, her sixth sense telling her Ruby wouldn't be far from it. As she approached it, eyeing up one of the marzipan fruits for herself, just to keep body and soul together, a young woman crossed her path. A certain young woman who was the last person she really wanted to see. Cressida plastered on a smile and greeted her with aplomb though.

'Hello, Cordelia, how are you?' Cressida ventured, though she had a hunch that the younger woman wasn't too impressed with her. She'd been to stay in Cordelia's family home, Ayrton Castle, in the summer and had discovered quite a few grim things while there – including the identity of a murderer. And

Cressida had most likely been the reason for Alfred leading poor Cordelia on in order to get information from her. All while Cordelia herself was setting her sights on being the future Lady Chatterton.

Tonight, Cordelia seemed unchanged since the summer, with long blonde hair that was neatly tied up in an elegant swirl and set off by her primrose-yellow satin evening dress. She'd daringly gone for a new-season fashion design that finished just on the knee, with a sparkling fringe down to her shins. Cressida remembered that Dotty said something about Cordelia and Victoria being thrown together due to an inheritance – which made no sense whatsoever – so despite her awkwardness in seeing her, Cressida decided she really should hear what Cordelia knew about their dead friend. If they had been thrown together so much in society, Cordelia might be one of the few people here who would have noticed Victoria was missing. She was proved right when Cordelia asked her that very question.

'Have you seen Vix Beaumont? She was meant to meet us all back in here, escaping from that husband of hers, but no one can find her.'

Cressida's heart fell. Once again, she had to tell someone that a person they knew and cared about was dead. She wondered who would tell the rest of Victoria's family – her mother and father, the sister who was due to start her debutante year next summer. They'd be a family waking up to the most terrible news on Christmas morning, assuming the policeman's knock hadn't come already. Cressida felt ill at the thought of it.

'Hello, did you hear me, Cressida? Have you seen Vix?' Cordelia spoke to her again and Cressida blinked back a tear or two that had sprung up as she thought about those who loved Victoria. And whether Victoria had been a close friend or just a well-known acquaintance of Cordelia's, Cressida was quite sure she herself was the last person from whom the younger woman would want to hear the news. But alas, fall to her it did. She braced herself and told her.

'I'm so sorry, Cordelia, I have the most awful news. Victoria's been killed.'

'Killed?' Cordelia took a step back and almost knocked over a waiter who was skilfully carrying a tray of cocktails to a table. Cressida mouthed an apology to him.

'Yes, I'm so sorry. She's dead.'

'But I just saw her. Not long ago. Killed? What happened?' Cordelia looked about her and found a chair nearby and collapsed into it.

'She was murdered.' Cressida sat herself down next to Cordelia, placing her handbag on the white tablecloth of the table next to them.

'Murdered?' She said the word as if it were foreign to her and she was unsure of the sound of it. 'How?'

'She was hit over the head and then drowned in the fountain outside,' Cressida replied as she stretched out a hand to comfort the younger woman, but Cordelia flinched her arm away. A sneer came across her face.

'And I suppose you're trying to solve it?' Cordelia pinned her with a gaze, her light blue eyes looking rather fierce in the glittering lights of the ballroom.

Despite Cressida's jealousy over anyone who might be a rival for Alfred's affections, she fought back with kindness. 'Yes. And I'm so sorry for your loss. Dotty said that you and Victoria were friends.'

This approach took the wind out of Cordelia's sails rather. She uncrossed her arms and fiddled with a diamond bracelet. Then, to her surprise, Cressida noticed her bottom lip start to tremble. 'Thank you. And I'm sorry for snapping. Mama says I shouldn't have been cross with you this summer when you left and took Lord Delafield with you.' She cocked her head and looked behind Cressida to where Alfred was peeling a prawn at the buffet table, and instead of eating it, handing it down to Cressida's podgy little dog at his feet. 'It was my first time being match-made and I didn't really know what to expect.'

'That's all right. And it's never fun having a murder in the house either, I can quite understand.' Cressida paused.

'Mama still has nightmares about it all. She and Pa are at loggerheads, she wanting to sell Ayrton Castle and he determined to stay. Thank heavens they sent me down to London for the winter to stay with Aunt Phoebe and Uncle Claude. Though I feel like I've brought the Scottish weather with me.'

'You have indeed,' Cressida agreed, pleased that although the weather outside was frosty, Cordelia had started to thaw. She knew she had to get some answers though, so despite wishing she could continue with the pleasantries, she asked, 'Cordelia, did you know much about Victoria's relationship with Clayton Malone?'

The corners of Cordelia's mouth turned down and she glanced around her. 'How did you know about that?' Her voice was almost a whisper.

Cressida almost laughed in shock, though stifled it well. 'I think *everyone* knew about it... we all suspected, at any rate. But look, I've just been speaking to him and he was as shocked as you. He was only seeing her tonight to return some letters.'

'That's true.' Cordelia didn't seem to mind talking about it now she knew it wasn't a secret. 'Victoria confided in me about Clayton, about how grateful she was that he had agreed to return the letters, as she was going to do for him. But then she was the one who broke it off, and, of course, you can't rely on a man being so gentlemanly.'

'Hold on a tick, did you say Victoria was the one to break it off? Clayton told me that he had done the right thing and ended it with her before they got caught. Said he wanted someone on his arm who he *could* be seen with.'

'Oh, did he?' Cordelia's interest piqued. She pulled the tops of her lemon-yellow satin evening gloves higher up her arm and adjusted the diamond bracelet on her wrist.

'Yes, he did. So are you sure Victoria was the one to break it off with him?'

Cordelia, who'd got lost in her own reverie, looked up at Cressida. 'Hmm? Oh yes. She told me all about it. Said she had to break it off with Clayton as it wasn't fair on Lord Beaumont. She said her husband knew nothing about it. Oh dear, do you think he did? Do you think he mur—'

'I don't know. Let's not leap to any conclusions. I think he might have known, but he has an alibi.'

Cordelia frowned. 'Hmm. Victoria was convinced he had no idea. She said he only reads the *Racing Post* and *Country Life*. So he'd never have seen her and Clayton in the gossip rags – he simply wouldn't have read them.'

'I fear he might have done. Ottoline Spencer, a family friend of theirs—'

'Oh her.' Cordelia rolled her eyes. 'Whatever she says, don't believe a word of it. Victoria was convinced she was after Lord B for herself.'

'Ottoline does seem very fond of Lord Beaumont, it's true,' Cressida thought out loud. 'But as she hinted to me, in not a very subtle way, Lord B might have been on the brink of divorcing Victoria anyway. Hence why I'm sure he knew about her affair.'

'Divorce? Hells bells. Poor Victoria. She never mentioned that. No wonder she was so keen to give him an heir. Then he would never have divorced her. That's all these old codgers really want. A little version of themselves to send off to boarding school and then the army and eventually inherit.'

Cressida thought of the gynaecologist, the man who had been dancing with Victoria shortly before her death. Could she have been seeing the doctor for that very reason; she needed an heir for her husband to fend off divorce?

'It's rather rude of me to ask, but did you know how Victoria was getting on with that? Was Lord B able to, well, get the job done?' Cressida hoped she hadn't shocked the young debutante. This was all rather salacious talk for such young and inexperienced ears.

But Cordelia surprised her. Perhaps she'd also had a cousin who'd encouraged her to look up some top-shelf books. 'Well, Clayton couldn't help, could he? Hence why she had to break it off with him. There'd be every chance that the baby would look like him and then everyone would spot a mile off that the baby wasn't Lord Beaumont's. Such different men!'

'Yes, with Victoria and Lord B both having blue eyes, and Clayton having such dark brown ones and darker colouring... yes, I see. There'd be a risk the baby would look like him.'

'Yes, exactly,' Cordelia nodded. 'I hear Victoria had been advised on some course of action and was seeing a doctor about it.'

'A Dr Hart, was it?' Cressida asked, lining up the pieces of this mystery in her mind like a patterned wallpaper.

'That's right. She was a patient of his. Though rumour has it that she'd had quite the falling out with him. I suppose patient and doctor boundaries can blur when the treatment is quite so personal. It must be desperate not to be able to have a baby when your marriage and whole way of life depends on it. Dr Hart has a great following apparently, though I haven't really looked into it, for obvious reasons.'

'I'm sure you'll find someone soon,' Cressida reassured her, though regretted her glibness when a roll of Cordelia's eyes reminded her of the faux pas at Ayrton with Alfred. Her Alfred.

Cordelia, however, then crossed her arms and cocked her head on one side. Cressida couldn't help but glance to where Alfred was standing. Ruby tucked under one arm, as he chatted to George and Dotty. She quickly returned focus to Cordelia and smiled in a sort of apology. Cordelia had, after all, set her sights on him herself this summer.

'Oh, don't worry, I've found someone rather dashing, and although Mama isn't one hundred per cent on board, he has got prospects,' Cordelia said, as if describing a business venture.

'Oh yes, I remember. Dotty mentioned it. An artist is he? Marcus Von Drausch? I know the name, but I can't place it.'

'From *The Tatler* perhaps?' Cordelia said, her chin raised as she paused to let the mention of the well-known society magazine take effect. 'There was a rather fun piece about him in November's issue. He's quite avant-garde and all that, but from a good family of course.'

'Of course. Austrian?' Cressida asked vaguely, thinking she should really be cracking on with finding this Dr Hart chap and discovering more about his falling out with Victoria. However, she realised it would be rude of her leave the conversation with Cordelia so abruptly, especially as bridges were being built after the summer's catastrophic visit to the young socialite's family castle.

'Far back on his father's side, I think. His mother's a Beaumont though,' Cordelia had carried on, and suddenly had all of Cressida's attention again.

'A Beaumont? Like Victoria?'

'Well, like Lord Beaumont really. Marcus is Lord Beaumont's nephew. Hence his prospects. Obviously, one hopes he'll become ludicrously famous for his amazing talent with a paintbrush, but that's not the only thing. And now poor Victoria's dead... oh gosh.' Cordelia stopped abruptly. And Cressida remembered what Dotty had said. *Cordelia and Victoria had been thrown together due to an inheritance...* Marcus was Lord Beaumont's heir! She mentioned this to Cordelia, who nodded, then carried on. 'I suppose you think this gives him a motive, but he's not the murdering sort. And nor am I, before you ask.'

'But the estate and titles are entailed on him – so he is the heir while Lord Beaumont has no children of his own? And with Victoria gone, it's looking less and less likely that it'll happen,' Cressida mused out loud, much to Cordelia's annoyance.

'Don't go thinking he'd do anything of the sort. Anyway, we've been here in the ballroom all night.' She looked around but couldn't find her beau. 'Well, he's around somewhere, and I've been here all night too.'

Cressida reached out and squeezed Cordelia's shoulder. 'Don't worry, I won't go accusing Marcus of doing anything. Now, I must go, I need a word with that Dr Hart.'

This mollified Cordelia, who shrugged off Cressida's reassuring hand and headed back into the party. Cressida's other hand had been behind her back the whole time, however, and as Cordelia disappeared into the crowd, she gently uncrossed her fingers. She couldn't promise that she wouldn't accuse the heir to Lord Beaumont's estate of murder. She couldn't promise anything at all.

19

With thoughts of heirs and inheritances dancing through her mind, Cressida left the ballroom. She needed space away from the loud music and excitable dancers and she wanted to share her thoughts with DCI Andrews. No doubt Andrews would be interested in what she'd found out. Not much of it made sense to her at the moment, but there was something reassuring about him and Kirby writing down the things she said, as if by doing so it cemented the ideas further in her mind too.

Like painting swatches on a wall to see which colour works best, she mused, as she followed the ornately decorated corridor from the ballroom to the billiard room, hoping that DCI Andrews had returned there. She reached the heavy, painted wood door and pressed her palm against it, ready to push. But just before she did, she leaned in and allowed her ear to cup against the door. She could hear voices. One she very much recognised as being Andrews, the other, she wasn't so sure. But what she was sure of was that there was no way she could garner anything from out here. The big band music from the ballroom, horns and trumpets blaring, filled every sound wave.

She would have to go into the room if she wanted to find out who was in there with Andrews.

Knowing full well that her presence would effectively end any interview that was going on, she paused again before opening the door. She knew Andrews was planning on inter-viewing the staff to check that no one had absconded in the small window of time between Victoria's murder and Dotty's scream. But he was last seen heading towards the kitchens to do that, and he'd interview those staff – the chefs and busboys – there, not here in the billiard room. He must be interviewing a fellow guest. A suspect.

Cressida bit the inside of her cheek. Usually, she'd find something to hide behind so she could listen in, or a convenient pipe that could carry the sound of voices from a police cell to another, or even fashion some sort of listening device like her friend Minty O'Hare used to do at boarding school to spy on matron. She sighed. None of these options was available to her. While she pondered what to do, she heard footsteps on the other side of the door, then she leapt back as the large brass knob started to turn.

She quickly turned and positioned herself a few steps away from the door next to a narrow console table on the other side of the corridor. She tried to look as nonchalant as possible, pretending to admire a Christmas display of silver-painted twigs, holly, ivy and hellebores while actually looking in the gilt-framed mirror that hung above it. In the reflection, she saw the door to the billiard room fully open and Clayton Malone walk out. Cressida watched as he strode off down the corridor in the opposite direction, and taking this as an invitation to enter the billiard room, she took a deep breath and strode in.

'What ho, Andrews, I see you brought Mr Malone in for questioning. I must say I thought he gave quite a compelling case for his innocence, if not much to go on alibi-wise.'

'Miss Fawcett, I... How did you know all of that already? No, don't tell me, you've already spoken to him and—'

'And know all about the letters, the affair and his side of the story regarding their break-up, yes.'

Andrews shook his head in bewilderment. 'Then you'll know as much as I do. These letters going missing is a bit convenient for him, don't you think?'

Cressida frowned. She'd never doubted his word on them being stolen. 'You're suggesting he might have just hidden them? And made up a story about them being stolen so as to move suspicion onto someone else?' Cressida thought back to how genuine he'd seemed while Andrews continued.

'Exactly. To distract from the fact he found that incriminating champagne bottle neck in his coat pocket.'

Cressida's frown eased as another thought came to her. 'I don't think that would be the case, actually, Andrews. He started telling me, in a rather frustratingly roundabout way, about the letters *before* he came upon the bottle neck in his pocket. And, what's more, I have it here.' Cressida opened her bag and carefully removed the sharp-edged broken bottle neck from her bag.

Andrews's eyes widened at the sight of it. 'Miss Fawcett, what have I told you about tampering with evidence?' He ran a hand over his brow as he flicked a handkerchief out of his pocket and carefully picked up the bottle neck to look at it.

'I know, and sorry. But would you rather I left it with him? If he's the murderer, then he could have got rid of it and it would only have been on my word that it ever existed. So, I took it off him just in case. Thought you might want it for one of those little brown evidence bags of yours. Any fingerprints of his on it can be explained away, though, as I saw him touch it myself when he found it in his pocket.'

'Another convenience for him,' said Andrews, with a quick raise of an eyebrow.

'I suppose so. He seemed genuinely shocked when he found it, but I did notice some blood on his cuff before I saw him touch it. And, as I'm sure you know having quizzed him too, he doesn't exactly have an alibi.' Cressida thought out loud. 'But the thing is, Andrews, he also doesn't have the best motive. He told me he had ended it with Victoria and they were exchanging their love letters in as amicable way as possible.' She paused, having found herself pacing the room alongside the large baize-covered table. She turned and looked back to where Andrews was leaning on the green, his hands splayed. She continued, 'Although Cordelia Stirling – do you remember her? From Ayrton Castle? Pretty, I suppose, though unremarkable...' Cressida pushed some of her own blonde hair back behind her ear. 'Anyway, Cordelia said that it was Victoria who ended the affair with Clayton—'

'Giving him a motive,' Andrews said, as if Cressida had given him the final piece of the puzzle.

Cressida, however, wasn't so sure. 'I'm not denying it's a strong case against him, but there are other motives to consider too. What if those letters were stolen, as Clayton says? Apparently there were some quite damning things said in them about Lord Beaumont – things he wouldn't want getting out. Suggestions over the death of his first wife, for one. Apparently she fell off a horse while out riding, but Clayton seemed to think that Victoria had uncovered something about it all, and it didn't look good. And did you know that if Lord B dies without an heir, the whole estate goes to some artist called Marcus Von Drausch? Who, conveniently, is in Cordelia Stirling's sights.'

Andrews waved his hand to slow her down. 'Hold on, Miss Fawcett. What's all this about heirs?'

'Well, if it isn't the spouse – and I'm not saying it isn't, but with a gouty leg and a decent alibi, it's looking unlikely. And it isn't the lover, which, again, it could be, but let's give Clayton the benefit of the doubt for now. Then isn't a murder like this usually something to do with money? And the biggest motive of the lot in that case belongs to Marcus Von Drausch, the heir apparent, as long as Lord Beaumont doesn't have a child. And with a nice young wife by his side, that was still a possibility. She was even seeing a Harley Street specialist about it.'

'Who told you that?' Andrews quizzed her.

'Cordelia Stirling...' Cressida gasped and then screwed up her brow as she thought. 'Oh, by Jove. Of course, Cordelia could have told Marcus about Victoria's trips to the Harley Street specialist and that there was every chance now that Lord Beaumont would have his own heir. But with Victoria gone, and the ageing, gouty lord, simply becoming less of a prospect for husband-finding-mamas the world over, well, Marcus is then set to inherit everything – Beaumont Park, the estate, the titles.'

'I see.' Andrews flicked open his notebook and made a few notes, then added, 'But wouldn't he kill Lord Beaumont instead? Why risk killing the wife? There's every chance Lord Beaumont could marry again, especially if he's determined to sire an heir.'

Cressida couldn't help but pull a face that showed her distaste for the prospect of whichever poor bride that dubious honour might fall to. Then her look turned to one of deeper concern. 'Not if the current Lady Beaumont *was* pregnant. If that were the case, then the unborn child would be the heir.'

'I see. And was she?' Andrews asked.

'I suppose we won't know for sure until the post-mortem. But I'll keep digging and see if I can find out. Her doctor, Dr Hart, is here tonight. He's next on my list of people to quiz.'

'And it looks like Kirby and I might have to find this Von Drausch chap. He's here tonight, I take it?'

'Apparently so. Cordelia said he was. And Andrews...?'

'Yes?' The policeman looked cautiously at Cressida, a note of resignation in his voice.

'Could I possibly sit in on the interview? I'd so love to hear what Marcus has to say.'

'You're not thinking of interviewing him yourself?' Andrews raised an eyebrow.

Cressida crossed her arms. 'I'd be happy to, but for two reasons. One, I'd like to see how he responds to a proper copper asking him all about the inheritance—'

'Fair point,' Andrews conceded. 'I can see it would be strange to have a civilian poke her nose into his financials. And the second?'

Cressida looked at her watch. 'The second, Andrews, is that we have less than two hours left tonight before the ball is over and the hunt for Victoria's killer gets even harder. We have to work together. We have to find out who killed her.'

20

DCI Andrews sighed and stood back from the table as he considered her proposal. He was about to give his answer, when the brass knob turned and the large wooden billiard room door opened. 'Kirby,' Andrews greeted his sergeant, who came into the room with a snortling pug in his arms.

'Oh and Ruby, how lovely.' Cressida took her small dog from Kirby's awkward grip on her. 'Where did you find her? I thought Alfred had her?'

'He did, miss. Lord Delafield was at pains to convey that he was in control, with total mastery of the situation, however he did ask that I take Miss Ruby here with me. He said he'd been getting funny looks from some of the older guests as Miss Ruby had decided that the nativity scene set up under the Christmas tree in the lobby would make a good bed for the night.'

'Awkward perhaps, but quite right. Why was Alfred so bothered about it?'

'It appears she felt that the nativity scene was the perfect spot to such a degree, miss, that she had ousted the baby Jesus himself onto the straw-strewn floor and had taken up residence in the manger. Seems she'd stolen a hotel napkin and had taken it into the manger with her. They're navy blue, miss, so you can imagine the way it looked. Very holy.' Kirby handed the bulky little dog over to her mistress with one last thought. 'If you'll permit me to express, miss, she really has got quite, well, *gainly* of late.'

Cressida looked fondly at her little dog and the two frog-like eyes blinked back at her. Those were merely rolls of puppy fat, surely? But then, she was almost two years old now.

'Making herself at home in the manger, you say? Ousting our tiny Lord and Saviour himself?'

Kirby nodded as Cressida narrowed her eyes and thought back to the weekend she had spent at Totteridge Hall a few weeks back, where Sir John Totteridge's corgis had quite the liking for young Ruby.

'Ruby?' Cressida held her up in front of her. 'Ruby, do I need to give you a lecture on the birds and the bees? Or is it far too late for that? Has the metaphorical horse bolted long before I got to the stable door?'

Cressida rolled her pug over in her arms and for the first time really looked at her belly. It was indeed far, far larger than usual and there was a definite change to her undercarriage. A snort from Ruby pre-empted a movement from under her skin and Cressida almost yelped in shock.

'Oh, you silly thing. You are pregnant! Putting your carnal lust above your figure. What will Mama say! And if dear Lord Canterbury were still here... he'd be most disappointed! Oh but, Ruby, are you really? Am I to become a grandmother at just twenty six? And after all I've told you about holding out for the right man.' Cressida held Ruby close to her again and rubbed her cheek on the soft velveteen fur between her ears. Ruby grunted with some satisfaction at the attention. Then Cressida cradled her again, mesmerised by the gentle undulating beneath the now-strained skin of her dog's stomach. 'What would they be called? Porgis? Cogs?' She shook her head.

'Right you are, sir,' Kirby said, and Cressida looked up from talking to her pregnant pup to see Kirby once again leaving the room.

'Andrews?' she queried.

'I've sent him to find Von Drausch. Which should give us just enough time to conceal you, and the mother-to-be – congratulations by the way – behind that curtain.' Andrews pointed to the window and Cressida almost laughed. It wasn't long ago that she'd feared for her freedom as she'd wondered if getting caught spying on Andrews' interviews would lead to a custodial sentence. That he was now pushing aside the floor-length curtain of the billiard room to reveal a deep windowsill seat was marvellous. And although Cressida couldn't help but think about her forthcoming litter of tiny porgies and cogs, she nodded enthusiastically as Andrews closed the curtain on her and they waited for Marcus Von Drausch to arrive.

A few moments later and Cressida, who had settled herself and Ruby onto the velvet cushion on the windowsill, and spent a moment gazing out to the snow-covered road, heard the sound of the door opening and Andrews greet the interviewee. Kirby had arranged the furniture to give them all a place to sit, and Cressida noted that the three men in the room would be a heck of a lot more comfortable than her and her poor pug – in her state too! – but she swept those thoughts from her mind as she made the best of the cold, hard window seat and listened in, first to the pleasantries and then to Andrews getting down to business.

He approached the matter of the entailment first and Cressida concentrated in order to catch every word. Soon, Andrews posed the question that had been on both their minds.

'Mr Von Drausch, your inheritance gives you a very good motive for killing your aunt. Do you have an alibi for the hour between six thirty and seven thirty this evening?'

'Kill Victoria? *Mon dieu!*' Cressida could hear the affront, but without seeing his face, she couldn't work out how genuine it was. In fact, she couldn't picture him at all, having not met him before.

She tried to remember the photograph that was attached to the article she'd read, but all she could picture was a man in an artist's cape, with a beret positioned at a jaunty angle on his head. She doubted he'd be in such attire tonight, but it was the only image in her head now as she listened in as he continued.

'Of course I have an alibi. I was in the bar and the ballroom – a whole gang of us. Seven-ish, you say? Ah yes, I remember now as the traditional dances had stopped – the waltz and what have you. I glanced up at the clock above the stage just as the band started up with the full pizzazz. Horns and drums and all. Bit of jazz. Nothing like the Paris clubs, you know, but not bad, not bad. That was on the dot of seven, then I went to the bar to buy some champagne – I'm sure one of the barmen will vouch for me.'

'Champagne?' Andrews quizzed, just as the thought had come to Cressida's mind. 'Celebrating something? A new-found wealth perhaps?'

'I take offence at that, sir. Can a man not buy a bottle of champagne at a ball without it being questioned? It's Christmas, after all.'

'By the bottle you say?' Andrews pushed and Cressida leaned as far towards the room as she could without disturbing the curtains or causing Ruby to yelp. She rubbed her pup's inflated belly, feeling the gentle movement within as she listened.

'Of course by the bottle, it's Christmas Eve. Why?'

'Because Victoria Beaumont was killed by a blow to the head. The most likely weapon being a champagne bottle.'

'*Mon dieu*,' Marcus repeated and Cressida rolled her eyes at his pseudo-French mannerisms. His artistic training had obviously taken him to Paris, but would his artistic temperament make him more likely to commit murder? She was a little taken aback, however, by what he said next. 'What brand was it? A Grand Marque, I assume? What do they sell here? There are two growers, I think. Tell you what, I'll tell you which one I prefer and if it's a different label to the one you found as the murder weapon, then it can't have been me.'

'I'm not sure that would stand up in a court of law, but by all means, which brand did you buy?'

'Pol Roger, of course.'

'Hmm,' Andrews made the non-committal noise, but Cressida took it to mean that the bottle by the body hadn't been from that famous champagne house. She listened as Marcus spoke on, more confident now perhaps that he had proven his innocence.

'You called her my aunt, but she's only that by marriage, of course. And the same age as me – younger perhaps! Uncle Peter is so much older than her. Not like Aunt Caroline, his first wife. She was more aunt-like really. I liked Aunt Caroline.'

'But not Aunt Victoria?'

'Oh, do stop calling her that. It's ridiculous. And of course I liked her, but it was odd, a woman her age being married to Uncle Peter. Aunt Caroline was at least only a decade or so younger, not four!' He scoffed at the idea of it.

'Lady Caroline Beaumont died prematurely too,' Andrews reminded him. 'Riding, was it?'

'Yes, riding. That set are very horsey over there in Worcestershire. But Aunt Caroline found it hard to keep up at times.'

'Was someone with her when she died?' Andrews asked and Cressida listened intently.

'I don't know. I think so. I know the news came back to the house pretty smartish, as my mother – Uncle Peter's sister, Patricia – was there and she said it all came about very quickly. Poor Aunt Caroline was dead as soon as she hit the ground apparently. A broken neck.'

'And with her gone, and the second Countess of Worcester now dead, it's looking likely that the estate will fall to you.' Andrews pressed the point home.

'Well, yes, but look here,' Marcus said, 'I don't want it. Well, I mean to say, I will take it on, if I must, that's my duty, but it's not my dream. Everyone assumes the only thing one might want from life is a title and grand estate—'

'I know plenty of people who do,' Andrews told him. 'And plenty of people rotting in jails as they tried to come about them by nefarious means.'

If this was meant to unsettle Marcus, it worked.

'Look here, I'm not one of those felonious fellows. I admire Uncle Peter, and I really liked Aunt Caroline. Even if I didn't have much to do with Victoria, I wished them all well. The last thing I want is to be responsible for a vast estate like that. I'm an artist,' he said with emphasis. 'An artist. I need space and creative freedom—'

'Which surely a large estate and associated income will provide?' Andrews queried.

'Bah,' Marcus was quick to retaliate. 'I already have enough income. I have an inheritance from my mother, and the Von Drausch family money too. What need have I for the daily toil and ins and outs of running an estate? Uncle Peter moans about it every Christmas. He says his ledger is never empty, with jobs infinite in their scope, from working out where to coppice the hazel next to refencing the sheep fields. Liaising with the tenants and tenant farmers, going to market and planning where to sow what and when. He has to actually know about *pigs*. Perish the thought. Then there's the legal side of things, it's like stepping into being a *grand fromage* at a city enterprise. Business, that's what it is, running an estate like that. And I have no wish for it.' He took a breath, then continued, his voice quieter. 'You know I knew Victoria during her debutante year? I was back briefly from an artistic retreat in Buenos Aires just as the season started and remember quite clearly chatting her up one night, but her being much more interested in what I had to say about my aged Uncle Peter, recently widowed and all that. He'd already been eyed up by some other Mama after a fortune and title for her daughter, but Victoria made a beeline for him. After that, I barely saw her the whole season. I headed back to Argentina for another month or two and found out by cable that the old boy had married her.'

Cressida could hear the scribbling of Kirby writing this all down and couldn't blame Andrews for closing up the interview and dismissing Marcus Von Drausch from the room. He'd all but talked himself out of the frame, especially if his alibi could be backed up by whichever barman was working the Belgrave Bar at that hour.

Once the door to the billiard room had opened and closed, and Andrews had called to her, Cressida reappeared from behind the curtain, Ruby in her arms.

She shrugged her shoulders at Andrews. 'Dead end there then?'

'Not necessarily,' Andrews replied, leaning against the billiard table. His elbow accidentally knocked one of the balls and it ricocheted off the cushion and across the green baize.

'But he sounded very sure that he really didn't want the Beaumont estate,' Cressida argued, catching the ball before it hit the pocket.

'He did, indeed.' Andrews crossed his arms across his broad chest. 'Call me a cynic if you will, but I'll believe that when I see it.'

'Well, fair enough. As you say, he talked a good game, but it might be that he was bluffing. The champagne thing though, that was pretty clever of him. And goes someway to ruling him out, doesn't it?'

'I'm not so sure, Miss Fawcett.' Andrews uncrossed his arms and pushed himself off from the baize-covered table. He put his hands in his pockets and faced her straight on. 'You see, the champagne bottle he said he bought, well, he was right, it wasn't the brand we found under Lady Victoria's body.'

'So he's innocent then?'

'Not necessarily.' Andrews scratched his salt-and-pepper-flecked beard.

'Oh,' Cressida said, perplexed. 'But...'

Andrews exhaled, then explained. 'Did you notice he led us down that avenue? He brought up the "what Grand Marque was it" conversation. Of course, if he is the murderer, he'll know which brand was found under Victoria's body and say the opposite. Perhaps if I'd asked him point blank, I would have put more credence on his answer, but because he seemed to come prepared with that little play, I'm not so sure. I'll make sure Kirby keeps an eye on him for the rest of the evening. But as far as I'm concerned, Marcus Von Drausch is very much still in the frame.'

Cressida nodded. Could it really be as simple as someone killing to gain such a massive fortune? Perhaps. Murders had happened for less. 'But,' Cressida continued her thought from moments before, 'you let him walk out of here, Andrews? If you think he has motive and opportunity, why not arrest him?'

Andrews sighed. 'Because I need more than a hunch to make an arrest. There's no evidence yet that Mr Von Drausch did it. He didn't have the bottle neck on his person – that was Clayton. And despite that whole thing with the champagne, well, it could just be that – a privileged young man who thinks he's been awfully clever proving to me that he drinks the un-murderous brand of bubbles. I need more than that to make the arrest.'

'I see. And we only have—'

Andrews frowned. 'Less than two hours to go.'

21

Once Cressida had compared notes with Andrews, she left him and Kirby to cogitate and write up their jottings. She'd told him about Dora, too, and although she didn't believe she could have done it, she'd mentioned the missing beads from her dress that she'd noticed. Andrews had sent Kirby off on the thankless task of looking for them and Cressida had felt bad about that, it being her lead and her idea, but she was grateful that she didn't have to head out into the snow. The flakes were really coming down thicker and settling in enormous drifts now. The billiard room's windows faced away from the courtyard and onto one of the side roads near the hotel, but she'd seen the thickening carpet of white covering the pavement and road. There would be no sign now of those footsteps in the dusting she'd seen earlier. And since then, time had crept on. The hands on Cressida's watch pointed to twenty minutes past ten o'clock. The evening would soon be gone and she'd be nowhere nearer to finding out who killed Victoria if she didn't start getting some answers. The doctor, a certain Dr Hart, seemed to be the next clear person of interest and so she headed into the ballroom, weaving her way through the throng of party-goers as she sought him out.

Although she spied many a handsome blonde and blue-eyed man among the dancers and drinkers, she knew almost all of them. None were the doctor she was looking for. Cressida left the ballroom, with its dancers oblivious to the murder investigation going on around them, and headed back towards the ornately decorated passageway that ran the length of the ballroom. She knew the cosy, firelit smoking room with its pretty mantel garlands and glittering candelabras led off it, as did the billiard room which had been made into Andrews's makeshift office. She walked past them both, wondering if there was another room down this way, but with Ruby getting heavier by the moment it seemed, and nothing else but kitchens and the ladies' powder room down this way, she decided it was a lost cause.

The ladies' powder room, however, was of interest, and as she put Ruby down and rubbed her heel from her pinching shoe, she realised that all that champagne earlier in the evening had finally caught up with her.

Hadn't Cordelia said that Victoria had swayed off in the direction of the ladies' powder room after she'd downed that martini? Perhaps Cressida could answer her call of nature and carry on the investigation all at once.

Cressida thought through everything she'd found out so far. That she was doing this thinking while on the lavatory was neither here nor there, though she did appreciate the relative peace of the exquisitely decorated cubicle.

She could still hear the music from the ballroom, though it was muffled and distant thanks to the thick wooden doors of the separate lavatories and main powder room, not to mention the soft furnishings that turned the area around the basins and mirrors into more of a boudoir than a bathroom. She'd felt quite comfortable leaving Ruby atop one of the pink velvet-upholstered stools that sat in front of a row of mirrors, with the friendly-looking lavatory attendant lavishing attention on her.

Cressida's list of suspects seemed to be growing by the minute, yet she could also start to cross off some with alibis. There was Lord Beaumont, who had at least one clear motive and seemed nonplussed that his wife was dead, but he and Ottoline Spencer were together in the piano bar at the time of the murder. And Ottoline might have a motive if she were in love with her friend, but she had insisted that Cressida investigate, which would be a very strange thing for a murderer to do.

Then there was Clayton Malone, who possibly had a motive if Victoria had been the one to break his heart, no alibi to speak of and the champagne bottle fragment found in his coat pocket. But he had seemed so sad to hear of Victoria's death. Was someone trying to frame him?

Everyone knew Dora Smith-Wallington wouldn't hurt a fly, but she did point out that Victoria's handbag was missing, and Victoria did have a very nasty go at her. Could that have prompted an uncharacteristic and violent outburst? But no, she had an alibi too, if her cousin Simon were to back her up.

Now Cordelia... she was at pains for her beau, Marcus Von Drausch not to be suspected, even though he'd inherit everything once the earl croaked. She herself might have wanted to help his inheritance along a bit, too. She certainly knew it was on the cards and she did admit to Marcus having prospects.

And even though Marcus himself swore blind that he wasn't interested in inheriting his uncle's estate one day, well, words and deeds were often quite different things.

And then, of course, there was this Dr Hart. A Harley Street clinician with a specialism in fertility. Cressida couldn't stop thinking about the looks traded between him and Victoria on the dance floor only moments before she was so brutally killed. She also kept going back to those footprints in the snow that led to and from the body in the fountain. Something about them still bothered her and she couldn't put her finger on why.

Cressida sighed. She was no further towards finding out *why* Victoria had been killed. If anything, she was more confused than when she'd started.

She waited while the voices she could hear in the powder room outside drifted off and let herself out of the cubicle. Heading directly to the basins, she nodded a hello to the young attendant, who was neatly dressed in navy blue with a white pinafore. She was pretty, with reddish-strawberry-blonde hair that was tucked up into a starched, frilled band. She handed Cressida some hand-soap and a towel once she'd rinsed the soap away.

'Thank you,' Cressida said, then remarked on the soap. 'It has a lovely scent to it, like sandalwood or cedar. Smoky, like Lapsang tea. Is it from a London stockist?'

'I believe it's Palmolive, miss.' The attendant bobbed a curtsy. 'But blended especially for the Mayfair by their master soap-makers.' She obviously took pride in her employer and Cressida smiled at her. She smelt her hands, but the scent had faded to something more floral. It was nice to have these few peaceful moments.

She exhaled and looked around her. The powder room was so elegantly furnished that even the windows had beautiful silk jacquard curtains hanging at them. Cressida instinctively moved towards them, her hand outstretched ready to feel and, secretly, judge the quality of the fabric. As she twitched the curtain back to appraise the lining, she realised where she was standing. The ladies' powder room faced the courtyard, its window an eye directly onto the fountain in which Victoria was found dead.

Cressida flicked one of the large curtains back and stepped into the window alcove, shivering as the air cooled around her.

Curtains were such wonderful insulators, especially beautifully interlined ones such as this, and she could understand why the attendant would close them to keep the chill away from the ladies who were powdering their noses. When they were open, however, anyone in the powder room would have seen the courtyard, as she could now, in all its twinkling glory. And, more importantly, anyone looking out would have had the best view of the fountain. The murder scene.

Cressida slipped back through the curtains and smiled at the attendant again. She hated the way that these hard-working young women, just like the maids in the large country houses that she visited, were so often ignored and deemed nameless. And she'd come to realise over the years that it was household servants that always seemed to know what was going on – far more than their compatriots 'upstairs'. She assumed a hotel like this would be much the same.

She smiled at the powder room attendant and introduced herself. 'I'm Cressida Fawcett, by the way. Merry Christmas and all that...' She waited.

'Violet, miss. And happy Christmas to you too.' Violet bobbed another curtsy.

'Oh please, no need for that. You'll need new knees before you're fifty at that rate.' This made the attendant giggle and Cressida carried on, now the ice was broken. 'Can I ask you something? Something about a young lady who was in here earlier?'

'Which young lady would that be, miss? There's been so many in and out of here all evening.'

'Lady Beaumont – long blonde hair, blue dress. She was found dead in that fountain out there...'

'Oh yes, miss. Terrible thing that was.' Violet shuddered.

'You've heard about it then?' Cressida said. Of course the staff had all been informed. Informed and commanded to stay put.

'Yes, miss. Poor Lady Victoria.' The attendant wiped a cloth around the taps by the marble-topped basin. Something about her use of Victoria's name made it sound like she was more familiar with her than just hearing about her murder.

'It sounds like you knew her? Had you met her before? I believe she was seen heading towards this powder room just before she died.'

'Yes, miss,' the attendant nodded her head enthusiastically. 'All of that. She had been in before, and I always thought she was such a striking lady, with all that lovely blonde hair. Like a princess – as well as a countess, of course. And she was always polite and said hello. Unlike some ladies who don't introduce themselves – not that I expect it, mind, but I gather their names from their conversations and I keep a copy of *The Bystander* under the basins here so I can see who's who, if you know what I mean.'

'I'm glad Victoria was nice to you. I always remember her being quite talkative too.'

'Well, that's why I was surprised tonight as she was not so friendly.' Violet fiddled with her starched white headband and looked a bit awkward, but she carried on nonetheless. 'Her lady-ship was a bit – if you don't mind me saying – worse for wear. And very cross about something.'

'Did she by any chance have her evening bag with her when she came in?'

The attendant thought for a bit. 'No, now you come to mention it. I usually note the bags, miss, as the ladies, like yourself, like to leave them on that armchair there while they do their business and I keep an eye. She didn't have one on her.'

'And did she meet anyone in here?'

'Well, there was a crowd of young ladies in here, you see. All of a sudden, they came in. One of those dance numbers must have come to a close and they came to dab their faces with tissues and gossip about their young men. I like that bit, the listening in.'

Cressida smiled at her. She thought if she were a powder-room assistant in a hotel like this, that would be her favourite part of the job too. 'Would you recognise any of those ladies, do you think, if you saw them again? I mean, if I were to meet you in the ballroom in a few minutes and we had a look, would you be able to point them out to me?'

Violet looked abashed. 'Oh, I better not leave my post. Mr Butcher says we all have to be the best we can be tonight and not get all silly over the murder and try to leave or anything like that.' Dedication to duty turned to disgruntlement with a sigh. 'Though it has been ages since I've had a break. Susie Potts was meant to come and relieve me an hour ago and she hasn't showed.'

'Not left the hotel, I hope?' Cressida wondered out loud.

'Oh no, miss – more likely she's been delayed with the turn-down service upstairs for the overnight guests. We like to leave little presents for them on their pillows and I think Susie was doing that tonight. So, I better not leave here, miss. Mr Butcher was adamant we all stick to our posts.'

'Well, yes, he's right, of course,' Cressida agreed, 'but this wouldn't be leaving. It would be helping the police.'

'The police?' Violet straightened her pinafore and her starched white cotton headpiece, suddenly looking alert again. 'Are you working with the police then?'

'Yes, I am. But I feel as if them marching you to the ball-room and asking you to point out the ladies who were in here at the same time as Lady Beaumont would put people on edge.'

'I see miss, yes. I understand.'

'But if you were to meet me there, it would look far more subtle. As if I were asking you about something hotel-related, you see?'

'Yes, I see miss. I'll do it.'

'Oh, wonderful! You are a treasure, Violet. Meet me by the door to the ballroom in about five minutes?'

Violet blushed a little, but looked more confident. 'Yes miss. Anything to help the late Lady Beaumont.' Her face saddened and Cressida realised that Victoria's death would have an impact on so many people. Murder really was such a vile business.

She reached over and handed Violet a tissue to dab her watery eyes.

'Thank you, miss. I know it's not my place to get all weepy about it, but she was such a nice lady. And to think of her now, down in the cellar on her own, in that nasty, damp place – oh, it quite gives you the shivers.'

'I know. It's ghastly,' Cressida agreed, but Violet's words had reminded her that Victoria, deceased though she was, was still, in some ways, very much with them. An idea came to her. 'Can we make it fifteen minutes, Violet. Meeting in the ballroom, I mean? By the door to the piano lobby perhaps? If you get there before me, do make some excuse as to why you're loitering. Tweaking the baubles perhaps or checking there's enough mistletoe for midnight.'

As Violet nodded, Cressida squeezed her arm in thanks. And then she picked up her handbag, and Ruby, and left the powder room. She caught a whiff of the smell of smoke again just briefly as she heard a lavatory flush, and she left before whoever it was could waylay her. Because Violet's words had given her an idea.

It was time to see what Victoria had to say for herself.

22

In the corridor outside the powder room, a huddle of ladies giggled their way past Cressida and she nodded a hello to one of them she remembered from one of Pinky Netherton's parties. Cressida remembered for a moment that hardly anyone else here knew about Victoria's death. It was still just a Christmas ball for them, with all the glitz and glamour that involved.

'Coming through!' a waiter called out, causing Cressida to step aside as he swerved between the hotel guests with a tray held high above his head, full of empty bottles and glasses.

Cressida glanced at her watch. It was almost half past ten. Time was pressing, but the good thing about a dead body was they tended not to go anywhere. These waiters certainly did though, and with an empty champagne bottle the murder weapon, might these chaps carrying trays of them have an idea of how it was come by?

Victoria down in the cellar could wait a moment or two longer, Cressida thought as she changed her mind on what her next move should be.

She looked both ways down the corridor, and with Ruby still in her arms and taking care not to step into the path of either a waiter or another gaggle of giggling women, she headed towards the beating heart of the hotel – the kitchen.

Busboys and waiters clattered in and out of the flip-flap doors that led to the kitchen and Cressida had to squeeze herself against the wall in order to not get in their way. She did notice how they worked though, with waiters bringing back trays of empty glasses and bottles and depositing them on tray tables just inside the door to the kitchen for the busboys to collect and take further in to be cleaned and sorted. Waiters with trays of full bottles and sparkling glasses always took precedence through the doors – fresh champagne was essential for a successful evening.

Cressida put Ruby down and let her wander off. Then she waited a little while until one of the trays of empties had been deposited and then tested out how easy it would be to nab one of the bottles. Very, it seemed, with no more than a quick dip through the doors and a swipe off the tray. Plus, where would the harm be in stealing an empty bottle? No one would mind, though it might look a little odd. Cressida was frowning and holding an empty bottle when a kind-looking busboy, who must have been barely halfway through his teenage years, slipped out of the kitchen and spoke to her.

'Are you all right there, miss? It's just I sees you hanging around and then nabbing that bottle, which is empty by the way, miss, and then just standing there and looking at it, like.' The young man – boy even – wiped his hands on the tea towel that was tucked into his apron tied around his waist and looked at Cressida expectantly.

'You are kind to notice. I'm quite well, thank you.' Cressida felt rather foolish but wasn't going to let that get in the way of a chance to investigate. 'So you definitely saw me take this from just inside the door there?'

'Yes, miss, and very natty you were too.' He grinned at Cressida.

'Natty, ha. Yes. I'm not a stranger to a champagne bottle.' Cressida weighed it up in her hands, then passed it back to the boy. 'Here, I don't need it. But I was wondering, did you see if anyone else popped in earlier to do the same thing?'

The boy shrugged and shook his head, so she tried to pin it down further.

'About two and bit hours ago? No?'

'No, miss, I didn't see anything, but we did notice a bottle go missing. An empty one. Monsieur Claude likes to count them in.'

'Who's Monsieur Claude?' Cressida asked. 'And why does he count the empties?'

'He's our somm— miss. Don't ask me how you say the real word. Smellier? Something like that.'

'The sommelier,' Cressida helped him along, slipping into a French accent as she did. 'Chap in charge of the wine. Yes?'

'Yes, that's right. And he likes to count the bottles and the corks. So he can tally them up against the bar bill and keep tabs of stock. Some of these champagnes,' he whistled. 'More than a month's pay for me!'

Cressida nodded, never more aware of her own privilege. Some nights she'd think nothing of drinking gallons of the stuff and she suddenly felt very bad about that fact. But she pushed the feeling down as she concentrated on the matter at hand. 'Did you see anything at all around the time the bottle went missing?'

'Like I said, miss, I didn't see anything.' He crossed his arms. 'And should I be talking to you? I probably shouldn't, miss. Is this about the dead lady in the fountain? Are you the police?' He looked at her askance.

'I'm not the police, no, but I am working with them, and yes, this is about Lady Victoria Beaumont. Anything you can remember would be so very, very useful.' Cressida stopped short of fluttering any eyelashes at the young lad, but hoped a bit of the old Fawcett charm might work wonders.

Luckily, it did.

'Well, there was something odd. Not me, but Eddy in the kitchen said he heard something, and it made us laugh, and that was about the same time as the bottle went as I remember it as Monsieur Claude told us off for laughing, like, but he was just in a mood as his corks and bottles suddenly weren't adding up.'

'What were you laughing about?' Cressida asked. This could be most interesting.

'Well, it seems a bit silly now.' The lad shuffled his feet and Cressida could see colour rising in his cheeks.

'Honestly... sorry, I don't know your name?'

'Jim, miss.'

'Honestly, Jim, nothing you could say could possibly ever sound so silly to me. And if you're worried that it's rude, well, all the rude words, I've heard them, I promise. And the less rude, but just silly ones, too. And the French ones. And a few in German too. And especially the Anglo-Saxon ones.'

Jim snorted a laugh. 'All right, miss, well, the thing was, Eddy was laughing as we saw, just a glimpse through the flip-flap door, some nice lady, but she looked pickled, zozzled, fried to the hat, you know?'

Cressida did know, for in her relatively short lifetime, she had been all of those things, and more. She nodded encouragingly and he carried on.

'But she just said the word pongy, like whiffy, you know, but in her posh voice... "Pongy".' He did an impression, with his head held up and two fingers clamped on his nose, flattening the last syllable. 'But slurred like. We thought she'd spent too long in the powder room perhaps, or didn't like all that French perfume she no doubt wore.'

When he'd finished she smiled and thanked him. 'You've

been most helpful Jim. When DCI Andrews comes to speak to you, do mention this.'

'Do you think it's important to the dead woman, miss?' Jim looked more serious again. 'Was that her? Saying pongy?'

'I don't know. Perhaps.' Cressida nodded to him as a call from the kitchen sent him running back in.

She stood for a little while longer contemplating what he'd said. A drunk lady – and Victoria had by all accounts been that – talking about something smelly. No, *pongy*. And that was around the same time that the empty champagne bottle was stolen.

If only Jim had seen who had taken the bottle, she could confidently be wrapping this whole case up; but, for now, all she had was that one word. Pongy.

And an appointment in the cellar with Victoria.

23

Cressida's mind was reeling, and not in the way it usually would be at this stage of an evening when she'd be tucking into something rather refreshing and fizzy or chilled and shaken. She was pleased, though, when out of the corner of her eye she saw a plump little pup waddle towards her, from the direction of the billiard room.

'Oh there you are, Ruby,' she said as she moved away from the flip-flap door of the kitchen towards her pup. She picked her up with a certain amount of effort. 'How did I not notice that you were with child? Or pup? Or pups, more like, by the look of you. Which one of Sir John's corgis was it? Dylan or Daffyd?'

Cressida nuzzled her small dog and carefully let her down again. She looked around at the passageway, which was less formally decorated here than the end closer to the ballroom and ladies' powder room; emptier too. She noticed another group of young ladies head into the powder room further up the corridor, so pressed together she couldn't recognise any of them, though a flash of sparkle in one of their headpieces caught her eye and it reminded her of Victoria and how pretty she'd looked in the Beaumont tiara on her wedding day.

Oh, Victoria... I will find out who did this to you. Cressida made the vow as she checked her watch. She didn't want to keep Violet waiting, but she felt that the poor girl probably deserved a few minutes away from her post and pretending to zhoosh up some mistletoe while getting to see the ballroom in full swing would be nice for her. Or perhaps those young ladies who had just gone into the powder room would keep her occupied. Either way, Cressida felt she still had time to quickly see if she could glean anything from Victoria's body; she doubted she'd want to spend too long down there anyway.

She glanced up and down the passageway and luckily it only took a few moments to spy the discreet brass plaque with a word engraved upon it.

Cellar.

Cressida looked about her, waited for the scurrying serving staff to disappear back into the kitchen and then with a turn of the brass knob gently pushed it open. She was somewhat shocked at the rush of cool, damp air that greeted her. Ruby whined a little and sat back on her haunches, and Cressida looked down at her.

'Not like you to shy away from an adventure.'

Ruby, could only reply by snorting and snuffling, but while doing so, she stood up again and bravely walked through the door. With Ruby now as her guide, and showing Cressida up somewhat, she followed her in.

The door led almost directly to a narrow staircase that, while carpeted and decorated much like the passageway outside with plaster mouldings and gilt Rococo flourishes, gradually lost its gloss as it curved its way down quite steeply. Carpet turned to well-worn wood under her feet and the walls went from being like those of the hotel above to rough-hewn brick and stone.

This cellar entrance was obviously meant to be seen by the paying guests of the hotel, perhaps even included as part of a tour, or if residents or diners had special bottles of wine they wanted to see, but as the stairs reached the cellar itself, they had to become more workaday. And the air became mustier and danker, as all good cellar air was.

Cressida paused to acclimatise to the gloom, before realising that there were electric lights installed. She flicked the switch, grateful for the foresight of the hotel owners to bring this modern convenience all the way down here.

Many country houses still relied on candles and oil lamps at their extremities, but the bare electric bulbs that now illuminated the bins of wine made navigating her way around the cellar a little easier. And it wasn't long before Cressida had found the trestle table, quickly erected, that was now the impromptu mortuary slab for Victoria, Lady Beaumont, Countess of Worcester.

Cressida took a breath and moved closer towards the shrouded figure. Her family motto went along the lines of fortune favouring the brave, though with something derogatory added in about the French that she never really understood. 'Never mind the French,' she muttered to herself, noting the cases of the finest Bordeaux and Burgundy wines around her. 'It's Dutch courage I think I need right now.'

The area of the cellar she now found herself in was more spacious than the part she'd first encountered, and the extra space was taken up with thick wicker baskets that looked like something that might dangle from a hot-air balloon. In an understandable diversion from going straight up to the dead body, Cressida peered into one or two of them.

Some were empty, bar the straw that had obviously been cushioning whichever fragile goods had been transported in them. These were perhaps the grocer's baskets – though vastly bigger than anyone would see attached to a bicycle or on a handcart – in which the easily bruised fruit and vegetables arrived for the hotel's kitchens. And those kitchens, if Cressida's calculations were correct, were directly above her now and could no doubt be accessed from one of the other steep staircases she could see spiralling away from this central atrium area, with its vaulted, low ceiling.

A wide ramp led up to what looked like a hatch and Cressida assumed that this was how the large hampers and various kegs of beer and cases of wine came in and out of the cellar. And how Victoria would eventually leave once the mortuary was open after Christmas.

Hearing a slow, but constant drip somewhere in the cellar reminded Cressida that time was ticking. She could put off examining her old friend's body no longer.

She put her handbag down on top of several stacked cases of wine and told Ruby to remind her to pick it up once she was done. Then, with another bracing inhale, she moved towards the trestle and gently lifted the corner of the pristine white sheet that had been laid over the murdered young woman.

Cressida had already seen Victoria's dead body of course, with the water of the fountain bubbling and coursing over her, but she hadn't anticipated how peaceful she now looked, lying here, her eyes closed and her body at eternal rest. There was a knock to her head, and still a trace of blood, though the waters of the fountain had done much to wash that away. It looked severe though, a real whack that could have easily resulted in the killer having a spray of rust-like blood catch on their cuff. Much like she'd seen on Clayton.

'You poor thing, Victoria, killed like this and left in that cold fountain...' Cressida tailed off. She still had the white sheet in one hand, but with her other she gently moved Victoria's still wet hair from around her neck. Her silk and pearl choker had come loose and a few stray threads indicated where pearls were perhaps lost forever in the fountain or flowerbeds. But as the choker fell away, it revealed something else. 'Well, I'll be blowed. Ruby, you will not believe this.'

There was no answer from her dog, but Cressida barely noticed. She moved her head so that she blocked less of the electric light bulb's glow and muttered again under her breath.

'It wasn't the bottle...'

Because what Cressida had just noticed, what the now loosened pearl-encrusted choker had been concealing, was that Victoria hadn't just been hit over the head.

She'd been strangled, too.

Cressida stared at the red mark around Victoria's throat. She could see how she – and the police – had missed it before, the choker would have covered it up completely. She would have to tell Andrews about this as a matter of the utmost priority.

The red welts were distinctive too. It wasn't just a piece of cord that had strangled Victoria, or the choker itself, but something more substantial, something twisted and thick. The glimmer of recognition – its thickness, its weave – set something off in the corner of Cressida's mind, but like all the threads that she just couldn't quite grasp, it was lost to her before she could pull it and work out what it was that was niggling her about it.

With one final look, and a gently mouthed 'goodbye' to her friend, Cressida let the sheet fall back over Victoria's unflinching face.

Then, in some gruesome mirroring of the act, she suddenly felt the suffocating crush of her own face being smothered by a cloth.

Cressida tried to breathe, but the harsh sacking sucked in hard to her lips and nostrils. She scratched at the rough cloth as best she could with her satin gloves, but could get no purchase on the taut fabric. Flailing her arms, she tried to reach behind her to stop whoever was pulling her backwards, her neck straining against the force that had caught her so unawares. She couldn't scream. She could barely make a sound as her whole body was pulled back, her silk-covered evening shoes offering her no grip, though she kicked out and scrabbled against the hard flagstones of the cellar floor.

The sacking reeked and she choked on the sickening taste and smell of must, mould and an old smokiness. She could hear something too – a snickering sound. A laugh almost, though whether it was male or female she couldn't tell as her ears rushed with white noise as panic set in. She wanted to vomit and scream and thrash around but found she could do none of these as she slowly ran out of fresh air.

Was this it? Had her investigating finally brought her to the stickiest of ends?

Cressida felt the last of the air in her lungs and closed her eyes.

24

Cressida's breath laboured as she found it harder and harder to get any air through the taut sack across her face. Then, just as she really thought the end had come for her, she was released. All at once, the cloth felt looser around her face, yet she was disorientated and dazed and a hard push saw her tumbling over a waist-high firm but narrow edge that dug into her back as she flipped over it, landing painfully among hard, bumpy items. The darkness that had enveloped her as she'd been captured remained. The smell of fresh straw was unmistakable; she was in one of the large wicker hampers that lined the walls of the cellar.

'Help!' Cressida yelled, pushing the sides and lid of the hamper, desperate to escape. She righted herself, thankfully having just enough room to move herself around inside the large basket and then tore off the cloth that had been over her head. She felt rather than saw what seemed like a heavy weight lift off the top of the hamper, but to her annoyance the wicker lid was now securely fastened by the sturdy leather straps she'd seen from the outside. There was no way she'd be able to weave a finger or two through the very narrow gaps and do anything about undoing them.

She was stuck.

'Help! It's just me, Cressida!' she called again, hoping that her assailant might change their mind or have captured the wrong person, though she knew that was unlikely. 'Help...' Her voice was quieter this time, the shock of what had just happened washing over her. Who was it? And why did they attack her?

She felt her legs and arms, but despite what would be nasty bruises, there were no breaks nor could she sense any long-term injury. She gingerly searched around her through the straw and realised that the uncomfortable lumps, that were bruising her further no doubt, felt like ceramic basins wrapped in string and cloth. Then it came to her; plum puddings!

She was in a Christmas hamper, like a large version of the ones her family received from Fortnum & Mason each year. So, she wouldn't starve if she were to be here for any length of time, that was one thing, and she was unharmed, so it could be worse...

She shivered as another thought came to her. The person who pushed her into the Christmas hamper was more than likely the murderer. Did they think they'd killed her? Or were they disturbed in the act and planning on coming back, before anyone could find her, and finish her off...

'Help!' Cressida yelled again, and then 'Ruby!' as if the small dog could aid her in anyway at all.

She moved around inside the hamper, rustling bits of straw as she did so and no doubt causing a few squashed plum puddings in the process. Finally, though, despite barely getting her breath back or her heart rate anywhere near normal, she managed to get herself into a crouching position. She had to be prepared to leap out of the hamper as soon as the lid was opened, plum pudding in its sturdy ceramic basin to hand, as she doubted the killer would come back and allow her time to get her bearings before administering a deadly blow. She tried to stay still and quiet, not helped by the tickling of the straw near her undercarriage.

Armed with Christmas pudding, Cressida waited.

And waited.

And waited some more.

She felt terribly guilty about standing up poor Violet. Fifteen minutes must have long since passed. She would have to apologise to the poor girl and convince her to come with her again to the ballroom when she got out of this puddingy predicament. The only positive she could think of was perhaps Violet might cotton on to something being wrong and alert Andrews. Cressida crossed her fingers under the ceramic pudding basin she was prepared to use to meet her foe. She strained her ears, desperate to hear any movement around her that might be a waiter or Monsieur Claude the sommelier coming down to the cellar. Or even Ruby, who she hadn't seen nor heard since she'd examined Victoria's injuries.

'Ruby!' she called again, suddenly fearful that the small dog might not have survived the assault as well as she had. *If something has happened to her*... Now Ruby was expecting pups, a fierce protectiveness, even more than usual, enveloped Cressida.

She called out again, her voice even more desperate now. 'Ruby!' But there was nothing, and now the crouching position she had concertinaed herself into was making her calves and feet ache and the heavy ceramic pudding bowl with its dense suet contents was a strain on her wrists. The straw was getting no less scratchy. And worse, although she couldn't see it, she knew the minute hand of her watch was ticking along, just like that drip somewhere deep in the cellar. She was losing precious investigating time.

As she was about to shuffle around to try to settle herself

into a more comfortable position, Cressida heard a noise. Foot-steps and a murmuring. She braced herself, ready to leap out and surprise her assailant.

The footsteps were coming down the stairs. Heavy – a man perhaps? Had it been a man who had pushed her into the hamper?

She recalled the smell of smoke when she'd been suffocating in that sacking. Was it cigarettes? Lord Beaumont with his constant cigar, he reeked of smoke, and Clayton Malone had smoked in front of her too. Not to mention Dora and her cousin and all his friends around that table. The doctor, only spied from afar, had had a cigarette in hand when she'd seen him. Even the smell of lingering smoke in the powder room... Violet? Could any of them have been her assailant? And now they were back to finish what they started.

Cressida held her breath. The footsteps neared. Definitely heavy. Definitely a man. She gripped the plum pudding basin tighter and waited for them to get closer. Just as her heart felt as if it was about to burst out of her chest, the footsteps paused.

Was this it? Was she about to face down the murderer?

25

Cressida held her breath. The footsteps started again and came ever closer. Again, they sounded heavy, like a man but in dress shoes, not boots. So there was no chance it was Andrews or Kirby – the cavalry in this case. A man in evening wear then – a guest. She concentrated on those footsteps, as they approached. But then, what was that she heard? A scampering? Little claws clattering on stone. And was that the sound of a pipe being dropped and an 'oh dash it all' from a voice she knew oh so well?

'Alfred? Alfred! Is that you?' Cressida called out and, letting the plum pudding basin clatter to its fellows in the straw, hammered as best she could on the side of the Christmas hamper, rocking it to show him which one she was in.

'Cressy?' The voice, Alfred indeed, sounded astounded. 'Cressy, is that you?'

'Yes! Yes, I'm here! In this hamper. Let me out, oh please, please!'

'Hang on a tick, old thing... Oh creepers, is that Victoria on the... Oh hells bells, what on earth are you doing down here?'

'I'll tell you everything once I'm out of this blooming basket!

I've got a yule log protruding right up my... Quick, Alfred, please!'

She could hear him scrabbling with the straps and cursing as the buckles slipped in his fingers. What relief then, moments later, when the light from the single bulb hanging from the cellar's ceiling cut through the darkness and silhouetted in front of her blinking eyes the most welcome shape.

'Oh, Alfred,' Cressida wanted to both cry and throw her arms around him in relief. She settled for taking his helping hands and letting him guide her out of the sturdy hamper.

'Here you go, old thing,' he said, when she was finally standing, albeit slightly wobbly, on the firm flagstones of the cellar floor. His gentle tone and concern quite disarmed her and she felt herself leaning into him. Alfred, his hands still in hers, let them go, and Cressida felt, in that moment, a horrible wash of rejection.

Perhaps Alfred didn't feel the way she hoped he might do? She'd barely seen him over the last few months, what with one thing and another. Perhaps he'd changed his mind and he wasn't interested in her as anything other than a friend?

But just as her thoughts were convincing her of his apathy, she felt his hands, those very same ones that had just released hers from his grip, gently hold the tops of her arms, and they pulled her closer into him. And she felt them press against her back, holding her safely and strongly as she rested her head against his chest.

Cressida stretched her neck and looked up at him, worried that she might not be able to discern any feeling at all in his face and fearing that this was just a friendly hug. The flickering light from the bulb made it tricky to make anything out, but just as she was wondering if Alfred was only trying to comfort her, she felt his head tilt down towards her and their lips meet in a kiss.

Although Alfred's kiss had come quite unexpectedly, and although not unwelcome – *not unwelcome at all* – it did confuse matters and had taken up quite some moments of their precious time. Still, despite the fact there was a dead body behind them, and they were in a dark, dank cellar, Cressida relished still being held in Alfred's arms. So much so, she decided that she rated this experience even better than when the head barman at the Savoy had named a martini after her, and therefore one of the best moments of her life.

'How did you find me?' she asked, forcing herself to pull away from him just a fraction, so that she could look into his face and not speak muffled against his chest.

Alfred shifted his weight too, just enough to move one hand from her back and gently pull a piece of stray straw out of her hair. 'Well, that's simple,' he said, glancing down to the patiently panting pup sitting by their feet. Two globe-like dark eyes blinked up at them. 'Ruby found me.'

'Ruby? Oh, Ruby!' Cressida released herself from Alfred's arms and reached down for her dog. 'I feared she might have been done in by whoever attacked me. But you're here, you clever little pup.' She nuzzled her face against the soft, velvety fur of her darling dog. Then she looked back up at Alfred. 'But how did she help you?'

'Had a set-to with my ankle again.' Alfred reached into his pocket and retrieved his slightly chipped pipe. 'I had a good look, but there were no morsels on the shoe this time. Couldn't fathom what the little thing was trying to do. But she wouldn't give up. Kept tugging at my trousers until it became quite obvious that she wanted me to follow her. Looked back every step of the way to check I was still with her. Then we got to the cellar door—'

'Did you see anyone looking suspicious as you approached?' Cressida asked.

'Afraid not, just tried to concentrate on not falling over Ruby. She's rather large these days, you know?'

'Yes. One is to be a grandmother...' Cressida shook her head. 'Porgis, I think. Or cogs. Anyway, carry on.'

'Oh well, congratulations and all that, old thing. So, I got to the door up there,' he nodded up towards the way Cressida had originally come too, 'had a shifty to see if I could see anyone of course, still wondering why your dog was so adamant I follow her. Assumed she'd lead me to some cache of sausages or a nice plate of shrimp, but here we are.'

'Here we are indeed,' Cressida agreed, her dog safe in her arms and the man she had come to love so very much with his arms once more wrapped around her. She let him kiss her again, then she pulled away with a sigh. 'Alfred, we can't do this.'

'I know, reputations on the line and all that—'

'No,' Cressida almost laughed. 'Not my reputation. I think that was blown the night I crept back to Chelsea at dawn with a string of onions, three shoes and that rather large Indian sapphire—'

'Joffe Nightingale did know how to throw a party back then. Shame he's in the—'

'Exactly. But what I mean is, it's not my reputation I'm worried about, but time slipping away from us tonight. We have to work out who killed Victoria before midnight, and that's only...' She looked at her watch, eliciting a grunt from Ruby as she did so, 'Oh, dear, just over an hour's time.'

'No, quite right. Duty first. Understood.' Alfred let her go and they stood awkwardly for a moment.

Cressida patted down her dress, checking for any other pieces of straw. In the light of the cellar's bulb, she noticed her lipstick smeared on Alfred's own lips. She pointed it out to him, then remembered she had a compact mirror in her handbag and reached across for it, luckily still where she left it on top of the wooden cases of Bordeaux wine. Once she'd checked her reflection in the smart little silver-cased mirror, she returned her focus to the case as Alfred then used it as he wiped the tell-tale red off his own face.

'Alfred, I arranged to meet Violet in the ballroom before I got, well, hampered. The poor thing will think I've stood her up.'

'Violet?' Alfred queried, handing the compact mirror back to Cressida.

'The assistant in the ladies' powder room. I thought it might be useful if she came to the ballroom with me to see if she could identify who was in the powder room at the same time as Victoria. It was the last time, I think, that anyone saw her. Violet said Victoria seemed drunk and not her usual self.'

Alfred nodded sagely. 'Best not keep her waiting. Once we get up there, I can wait outside and we can go with her to the ballroom.'

'Thank you, Alfred, and thank you for rescuing me, I don't know what I would have done without you finding me.'

Alfred smiled at her, then grinned. 'When you were hampered.' He chuckled to himself. 'That's a good one, Cressy.'

Cressida narrowed her eyes at him. 'I know you, Alf, and I know that at some point in the not-too-distant future I'm going to be the butt of one of your rambling anecdotes.'

Alfred feigned outrage, then nodded. 'Too true, Cressy, too true. And I hope it's one that has one hell of an ending.'

Cressida so desperately wanted to lean back up towards Alfred and kiss him again, but as they'd both just decided, duty must come first. Not to mention freshly applied lipstick. So, after an awkward pause, they both said 'right' at the same time, and then bumped into each other as they headed towards the door. After one or two 'after you,' 'no, after you's, they were about to leave the cellar when a growl from Ruby held them back.

'Is she all right?' Alfred asked, and Cressida shook her head. She hadn't heard that sort of noise before and it was only when it turned into the sort of snuffling and snorting that she recog-nised from previous investigations that she let her breath out.

'She's onto something, I think.' Cressida grabbed Alfred's sleeve and pulled him around the other side of the trestle that had Victoria upon it. 'She has a very small – admittedly tiny really – bit of wolf in her and I'm sure this is how she tried to howl.'

'I remember from the Scotland Express. Very wolf-like,' Alfred agreed, watching the pudgy little dog wag her small pig-like tail as she nudged her nose against another of the wicker hampers in the cellar.

'It could just be sausages,' Cressida said, kneeling down to see exactly what Ruby was nuzzling against. 'She is eating for about nine now. But you'd think she'd be trying to jump into the hamper if that were the case, not squeeze down next to it.'

Ruby was indeed trying to wedge her head down between two of the Christmas hampers, and Cressida asked Alfred to help her shift one of them out of the way. It was full of Port wine and stilton cheeses, but this didn't seem to be what Ruby was interested in. As soon as her head could fit, she barrelled into the gap and started yapping and snorting again.

'Can you see what she's got?' Alfred asked.

'No and I don't have a torch.' Cressida looked about her for something that might help see further into the darkest corner of this already dark cellar. Just as she was about to start emptying every Christmas hamper in search of candles, Ruby edged her way out, bottom first, of the gap. And in her mouth was a white cloth, with red coursing through the folds of it. Ruby proudly dropped the clump of fabric at Cressida's feet and earned herself a kiss atop her head as Cressida knelt down and picked up the cloth.

But it wasn't a cloth at all. Cressida and Alfred both looked in horror as she pulled apart the three separate items: a pair of white satin evening gloves, much like her own, and a white handkerchief. But unlike any evening gloves Cressida owned, or any handkerchief she ever hoped to, these were covered in bloodstains.

She wanted to drop them in horror, but kept a firm hold despite her shivering and trembling hands. Then she turned them over and noticed something that was almost hidden under the blur of red blood on the handkerchief.

An embroidered monogram.

PB.

26

Back up in the corridor there was much better light thanks to the chandeliers, not to mention the myriad candles dotted around the side tables and in sconces on the walls, so Cressida showed Alfred the hanky and gloves.

'PB, that must be Peter Beaumont,' Alfred said. 'So it's true? The jealous husband is the murderer.'

'But he has an alibi,' Cressida mused. 'And I can't see him wearing these evening gloves. The hanky must be his, but the gloves are not.' She held them out in front of her. 'Almost every woman here tonight has a pair like these, but, of course, with dancing so much and eating the buffet, many of us have taken them off.'

'Not you though, and I must say, they look rather splendid,' Alfred grinned at her and Cressida was about to playfully tell him off for not concentrating on the case when suddenly a voice yelled from the other end of the corridor.

Cressida instinctively and quickly folded the gloves and handkerchief away into her handbag.

'Cressy! Cresssssssy!' Dotty came running towards Cressida and Alfred, George hot on her heels. 'Cressy!'

'Dot! What is it?' Cressida caught her friend in her arms as she barrelled into her.

Dot gave Cressida no time to tell her of her own plight, or recent abduction, before launching into a breathless explanation of her urgency. 'We don't know, not for sure, but it looks serious,' she panted, and gulped down some air, holding a hand to her waist to ease off a stitch. 'Sorry, running not my strong suit. Especially not after all the dancing.'

'What is it, Dot, what's the matter?' Cressida tried again.

George, who wasn't quite so out of breath, helped out his almost-fiancée and took over. 'We just saw your friend Andrews and his sergeant go at quick march towards the powder room.'

'The ladies' powder room? Why?' Cressida looked at Alfred, then back to the others.

'We're not sure.' Dotty had got her breath back. 'But they looked awfully concerned and had some other police with them, too.'

Cressida needed no more encouragement. With a quick thanks, she scooped up Ruby and hurried around in the direction of the powder room. She felt her spine tingle and it wasn't a good feeling. *Violet...*

As she neared, she could see what Dotty had been trying to tell her. She placed Ruby on the floor and walked slower, but still with purpose, towards the door to the ladies' powder room. A few disgruntled-looking women were standing close by, muttering to each other while taking the opportunity to catch their reflections in the large mirrors in the corridor. She didn't recognise them; they were a little older than Cressida and her friends, and although dressed in the height of fashion, a little more demurely than the shorter hemlines of the younger women.

Cressida edged close enough, pretending to look at herself in the mirror, too, in order to hear their conversation.

'... quite scared the life out of her...'

'... the poor thing... not very festive...'

'... they're saying... covered in blood... simply ghastly for her.'

'... poor Dora, what a way to ruin Christmas...'

Dora? Was Dora hurt? Or worse, dead? And even worse... if Victoria wasn't the only death tonight, and Dora was dead too, well... who next?

Cressida spun on her heel away from the gossiping women and with some urgency approached the policeman who blocked her way into the powder room. He looked as unhappy as you'd expect someone to be working on Christmas Eve to look and he stuck a raised palm out to stop Cressida in her haste.

''Scuse me, miss, but no further than this, please,' the policeman said, his bristly moustache moving more than his lips as he spoke. His brow was heavy too, made more so by the weight of the sturdy helmet upon his head.

'Officer, please, is DCI Andrews in there?'

The policeman shifted his weight, but otherwise stayed firm. 'He is, miss, but that's got no bearing on whether you can go in.'

'But I know him. And him me. I help him solve cases.' Cressida could hear how her words sounded – and the policeman snorted in a derisory way.

'I very much doubt that, miss. Detective Chief Inspector Andrews would hardly need a civilian helping him.'

'We're old friends. My father...' Cressida couldn't get the right words out, it seemed, and nothing was making any difference to the solid blockade of the policeman. Just as she was searching for something else to say, something to convince him to let her through, Ruby sauntered over and sat next to her. And then a very unexpected thing happened. The policeman went from being as tough as a cliff face next to the North Sea to 'coochie-coo'ing Ruby. Cressida almost laughed.

She picked up Ruby and offered her over to the policeman. 'She's called Ruby and she's a pug, would you like to hold her?'

'I know she's a pug all right, miss,' the policeman said, his voice, though still earthy and East End in accent, now softer and adulating. 'Look at that wide lower jaw, those button ears, that wonderfully undershot mouth and she's not apple-headed, no indentations. Lovely example of the breed. My little girl, Beth, would love one of these. My old mum used to breed them, you see, for the society girls, but we never could keep the pups, but now Beth wants one to remind her of her old nan.'

'Well, I'm afraid I can't give you, Ruby, she means the world to me. But she's in the family way, you know, up the duff. Wearing the bustle the wrong way round. In the pudding club. And I'm sure one of the pups could come Beth's way if you could just see your way...' Cressida nodded her head in the direction of the powder-room door.

'Would you? Really, miss?'

'Can't promise they're one hundred per cent pug, I think a Totteridge corgi had his wicked way with her last month, but what use is a pedigree these days anyway?'

'Exactly so, miss,' said the policeman, a world away, cradling Ruby like a little baby. Ruby was not complaining.

Cressida wondered for a moment if by entering the powder room she might never see her darling dog again, but she had faith that Dotty and Alfred would step in if the infatuated copper did anything as rash as steal her. So, with a whispered thank you to her small mushroom of a dog, Cressida slipped into the powder room.

As soon as she opened the heavy wooden door, Cressida came across a scene that was as ghastly as it was grisly. Andrews and Kirby were there, with another policeman, who started towards Cressida the moment she walked in, only to be paused in his tracks by Andrews.

To Cressida's relief, Dora Smith-Wallington was sitting on

the chair that was usually reserved for the ladies' handbags. She was alive and uninjured. However, she was weeping into a handkerchief. And Cressida could see why.

In front of the doors to the cubicles, lying on the floor, her legs and arms tumbled around and over her, and a blossoming red stain soaked through her pinafore, was Violet. And in the middle of that bloodstain, stuck straight into her stomach, was a large glass rod.

Cressida raised a hand to her mouth, then half-stumbled towards where Dora was sitting and crouched down next to her. 'Dora, what happened?'

'Miss Fawcett, please,' Andrews was by her side and placed a steadying hand on her shoulder. 'Let's give Miss Smith-Wallington some space, she's had a nasty shock.'

Dora didn't look up from the handkerchief that was both gripped in her hand and covering her eyes. She was shuddering with sobs.

Cressida let Andrews help her up, while not taking her eyes off Dora. Then she turned to Andrews with an idea. 'Dotty's outside if you think Dora would be happier with her, out of this...' she waved her hand towards the body on the floor, 'this scene.'

'That's a good idea. Kirby!' Andrews gave orders for Kirby to take Dora outside and make sure Dotty knew to keep her close and comforted. Then he turned back to Cressida. 'I don't know how you got in' – he raised an eyebrow – 'but now you're here, I'd appreciate your insights.'

'We were due a little tête-a-tête, Andrews, I've got quite a lot to tell you, as I'm sure you have too, but this... this is so terribly sad. Poor young thing. She seemed so sweet, and so proud to work here.' Cressida leaned against the basins; she needed the support as well as wanting to be as far away from the body by the lavatory doors as possible, while still being at the scene. It had really been a very trying night on the old knees, and she felt them quivering again as the shock of seeing another dead body set in.

Andrews stood next to her, his large, familiar presence a comfort, even if his dark green tweed, street-worn boots and grizzled beard looked so terribly out of place in a ladies' powder room. He was straight down to business, though.

'You'd met her then? Tonight?' Andrews automatically looked around for Kirby and his notebook, but, of course, he wasn't there. Instead, Andrews got his own out and licked the leaded end of a stubby pencil. 'Carry on.'

'Yes, I did. She was here, of course, earlier and we were talking about the soap's fragrance...' Cressida narrowed her eyes in concentration. She often thought of her deductive process as a loose thread that sometimes needed a tug to unravel the real story. And she felt this was very much a small, but not insignificant thread to pull. But she couldn't quite grasp it. She shook off the frustration and carried on. 'You see, I'd popped in for a pee just before I went down to the cellar to see Victoria—'

'You did what?' Andrews looked exasperated.

'Ah, yes. Well, I did say we had much to catch up on. And my visit to Victoria was part of that. And my abduction, if you can call it that. And daring rescue. Oh, and the gloves and bloodied handkerchief. Hmm, yes, quite a bit to tell you about really.' Andrews shook his head. 'But before I do, when did this happen?' She looked at the young woman on the floor.

Andrews flicked his notebook back a page or two. 'Between ten thirty and quarter to eleven o'clock. Miss Smith-Wallington couldn't be more exact, but she entered the powder room at about that time and was greeted by the attendant—'

'Fully alive, I assume?'

'Yes, fully alive. She locked herself into one of the cubicles to do her business and claims not to have heard anything else, except a thud when we assume the body dropped to the floor in front of, and blocking, her door.'

Cressida listened to what Andrews said, but her thoughts had caught up with her. She looked at her watch and remembered checking it the last time she was here in this powder room.

And then she realised the timing. It didn't matter that Cressida had been distracted by talking to Jim the busboy, and that she was attacked while down in the cellar. She would never have met Violet in the ballroom at about quarter to eleven, as by then Violet was already dead.

27

'So, what's all this about you being abducted? And a bloodied handkerchief? Gloves?' demanded Andrews.

Cressida briefly wondered if he was going to give her a grilling. She shivered as she thought back to those horrible minutes – though it felt like hours – when she was trapped in that hamper with its plum puddings and that rather uncomfortable yule log. And then there was the shock of finding the grisly gloves and hanky.

When she looked back at Andrews, she could see that his stern expression was tempered by a kindness in his eyes and she remembered how often Andrews worried about her, for her own sake, and for her father's, a man he credited with saving his own life all those years ago.

So, Cressida told him everything.

Andrews nodded along, until she got to the part when she was examining Victoria's body.

'You see, her choker had fallen away, Andrews, and underneath it, there was a very clear mark that looked to me as if she'd been strangled.'

'Strangled? But the knock to the head, the champagne bottle—'

'The top of which somehow ended up in Clayton Malone's pocket,' pointed out Cressida.

'And you're saying that's no longer the murder weapon?' Andrews shook his head. 'I don't understand.'

'I think it's still part of the murder, how could it not be? Victoria wouldn't hit herself over the head with a champagne bottle and then hide the broken top in Clayton's pocket while she was being strangled.'

Andrews rubbed his beard. 'Yes, I can't see that happening. And she was definitely hit by the bottle. So, what then? The champagne bottle was used to subdue her? Knock her out so that—'

'So that strangling her was easier.' Cressida could sense the thread dangling in front of her and tried to mentally capture it and unravel it. She posed another question, as much to herself as to Andrews. 'But why not keep hitting her with the bottle? Why then feel the need to strangle her?'

'To make sure she was properly dead? Taking no chances?' Andrews answered anyway.

'The cold water of the fountain would have done that, she could have drowned if she were unconscious, or the murderer could have just kept using the bottle. But she was strangled too, killed twice in a way... Oh, I need Dotty and her encyclopaedic knowledge of criminal psychology.'

Andrews crossed his arms and furrowed his brow. 'It just doesn't make much sense. But we must bear it all in mind. But back to these gloves and the handkerchief you mentioned?' Andrews asked and Cressida rootled in her small evening bag for the clues Ruby had found.

'Here. The handkerchief must be Lord Beaumont's, but the gloves, well, they're not his.'

'Quite.' Andrews nodded.

'Don't you think they mean a woman must be involved?' Cressida asked.

'There were no gloves found on Lady Beaumont. They could be hers, and it wouldn't be too much of a stretch to think that she might have been carrying one of her husband's hand-kerchiefs with her either, especially if she had recently been arguing with friends and ex-lovers. A bit teary, you know.'

'Or pongy...' Cressida whispered to herself, recalling Jim's words and thinking of a hanky's other use at times – to cover one's nostrils.

'What's that then?' Andrews asked and Cressida shrugged. She wasn't sure yet if her young waiter's words meant anything and she didn't want to try Andrews' patience any more than she had to.

'Oh, nothing. Just something I heard. Not to do with Victoria.'

'Hmm,' Andrews accepted the brush-off with good grace. 'Now, on to you being attacked. Did you see who it was at all?'

Cressida thought back to the rough-hewn sack that was pulled taut across her face and grimaced. 'No,' she answered him. 'But I did smell smoke. And Lord Beaumont's a smoker, as is Clayton...'

'Both worth bearing in mind, Miss Fawcett, when you're thinking things through. Pulling your threads.' Andrews folded up the gloves and handkerchief and placed them in one of the brown paper evidence bags she was now quite used to seeing. In her mind, though, these clues did nothing to clarify anything. They only confused matters.

A man's hanky and a woman's gloves...

A murdered countess and a murdered maid...

Two sets of footsteps in the snow, but only one pair of ruined shoes...

A blow to the head, but a strangulation too... not to mention a sharp glass rod through the body of a ladies' room attendant...

There was something gruesome going on at the Mayfair Hotel tonight. Something dark and sinister, and whoever was behind it had a dastardly motive. It was simply a matter of finding out what that motive was.

Before it was too late.

Cressida took a deep breath, then regretted it as the smell of blood mixed with the sandalwood and florals of the hotel's soap made her quite nauseated. She coughed into a tissue and dabbed her eyes which had started running. She half-stumbled back towards the basins and caught the edge of the vanity top to support herself. This night was full of ups and downs; in no time at all she had gone from the excitement of kissing Alfred and thinking she was on to a new lead to seeing the second dead body of the night. But there was a part of her – possibly the part inherited from all the Fawcett ancestors standing up to the French – that made her gird her loins and get a grip.

'I'm sorry about that, Andrews, I just had a funny turn,' she explained as the policeman came to her side. 'Was there anything else Dora said about the moments before she heard the thump? Did Violet call out? Was there a conversation about anything?'

'She says not, but then Miss Smith-Wallington was in deep shock, as you can expect. Such a nice young lady.'

'Yes, Dora's renowned for her niceness. Her forbearance is legendary. How she does it, I don't know. Carry on.'

'Miss Smith-Wallington said she tried to exit the cubicle and found the door hard to shift. In her panic, she rather "shouldered it open" and in so doing rolled the body of the young woman. Her screams were heard by ladies just outside the room and the rest you know.' He closed his notebook, then scratched his beard in thought. 'What we don't know, though, is what it is that's killed her.'

'Well, that glass rod, I should imagine, Andrews,' Cressida said, trying not to look at the gruesome scene on the floor.

'Yes, we can see that. But what is it? Where did it come from?' Andrews shrugged as he posed the questions.

Cressida looked at the poor dead woman lying on the floor, the strangely shaped glass rod sticking out of her stomach. It was sharp all right, and slightly tapered, but also undulating and very clear – where it wasn't smeared in blood, of course. The sight was horrifying, but Cressida steeled herself to look properly. And then it came to her.

'Oh, Andrews, I know exactly what that is. We've been walking past them all night.'

'We? I don't recognise it—' He looked confused as Cressida interrupted him.

'Yes, "we". All of us.' She shook her head in disbelief.

'Well then, what is it?' Andrews waited expectantly.

'That, Andrews, is a tree ornament. From the beautiful specimen in the main lobby, seen no doubt by hundreds of guests, tourists and day trippers since the tree was decorated. It's an icicle, I believe. The tree is adorned with them. And I bet if we ask the staff who decorated it to do a count, we'll find one missing.'

'An icicle?' Andrews rubbed his beard again. 'Well I never. You always wonder if you'll find a dead body mysteriously stabbed and the murder weapon just melted away. And it would be bleeding clever to use a real icicle for that very reason. But not a *glass* one.'

'As cold and snowy as it is out there tonight, Andrews, I should imagine the chance of finding a lethally long real icicle just when you have the opportunity to kill, well, that's hardly going to happen is it? But a handy glass one, just hanging in plain sight? That's much more convenient. Speaking of hands, are there any fingerprints?' Cressida, despite really not wanting to, peered in to look closer at the blood-covered ornament.

Andrews tutted and shook his head. 'No, no fingerprints that we can make out at the moment, though, of course, we'll take it back to the station after Christmas for analysis. But the blood is covering most of it and there just seem to be smears.'

'Let's hope your boys find something. It would be hard to wipe that clean and leave all that blood on it,' Cressida mused.

'Well, we did find something else. Not fingerprints, but something almost as personal.'

'Oh yes?' Cressida looked up from where she'd been staring at the poor woman on the floor. Having not wanted to look at her at first, she was now keen to make sure that no other important details were missed.

'Yes, you see there was something of interest found on the young woman's body here. A pack of letters.'

'Oh, really? Love letters?'

'Yes, now you mention it. Well, from what I could see from a precursory look,' Andrews confirmed. 'Love and gossip it seems mostly. But it means we'll be bringing Mr Malone back in for questioning.'

'Let me guess, they're addressed to him?' Cressida asked.

'Correct. Seems he's been a busy boy.'

'Can I see them? I'm not sure they'd be from Violet...' Clayton had never mentioned an affair with a member of the hotel staff. These had to be the ones that Victoria had written to him. But why did Violet have them?

Andrews reached down behind him to where one of the police's brown evidence bags was resting up against the floral curtain that hung under the basins and their vanity top. Opening it, he pulled out a stack of letters that were tied together with string, but with one already slipped out of the binding and opened on top.

'There,' Andrews pointed to the bottom of the last page of the open letter. 'Signed with a V. Do you think the rogue pushed his way in here, threw her letters back at her and did the deed?'

Cressida slipped another letter out of the pack. She felt bad reading this private and personal correspondence, but she had to know.

And she was right.

She shook her head. 'There, Andrews, see. Not V for Violet. These letters are signed V for Victoria. These are the letters stolen from Clayton. Addressed to him and written by Victoria Beaumont. He was meant to return them to her tonight. Here, look,' Cressida pointed to a phrase, 'she talks about "Peter being an oaf" and "Beaumont Park is so bleak in this weather, I miss the excitement of London". They're Victoria's letters.'

'What were they doing lying next to the victim here then?' Andrews asked.

'I don't know, Andrews. But I do know – now more than ever – that these two murders are linked. Whoever killed Victoria, killed Violet.'

'But why?'

Cressida could feel her eyes welling up as she spoke out loud what she was ashamed to say.

'Because Violet was about to help me unmask the killer. Someone found out, and they killed her.'

28

Cressida left DCI Andrews in the ladies' powder room and was pleased of the fresher air out in the corridor. Instead of sickly sandalwood soap and the metallic tang of blood, the space around her now smelt of pine needles from the boughs decorating the side tables and the sweet smell of candlewax laced with Christmassy cinnamon and nutmeg.

She paused, resting against one of the side tables for a moment, and took a couple of deep breaths. Poor Violet. Like Victoria, she too would have a family who would wake up on Christmas morning to the worst news imaginable. A mother and father, siblings, perhaps even a sweetheart.

Cressida wiped away a tear before shaking her head and bracing herself for the rest of the night ahead. She couldn't let these thoughts overwhelm her, not while the killer was still on the loose.

The burly policeman, still carrying Ruby like a cradled baby, approached her and Cressida sagged a little with relief. Seeing her dear pup so well looked after lifted her spirits.

She beamed at the constable. 'Thank you,' she said as she took Ruby from him, admittedly having to prise his hands away a little more forcefully than perhaps she thought she might have to. He really did *love* pugs... Once Ruby was back in her arms, she added, 'I won't forget about your Beth. If you think she'd really like one?'

'Cor, yes, miss, that would be grand.' He bowed his head in a quick thank you and then went back to standing sentry on the powder room door, only shifting once to let Kirby in to see his boss.

Ruby snuffled her approval and Cressida smiled at her.

'Using your womanly wiles like that, Ruby, I don't know...' Cressida gently told her dog off then looked up as Kirby appeared by her side.

'Orders to accompany me as I find Dora?' Cressida asked him, knowing the answer would be yes even before Kirby nodded as such.

'That's right miss,' he confirmed. 'Chief needs to inquire further about the scene she stumbled upon once she's less taken by the shock of it all, as it were.'

Cressida nodded. 'Dotty will have calmed her down. Let's find them.'

Together they searched for her other friends, eventually finding them, along with Dora, in the smoking room. Its wood-panelled walls and roaring fire were a comfort, and its air of gentleman's club was increased as Cressida noticed that Alfred and George were keeping a sensitive distance from the girls. Dora was sniffling into a handkerchief and accepting comforting pats on the back and the occasional 'there, there' from Dotty.

Andrews had allowed Cressida to take Victoria's letters but had also ordered for Dora to accompany Sergeant Kirby back to see him – something Cressida understood, but needed to delay just slightly. She had her own investigating to do first. She turned to speak to Kirby before he marched into the room behind her.

'Sergeant Kirby, would you mind terribly if I asked Dora a quick question? Andrews has given me permission.' She'd lost count of how many times she'd had to cross her fingers under the reassuring weight of Ruby, but she did it again now.

Kirby looked disbelievingly at her, but nodded nonetheless. 'Right you are, Miss Fawcett, if the boss proclaims it to be so, so shall it be.'

Cressida smiled, she was always fond of Kirby, especially when he used far too many words when one would suffice. What had Alfred called him once? The human thesaurus...

'Thank you, Kirby. I'll send her right out.' With that, she touched the young sergeant on the arm, watched as the pink flush spread over his cheeks right up to the wisps of ginger hair that peeped out from under this helmet, and gently closed the door behind her.

Dotty looked up as she walked in.

'Oh Cressy, thank heavens. Poor Dodo here is in bits. She's convinced she'll be arrested for murder.' Dotty gave Cressida a look, and being such old friends Cressida knew how to interpret it. She placed Ruby down and then crouched next to Dora.

'Dodo, please don't worry. DCI Andrews is the best on the force, and a personal friend. I assure you, he won't go around arresting anyone who isn't guilty.'

Dora took her hands from her face, which paled further as she looked up and met Cressida's eye. 'Cressida... you're here. Oh, thank heavens.'

'I came as soon as I heard.' Cressida gripped Dora's hand in hers, feeling the flinch as she did so. Dora really was on edge. 'Please, Dodo, don't worry. Just tell us what happened.'

'But there's no one to vouch for me,' Dora let Cressida hold her hand as she replied, her voice quiet and haltering. 'I found the b-body.'

'It's horrible, isn't it? A real shock to the old system. I

needed about forty martinis after I found my first dead body, isn't that right, Dotty?'

'Well, you almost got one of my ancestors smashed on your head too, but yes, I think you'd have preferred a few martinis,' Dotty agreed.

'So, you see, I know how it feels.' Cressida could feel her knees searing with pain. It wasn't so long ago that she'd been crouched in this same position in that Christmas hamper, waiting tensely for the killer to return. She gritted her teeth, determined to carry on. Comforting Dora was more important than aching knees. And more than that, needling out whatever she could from Dora about Violet's death was paramount. She took a deep breath, then carried on. 'Dodo, can I ask you something? DCI Andrews said you heard nothing before the sound of what must have been Violet's body hitting the ground. Is that right?'

Dora looked up at Cressida, her eyelashes wet with tears. 'Well, no...' She paused, a hiccough escaping through her ragged breathing. 'Sorry, I'm quite in bits.'

'Take your time, Dodo,' Cressida reassured her, though she shot a look at Dotty which indicated that time was very much of the essence.

'I did hear a voice...' Dora started, then hiccoughed again. 'Sorry.'

'Perfectly natural,' Cressida reassured her. 'I've been known to hiccough the whole duration of a wedding. But tell me more about this voice? Do you know who it was?'

'No, I didn't recognise it, so I suppose it might have belonged to that poor dead girl in there.' Dora clamped the handkerchief to her mouth as she hiccoughed again and then started crying. Dotty rubbed Dora's back, issuing 'there, there's, and eventually Dora carried on. 'I remember it was something about soap. Liquid soap from a dispenser, but it was just a burble, a really hurried sort of conversation.'

'Why didn't you tell DCI Andrews this when he asked you? Are you sure you didn't hear another voice, two people having a conversation?'

'I'm so confused.' Dora's eyes were wide, tears streaked from them and she was trembling. Cressida felt awful pressing her for more information, Dora was clearly in shock, but she simply had to have all the facts if this case was going to start making any sense at all.

'Was it a woman's voice?' Cressida asked, assuming it must be, if it was in the ladies' powder room.

'I... I suppose. I really didn't hear anything else except for that phrase about soap dispensers.'

'And you didn't hear the poor girl cry out?' Cressida asked, trying not to sound frustrated.

'No, that was the thing. Not at all.'

Cressida looked down at the letters in her hand. Andrews hadn't said where on the body they had been found. There was no blood on them, so they can't have been in the pocket of her apron.

Oh gosh... Cressida thought, seeing what she thought looked like a bite mark in the paper.

'Um, Dodo, when you found the body, these weren't placed in the victim's mouth were they?' She showed Dora the letters, which started off another round of tears. Through them, Dora hiccoughed a sort of yes. Then she whispered a confession.

'I did something terrible, Cressy. Something the police will never forgive me for.'

Cressida shot a quick look to Dotty, who raised an eyebrow in return. All unseen by Dora, who had covered her face in her hands. Her gloveless hands. Cressida thought back to the pair of white satin, bloodstained gloves she'd just found in the cellar.

Could Dora have been down there? Could Dora have pushed her into the hamper and then discarded her bloodstained gloves behind one of the large wicker baskets? Cressida looked at her. Her beaded dress still glimmered and glinted in the light from the fire and the lamps and candles in the room, but she was hunched over in the chair. Her plain navy blue shoes were kicked off and Cressida could see nasty red marks on her feet – the trouble with wearing ill-fitting shoes for a night of dancing. And she was trembling. Was it with shock, or with the fear that she was about to be found out? What was the terrible thing that she insisted the police would never forgive her for?

Cressida squeezed Dora's shoulder. 'What did you do, Dodo?' she asked gently. 'I'm sure it can't be anything too terrible.'

'They'll be so cross with me,' she whispered. 'What have I done?'

Cressida looked at Dora's bare hands again and couldn't shake the idea that she no longer had evening gloves on. But then a thought occurred to her, and she had to admit she was pleased of it, and rather blurted it out. 'Oh, but Dodo, you were trapped in the loo when I was in the cellar.' *And when I was attacked...* she thought to herself.

Dora looked at Cressida, raising her head suddenly from her hands and opening her eyes wide. 'Cellar? What are you talking about?'

'Sorry, Dodo, I was leaping ahead of myself. You being stuck in the lavatory just now, with the body blocking your way out, well, it means it couldn't have been you who pushed me into a hamper in the cellar. No need to look so worried, Dodo, Alfred rescued me.'

'Alfred did, did he?' she sighed. 'I'm so happy for you two.'

'Well, we're not an item yet.' Cressida felt a flush rise on her own cheeks as she looked across to where Alfred was standing by the fireplace, his gaze fixed solely on her. Cressida couldn't help but smile briefly at him, then turned back to Dora, who looked vexed. 'Dodo, tell me, please, before Kirby comes back in. What is it that you think the police will be cross about?'

Dora pulled her hands back to her face as if shielding the others from the memory she was recounting. 'I had to push the door so hard to open it and I think I rather tumbled the poor girl around a bit. My shoulder hurts from the effort.'

'That sounds understandable. What did you do that was so awful?' Cressida asked.

'The letters...' Dora lowered her hands from her face. 'I was the one who took them out of her mouth. After I'd got over the initial shock, of course. Which was ghastly.'

'Ghastly,' Cressida and Dotty agreed at the same time.

'But I had to take them out. It just looked so uncomfortable for the poor girl,' Dora continued, and although Cressida understood, she imagined the glass icicle in the girl's stomach would have looked a tad more uncomfortable. Still, it was clear Dora was beating herself up over this minor misdemeanour.

'I really wouldn't worry,' Cressida reassured her. 'If you like, I'll make sure DCI Andrews knows where the letters were, originally, and explain to him exactly why you moved them. That way he'll know all the salient facts and it explains it if he finds your fingerprints on them later when they're analysed.'

Dora nodded meekly. 'Thank you, Cressida. I knew I could trust you.'

'Of course, Dodo. And I hate to do this, but with Sergeant Kirby waiting to take you back to Andrews, can I just make sure I have everything correct?'

Dora nodded and Cressida continued.

'So, you were in the lavatory when you heard someone – most likely the poor murdered girl – mention a liquid soap dispenser, or something like that. You didn't hear her scream, so you think she had these letters shoved into her mouth when she was killed. Do you think that's a fair assessment?'

As Dora nodded, Cressida stood up, holding the letters out in front of her. Her knees clicked and she felt the flood of relief through her legs as Dotty offered some words of comfort to their shaken friend. Dotty then helped her up from the chair and on with her shoes. Dora winced as she pushed her feet into them, but, after a moment or two, nodded to Dotty and off they went in the direction of the waiting sergeant.

'One last thing, Dodo,' Cressida asked, making both Dora and Dotty turn around just before they got to the door.

'Yes, Cressy?' The unhappy girl sniffed, gripping her handbag tight to her chest.

'Where *are* your gloves?'

Dora looked at her hands as if seeing them for the first time, then paled further, though that barely seemed possible. 'I... I don't know... I had them on when I went into the powder room—'

'And no doubt took them off when you were in the cubicle,' prompted Cressida.

'Yes, of course.' Dora seemed genuinely confused.

'Did you put them somewhere? On the side perhaps?' Cressida received a glare from Dotty at this point and she wasn't sure why. Dotty knew she asked questions like this. But it surprised her when Dotty took over.

'Cressy doesn't mean to lead you in her questions. Do think clearly without any sort of prompt as to where they might be,' Dotty said confidently and Cressida realised her mistake. Dotty reading those detective books really was useful for their investigations. Perhaps she should give them a try too.

Yet, Dora merely shrugged and shook her head. 'I think they were maybe on the chair where I left my handbag,' she indicated the bag, looked inside it, then shook her head again. 'No, I didn't put them in there. Yes, I'm sure they were on the chair. I didn't realise they'd gone when I came out. Other things were...' she tailed off, staring at the floor as no doubt the image she'd seen flooded her mind again.

'It's all right, Dodo,' Cressida said softly. 'Thank you. Now,

Sergeant Kirby and DCI Andrews will look after you, I promise.'

With that, Dotty escorted Dora to the door and into the custody of Sergeant Kirby. Could Dora's missing gloves be the bloodied ones she'd found in the cellar? The timings couldn't work, but both seemed like important clues. Yet so were the letters she was holding in her hands. Would Victoria's own words lead her straight to her killer? Carefully, she undid the knot on the piece of string that held them together and started to read...

29

Despite the trumpeter giving a career-defining solo in the ballroom, Cressida and Dotty were sitting in a hushed, almost academic, silence in the smoking room as they read through the letters written by Victoria Beaumont to Clayton Malone. Alfred and George had left them to it, deciding their talents were best suited to keeping an eye on the guests in the ballroom and cajoling anyone who looked like leaving into one more drink, or one more dance.

Occasionally, Cressida would pass a letter over to Dotty, pointing to a phrase, and vice versa, as each found out more and more truths about Lord Beaumont and his first wife, Clayton Malone and, most importantly, Victoria herself.

'Look here, Dot.' Cressida thrust another letter towards her friend, who was stifling a yawn. Time was running out, but Cressida finally thought they were getting somewhere. The *why* perhaps. And the *why* should lead to the *who*. At least that's what Cressida hoped.

Dotty took the letter and peered at it, adjusting her glasses. She read aloud, '"Peter's doctor said his heart is weak and that he shouldn't exert himself. He mustn't overdo it, or he could keel over at any time. So, you'll be unsurprised to know that I've booked us a trip to Switzerland, and for both of us to try downhill skiing, They say it's *very* exhilarating!"' Dotty pulled a face at Cressida, who raised an eyebrow in return. 'Not a very wifely thing to suggest,' she agreed. 'She even underlined the word very. But listen to this one: "I wish Mrs Spencer would stop calling on us at every hour of the day. I believe that woman could sniff out a teacake at one hundred paces. She even stayed the night last Tuesday, claiming her car had a fault, though she motored off quite happily the next morning having done nothing to it." Sounds like Victoria didn't like Ottoline or think of her as a second mother and all that, quite as much as Ottoline insists,' suggested Dotty.

'Exactly. And there are more examples of it throughout these letters. Listen to this.' Cressida riffled through a few of the opened letters that were scattered in front of them and, once she'd found the one she was looking for, she read aloud. '"You know who called on me again today. She wanted to go riding. Peter says I need to be more gracious to her after what we did, but there's something about her that gives me the creeps. It's as if she feels she missed out on the golden ticket with Peter and now obviously she thinks it's too late for her, so she comes to Beaumont Park and insipidly sits around. I'm sure I saw her tamper with my saddle when we rode out yesterday and if I hadn't tightened it, I would have been a goner at the lower field fence. Just like Lady Caroline before me."'

'Ottoline?' Dotty asked, wide-eyed.

'Who else?' shrugged Cressida. 'But this is the one that really makes me wonder what's going on in that household. Listen to this, Dot, and remember Victoria is telling her lover this, so she'd have no reason to lie to him. And it goes along with what Clayton seemed to remember from the letters.' She cleared her throat, then quoted. '"Yesterday, I found a letter from Peter's first wife, Caroline. It looks like it was never sent, it was just left in what was her desk in the corner of the drawing room. (You'd think Peter would have cleared it out before he married me – a bit macabre for me to have to sit at the same desk as his late wife, don't you think?) Anyway, it was to Otto-line, asking her to teach her how to ride side-saddle. Due to her *condition*." That bit's underlined, Dotty. Then Victoria says that Caroline says, "I've never been confident on horseback, not like the Spencers and Bingley-Corbetts and I'd appreciate some help."'

'You said Lady Caroline died from a horse-riding accident. So perhaps she wasn't a very confident rider,' Dotty said.

'Or not in a condition to really be out in the saddle in the first place. There's never been any mention of Lady Caroline being with child.' Cressida looked over to where Ruby was lying, more rotund than ever, on the sofa next to her. 'I'd like to get my hands on the coroner's report. I'm sure there was one. Victoria mentions it in that letter over there,' Cressida pointed to one of the pretty pink-edged sheets, that was still lightly scented with lily of the valley. Dotty passed it over and Cressida found the paragraph and read from it. 'This is the bit, Dot. "I couldn't help having a look through Peter's drawers while he and Ottoline were taking one of their boring turns around the terrace"; she then breaks off and moans for a bit about how little there is to do in the countryside if one doesn't like gardening or riding, and how "you know who" is always popping in, then she continues, "and I'm worried Peter has lost, or destroyed, much of the paperwork surrounding Caroline's death. There was a folder marked for it, but so little in there. Just her will, leaving him everything."'

'That is macabre,' Dotty shivered. 'Imagine snooping around your husband's desk and even suspecting he might have had something to do with the death of his previous wife.'

'It doesn't look good for Lord Beaumont, does it?' Cressida remembered the monogrammed handkerchief in the cellar, covered in fresh blood, and frowned. 'Or his "friend" Ottoline, who seems to have a delicate little foot very firmly in the door.'

'But they both have an alibi for tonight,' Dotty reminded Cressida, putting down the letter she was holding and taking her glasses off to rub her eyes. It was getting late.

'I know. But it seems all wasn't quite as we thought at Beaumont Park, that's for sure,' Cressida replied.

The door opened and DCI Andrews appeared from behind it. Cressida could see his eyes sweep across the mess of letters that were all over the arms of the chairs and sofas, and decorating the Persian rug on the floor of the smoking room, much like the flakes of snow that now thickly covered the road and pavement outside.

'Miss Fawcett, Lady Dorothy.' He nodded as he came into the room. 'I see you've got to work.'

'Without a moment to waste, Andrews,' Cressida said, matter-of-factly, uncurling her legs from underneath her and helping Ruby jump off the upholstered sofa onto the floor to waddle over to her favourite policeman.

Andrews bent down and gave the small dog a stroke, before clearing his throat and standing upright again. Cressida smiled at him. He was a good egg was DCI Andrews, and no doubt had been working just as hard as she and Dotty had been. And now Cressida had to fill him in on what they'd discovered.

He listened with interest as she told him about the unhappiness in the Beaumonts' marriage and the suspicions Victoria had over the death of the previous Lady Beaumont. Not to mention the mystery of Dora's missing gloves. Andrews took it all in, jotting down notes as she spoke. Cressida concluded with, 'Can I beg a favour from you, Andrews? Can you look into Lady Caroline Beaumont – Lord Beaumont's first wife? I'd be interested to know the results of the coroner's inquest into her death, assuming there was one. It might be of great interest, especially if she was with child, as I think she might have been.'

'All boiling down to inheritance you think, then, Miss Fawcett?'

Cressida looked at him and raised an eyebrow. 'Money can be the root of all evil, Andrews, but let's just see, shall we? Whether Lady Caroline's will had any bearing on things, I don't know. Maybe we should be looking to what Lord Beaumont would stand to inherit from Victoria. I remember the general belief during our season was that the Fanshawes were very wealthy, from business links in the Midlands, but how much of that now goes to Lord Beaumont, I don't know.'

Andrews nodded and made another note.

Cressida continued. 'Is there a way of checking how wealthy the Fanshawes are? And what money Victoria took into the marriage? And do you have any news on the tree decoration?' she asked.

'Yes, and you were quite right. The head housekeeper here at the hotel was responsible for decorating the tree and she was good enough to take a look at it, despite it still being covered in blood. They were new this year, it seems, and she recognised it straight away. And seeing them hanging on the tree again for myself, well, let's just say, yes, you were right.'

'I knew it.' Cressida shook her head, the image of the young woman's frightful death still lingering.

'Discovering what the murder weapon was is darned useful, so thank you for that, Miss Fawcett, but sadly we're no closer to finding out who might have taken it from the tree. We're canvassing the staff in the lobby, of course, to see if they saw anything, but we still don't want the hundred or so guests here at the ball spooked and making a run for it.' Andrews scratched his beard as he spoke.

'Is everyone still buying the theft story? What about Violet's murder? Word must be getting round, surely?' Cressida asked. 'We're under enough pressure to get this solved by carriages at midnight.'

'So far, Violet's death has been explained as a tragic accident, helped by the fact that Miss Smith-Wallington was the
only witness and she has agreed to keep the truth to herself for
now. There's another ladies' lavatory the other side of the ballroom, so no one is inconvenienced.'

'I saw a few ladies hovering around the corridor when Dodo
was in the powder room with you, I'm afraid they were starting
to gossip,' Cressida told Andrews and his face fell.

With a sigh, he replied. 'Well, in that case we need to crack
on. I believe there was still a lead you wanted to explore. A
certain Dr Hart of Harley Street?'

'Yes, and even more so now, as from reading Victoria's
letters to Clayton, I wonder if Lady Caroline had been pregnant when she died. I don't know how this doctor might be
connected to Violet's murder, but it was clear that he and
Victoria had some sort of tension between them.'

'But I can't see how that would relate to Miss Violet's
murder either. I'm afraid we're going to have to dedicate police
resources to removing Violet's body to the cellar and gathering
evidence from the crime scene, not to mention getting witness
statements from everyone who was nearby when the murder
happened.'

'Let me handle Dr Hart then,' Cressida told him, standing
up and brushing down the silk of her dress. 'I agree, it's hard to
know how he might have had anything to do with Violet's
death, but I still feel he's worth talking to. And with time swiftly
running out, we must try every avenue.'

'Agreed. Thank you, Miss Fawcett, and good luck.' With
that, he gave her a quick bow of his head and a flick of his hand
as a sort of 'carry on' salute.

As he left the room, Alfred and George returned.

'Afraid to say it, ladies, but the party is beginning to wane in
there.' Alfred pointed his pipe stem towards the ballroom. 'No

one's attempting to leave yet, but there's definitely less dancing going on—'

'And most of the sausage rolls are gone,' added George, popping one into his mouth as he spoke.

'No wonder, George,' Dotty chastised him, though she lovingly held onto his arm as she manoeuvred him back towards the door. 'But let's see what's left. I want to put a plate together for Dodo. She looked awfully pale. And Kirby will be hungry too. I think they'd both appreciate a little sustenance. Is that all right with you, Cressy?'

Cressida smiled at her friend. Any idea that gave Dotty some time with George on this most unusual of proposal nights was fine with her. They deserved more than just the few minutes they'd had since he arrived back from Egypt. She nodded enthusiastically. 'I think it's better I find Dr Hart on my own anyway, bearing in mind the sensitivity of his business and all that,' Cressida agreed, happy that Dotty didn't argue this time. Instead, arm in arm with George she left to hunt down what was left of the buffet.

Alfred, however, raised an eyebrow. 'Sounds like the investigation continues? You don't think that being chucked into a Christmas hamper is a warning sign that perhaps the murderer doesn't want you poking your noble old nose into their business?' He leaned against the fireplace and looked contemplative.

Cressida let him think, though she had a sneaky look at her watch at the same time too.

Luckily, Alfred continued, 'It's just I'd hate it if something happened to you, old thing?'

Cressida looked at him and sighed. This was why she was always so cautious about getting romantically involved with anyone, let alone pledge one's life to them. It wasn't so much that they would curtail one's freedom, she realised, but that loving them made one just that bit more careful about throwing oneself in harm's way. Alfred was right, she had just been targeted by the murderer. But it could have been much worse.

She stepped across the fine Persian carpet and met him at the fireplace, touching his arm gently as she stood in front of him. 'That's just the thing, Alfred, being attacked like that, though jolly scary and not at all the sort of caper I was anticipating tonight—'

'Oh no?' He cocked his eyebrow at her again and she cuffed him on the arm.

'No. But don't you see, it means I'm getting close. Whoever it is would never have shoved me into that hamper of Christmas goodies if I wasn't on the right track.'

'That's where you're wrong.' Alfred's lack of agreement took Cressida by surprise and she wondered for a moment if perhaps he didn't understand her at all.

'I don't think so, Alf—' she started, but he interrupted her.

'No, I mean you're wrong to just say "I'm" on the right track. You've got us too. Dotty's inhaled those detective novels and I... well, let's just say I plan to be by your side for the foreseeable. So *we're* on the right track, Cressy, *we*.'

Cressida looked up at Alfred and grinned at him. Timings and murderers be damned. She definitely had time for a kiss.

30

'You don't happen to know where this Dr Hart is, do you?' Cressida asked Alfred once their lips were free to do talking.

'Charles Hart? That Harley Street chap?' Alfred asked and Cressida nodded.

'That's him. I glanced at him briefly earlier but haven't seen him since.'

'Charles Hart's in the Mutton Pie Club,' Alfred said matter-of-factly.

'Oh.' Cressida crossed her arms in front of her. 'I see.'

The Mutton Pie Club was a dubious dining society, and Alfred, along with several others of their acquaintance, was a member. They met in their London club and while wearing special cummerbunds or waistcoats decorated with a pasty-like frill on the golden-pastry-coloured silk, they ate several courses of pies. They drank and gossiped too, and although the outcome was usually nothing worse than a sore head, a feeling of being overly full for the next few days and a wish to see nothing pastry-covered again for at least a week, there had been some Mutton Pie Club evenings that had ended with a night in the cells for too rambunctious a member.

Cressida looked up at Alfred as he was telling her about one of these evenings involving, she assumed, Dr Charles Hart.

'... which made him convulse with laughter so the hinge broke and mushrooms went everywhere. Which just goes to show that just because a chap's called Guy and he's quite good fun, he's not necessarily great with fungi.'

'And this has to do with Dr Hart how?' Cressida asked, keenly aware of the time ticking away.

'Oh, he brought the mushrooms, Cressy. Did I not mention that bit? Excellent pie they made too. We'll never know if the elephants we saw were real, but the pastry was crisp as anything.'

'I see,' she said, this time with a touch more mirth to her voice. 'So you *know* Dr Hart. Can you help me find him? I was going to start looking for him in the ballroom, but then I—'

'You were hampered,' chuckled Alfred, who still found that amusing.

'Yes.' Cressida shook her head in resignation. Yet it was Alfred's buoyant sense of humour in any situation that she so admired in him. 'Will you help me find him?'

'Of course, Cressy.' Alfred's face softened. 'If I can find you in a locked hamper in the cellar of the hotel, I think I should be able to find a fellow Mutton Pier at a Christmas ball. And if I know Charles, I know exactly where he'll be.'

'Where?' Cressida asked.

Alfred raised an eyebrow at her. 'The games room. Fancy a flutter?'

'There he is.' Alfred leaned in close to Cressida, which set her goose pimples off again, and pointed to the same handsome blonde-haired man she'd seen earlier, both dancing with Victoria and when Dotty was telling her all about him. This time, he was standing by the roulette table that had been set up, along with those for baccarat, craps and blackjack, in one of the hotel's reception rooms just off the ballroom. 'Just like Hart to be at the gaming tables – bit of a risk-taker that one.'

'Oh really?' Cressida turned to face her friend, shifting Ruby's weight in her arms. 'Not sure that's an attribute one wants in a doctor.'

'Hmm, I see your point. Still, looks like he has plenty of happy patients.' Alfred pointed towards the man, who was surrounded by some of the most glamorous women in the room. As Dr Hart looked up from his gaming chips and noticed them, Alfred turned his pointed finger into a casual wave. 'Oops, sorry about that, old thing,' he whispered to Cressida. 'Looks like we've been spotted.'

'Don't worry, Alf. I'm keen to go and talk to him,' she said and they started to make their way over, threading through the gaming tables that were adding another touch of festive fun to the feel of the party, with their bright green baize, postbox-red squares and the giggling and carousing people all around them. Cressida whispered in Alfred's ear again as they weaved through, saying, 'And do you think they're really all his patients?'

Alfred paused a few paces away from where Dr Hart and his coterie were standing. 'You do know what sort of treatment Charles offers, don't you, Cressy?' He looked concerned, big brotherly almost, and Cressida could feel the blush rise in her cheeks. Alfred continued. 'Charles is a doctor of, well, of ladies' things...'

'Yes, I know, Alf.' Cressida whacked him with her handbag, which was easier said than done what with Ruby still nestled in her arms. 'Your sister filled me in all about his pioneering obstetrics and gynaecology. Or ladies' things, as you so coyly put it.' She raised an eyebrow at him and he nodded, then pulled a face at her, to which she almost responded with one of her own, but kept her mind firmly on the case in hand. 'I just wouldn't have thought his patients would be all too keen to socialise with him. It's all rather private what goes on in those appointments, I should imagine.'

'Well, he's obviously very good at his job,' Alfred conceded as they reached the doctor and his ladies, and he stuck out a hand to him.

Introductions were made, and Cressida hoped that her cheeks were less flushed than they felt. For, up close, Dr Hart was really rather dashing. He had baby-blue eyes, and blonde hair, but more than that: he was tall, slim and had cheekbones and a jawline that made him appear more like a movie star than a doctor. And he was dapper in his white tie and tails, but then it was a look that made the best of any gentleman. Dr Hart, however, looked like he might look equally as smashing in a potato sack.

'Merry Christmas and all that, old fellow.' Dr Hart gripped Alfred's hand, then took Cressida's hand in his and gently brushed it against his lips as he bowed his head down to do so. 'And a very merry Christmas to you, Miss Fawcett. A delight to meet you. Are you and Delafield here an item?'

'Well, we're...' Cressida flustered and she was grateful beyond measure that Alfred helped her niftily out of the spot.

'Actually, Cressida and I have our minds on something else tonight. We were wondering if you knew much about Victoria Beaumont, the Countess of Worcester.'

'Lady Beaumont? Why?' Dr Hart peeled himself away from the women either side of him and gestured for Alfred and Cressida to follow him a little way away from the group. 'Zsa-Zsa, put those chips on number 39, why don't you?' he called over to a giggling redhead, who waved back and whooped with glee as the ball was dropped into the spinner and the game started once again.

Once they were free of the melee, Cressida answered Dr Hart. 'We're wondering about how well you know her and whether she's a patient of yours?' she asked, still holding a now-sleeping Ruby in her arms.

'Why would you want to know that?' Dr Hart's eyes skittered from Cressida's to Alfred's faces. 'You know it's not my place to talk about patients.'

'Even when they're dead?' Cressida let her comment hang and studied Dr Hart's face. To her amazement, he betrayed barely a flicker of emotion at all.

'Dead, you say? That is interesting. How so?' the doctor asked.

'Tonight. Murdered here at the hotel,' Cressida informed him. 'And I don't mean to be rude, Dr Hart, but you don't seem too surprised?'

Dr Hart pulled a silver cigarette case out of his tailcoat pocket, removed a cigarette and tapped the end of it against the case. Alfred produced his lighter and lit Dr Hart's cigarette, while the doctor's face remained inscrutable. He inhaled, blew out a large cloud of smoke, then finally spoke.

'Murdered? That's even more interesting. I'm not surprised, to be honest. Lady Beaumont wasn't what she seemed.'

'What do you mean?' Cressida asked, tensing for the answer.

Dr Hart picked a piece of tobacco from his teeth, contemplating his answer. Handsome though he was, Cressida was beginning to dislike him intensely. There was something about the way he'd reacted to the news of his patient's death, and more than that, as if somehow in her dying some sort of balance had been tipped. As he kept saying, he found it all more 'interesting' than perhaps 'shocking' or 'terribly sad' like most people would.

Finally, he replied. 'Again, I'm not at liberty to divulge any details about my patients, living or dead. What is said, or done, in my consultation room stays there.'

'But did she ever say anything to you that might hint at what might have got her killed?' Alfred coaxed, but Cressida went one step further.

'Dr Hart, Scotland Yard detectives are here at the hotel now, investigating her death. I don't think they'll look too kindly on your reticence.'

At the mention of the police, a scowl fleetingly crossed Dr Hart's face. It disappeared as the redhead named Zsa-Zsa shrilly called him back to the gaming table.

'What you call reticence, Miss Fawcett, I will merely insist is professional discretion. Scotland Yard can ask me anything they want, and my answer will be that they should come back to me in early January with a warrant to search my office. For that is the only way they will get any patient details out of me.' He took another deep drag of his cigarette and flicked the ash on the floor.

'I understand,' Cressida said, and she felt rather than saw the look of confusion on Alfred's face at her letting the doctor go with so little fight.

After a very short, but very awkward, silence, Dr Hart gave a nod of goodbye to Alfred and another lingering, somewhat disconcerting, hand kiss to Cressida. Then he turned his back on them and headed back to the roulette table. He left behind him one very frustrated amateur sleuth and the persistent smell of cigarette smoke.

31

'Well, that was, in the words of my esteemed mother, a bit of something and nothing,' harrumphed Cressida as they turned away from the gaming tables, leaving Dr Hart to his bevy of ladies.

'Must admit, I was surprised when you said you understood his position. Not your usual gung-ho quizzing of a suspect,' Alfred said, looking Cressida squarely in the eye.

'I know. But, you see, Alfred, there was no point. If a man will need a warrant before he even speaks to Andrews, then there was no way he was going to break rank and speak to us about it. Something about Victoria's death riled him, though.'

'Yes, he didn't seem awfully surprised. In fact, he said he was the very opposite. Not surprised.'

'And he most certainly did not want to talk about her,' Cressida added.

'Got to respect a chap's oath and all that,' Alfred pointed out.

'I think that's the Hippocratic one about doing no harm,' Cressida replied. Then, in more of a mumble, 'I didn't realise there was one about doing no gossiping too.'

Alfred, who had heard what she'd said despite the mumbling, got his pipe out – the chip to the bowl be damned – and clenched it between his teeth. Cressida knew this was his way of neither agreeing nor disagreeing, and amicably ending the discussion. She put Ruby down, as the small dog had started to squirm, and was about to pose the question of what they were to do next, when she felt a light tap on her arm.

She turned around and was a little surprised to see a woman, slightly older than her, in her thirties perhaps, but as elegantly as dressed as anyone else in the room. Cressida recognised her as Lady Gorebridge, not someone she knew socially so well, but a familiar face on the pages of *The Tatler* and *The Bystander*, mostly renowned for her love of horses, racing and point-to-pointing – and also well known for marrying Lord Gorebridge, who was quite a few years older than herself.

Lady Gorebridge's hand hovered on Cressida's arm, then she removed it as she took in Alfred too. 'Quick word, if you have a moment?' Lady Gorebridge said, with a glance behind her to check on Dr Hart and his companions. 'Away from the crowd.'

Cressida nodded and followed Lady Gorebridge and her magnificent feathered headband just out of the games room and back into the ballroom.

'I saw you talking to Charles. Dr Hart, that is,' Lady Gorebridge volunteered. 'Though, I must say, I'd have thought your partner here was quite capable of doing the job himself.' She looked Alfred up and down.

Alfred looked confused. 'You mistake me for a doctor perhaps, madam?' he said, his pipe poised in mid-air. 'A flattering mistake to make, but sadly I am not.'

Lady Gorebridge squinted at him, sizing him up. 'No, not a doctor, sir. The other thing that Dr Hart does for us.' She pulled away from him, though laid her hand again on Cressida's arm. 'Perhaps we should speak alone.'

Cressida looked at Alfred, who nodded, then stepped away, allowing Cressida and Lady Gorebridge to speak more privately.

'I'm afraid that I don't know what you mean by that,' Cressida asked the older lady. 'Was Dr Hart of great use to you and, um, Lord Gorebridge?'

'Oh, you could say that, yes,' Lady Gorebridge laughed and nodded enthusiastically.

'Infertility can be such a painful issue, I suppose,' Cressida mused. 'That Dr Hart can help, and has treatments that can aid those women unfortunate enough not to be able to have children otherwise—'

'You do know what he does, don't you?' Lady Gorebridge interrupted her. 'His *special* treatment?'

'Well, I assume he helps with fertility. A new drug perhaps. I've not put much thought to it before tonight. I'm not married, you see, so—'

'Well, when you are, and if it's not to that very nice-looking, and dare I say it, virile young man, you might find you need Dr Hart's help. Particularly since you are blonde too.'

'Why would that matter?' Cressida was confused. 'Are blondes less likely to be able to have babies?'

Lady Gorebridge threw her head back in laughter. 'No, you innocent thing, you. Dr Hart's most popular treatment has nothing to do with the fertility of us women, but that of our husbands.'

'I don't understand...' Cressida looked over to where Alfred was entertaining Ruby with a piece of cheese. 'I thought he was a gynaecologist. Not a specialist in men's health.'

Lady Gorebridge took a deep breath. 'Let me explain it to you. And in so doing let you into the biggest secret in society today. Dr Hart helps women like us – and by that I mean women who have married men much older than ourselves – to have children. My own dear Rodney, for example, spent so long in the saddle back in the day that it meant he was fairly useless when it came to siring a foal of his own, if you catch my drift.'

'Oh gosh.' Cressida glanced over at Ruby, pregnant with pups, as the realisation of what Lady Gorebridge was saying came upon her.

Lady Gorebridge continued unabashed. 'You might think, well, siring foals is easy. Any *lover* of breeding could help you with that. But, of course, if I might continue the metaphor, sometimes pedigree traits must be maintained. Sires must resemble other sires, so that their foals may look alike, if you see what I mean.'

'Oh, I think I do.' Cressida took it all in while racking her brains to picture what Lord Gorebridge looked like. She hazarded that he was perhaps blonde and blue-eyed.

'As I said, my own dear Rodney was a little long in the tooth and hard in the saddle, but I heard from Margaret de Bouvet that Lydia Puck-Norton had used this wonderful doctor in London to help keep the family tree intact.' She looked rather coyly back in the direction of the roulette table. 'And she wasn't mistaken. Lydia confirmed everything, while holding her bundle of joy – a beautiful blue-eyed baby boy.'

Cressida by this point possibly had the widest eyes in the ballroom. 'Oh, I see. Gosh.'

'Gosh indeed. It's a very pleasurable treatment too—'

'Especially if you're a keen rider,' Cressida finished off her statement and earned an approving nod from Lady Gorebridge. 'Dr Hart must have a hand in almost every branch of the nobility,' remarked Cressida.

'A hand... or, indeed, something else.' Lady Gorebridge nudged Cressida in the ribs, confident now they were on the same page. 'Rodney was delighted when little Hughie came along, his heir. Blonde and blue-eyed just like him. And, of course, set to inherit everything. And me, as brood mare, duty done.' She paused, a flicker of mirth on her face. 'Although I have to admit, Charlie, our "spare", and Gertie, our little girl... well, they were just for fun really.' She pealed into laughter again and Cressida bit her lip to stop herself from giggling too. But as revelatory as this all was, and shockingly good gossip into the bargain, Cressida needed to focus on Victoria and her relationship with the doctor.

'Well, that all sounds very... intriguing,' Cressida said. 'I'll definitely bear it in mind as and when. Mama's always after me to find a husband and the young and fun ones are few and far between.'

'Oh, I thought you two were an item,' Lady Gorebridge gestured towards Alfred, her many diamonds catching the candle and electric light from the chandeliers in the ballroom. 'Actually, I did think it was a little odd, you approaching Charles with your young husband in tow, though the war wounded so many of our young men in ways we simply can't fathom.'

'Alfred was too young to fight,' Cressida corrected her.

'Well, whatever. We all do our best to keep it absolutely hush-hush of course. Especially from the husbands. They can be awfully sensitive. Oops.' She gestured to the half-full glass of champagne in her hand and shrugged. 'I've probably told you far too much. You mustn't say anything.'

'I won't, I promise.' Cressida raised a finger to her lips. She realised now why Dr Hart had been rather tight-lipped when it came to talking about his patients. In his line of medicine, discretion was absolutely key.

'Good, good.' Lady Gorebridge said, seemingly easily satisfied. *Much like she had been by Dr Hart*, thought Cressida rather crudely, as Lady Gorebridge carried on. 'So why were you seeking him out? I'm not sure if he does much else except for his special fertility treatment – not something you need at the moment, unless your mama has someone old enough to be your own father in mind for you. Who recommended him to you? It's always a personal recommendation. Not the sort of thing he advertises in *The Lady* magazine – though can you imagine?' She threw her head back, laughing again, then spread her hands in front of her and quoted as if from a billboard. 'Husband not up to scratch? Need that heir? Never fear, for Dr Hart has a very special remedy!'

'Gosh, that would be an advertisement indeed!' Cressida agreed, keeping her tone as light-hearted as Lady Gorebridge's. 'And yes, you're right. I was recommended. Though more for the future, just in case. Alfred and I aren't... well, who knows if I'll ever need the doctor's services, but my friend Victoria Beaumont certainly did.'

Lady Gorebridge stopped laughing and looked more acutely at Cressida. 'Victoria Beaumont, you say? Interesting.'

'How so?'

Lady Gorebridge's whole demeanour changed. She stood more stiffly and held her glass of champagne defensively in front of her crossed arms. 'Only that I believe she was one of his most recent customers. New to him too, of course, as one always is at the beginning. But there are a few return patients. Charlie's Old Girls we call ourselves, who have the spares to thank him for, as well as the heirs, and, of course, he opens up to us more than perhaps he should.'

'Oh yes? And did he mention Victoria? She was receiving the doctor's treatment, wasn't she?' Cressida felt like she was getting somewhere.

'Yes, yes she was. And successful too, I think. But Charles clammed up when he spoke about her to me. Now, I can't be sure, but in the same breath as mentioning her name, he also said that one of the ladies he'd been seeing recently had threatened to go to the press.'

'Ah. I can imagine that would be a big no-no. And you think it was Victoria?' Cressida asked.

'Well, he's barely taken on any new clients since Lydia's

twins. And some of us pay quite hefty retainers for his services and get to know the ins and outs' – Cressida blanched at that turn of phrase, but Lady Gorebridge continued – 'of everything that's going on. And Victoria Beaumont most definitely caused a raised eyebrow among our little circle. At least I'm assuming it was her. No one else new on the books, so to speak.'

'You said "threatened" him with going to the press, but I assume she hadn't, or else it would have spread around society – the country even – like wildfire. How had he managed to prevent her from telling all, I wonder?' A shiver of realisation went down Cressida's spine as she spoke the words out loud. What *might* he have done to stop her? And then another realisation that could link him to both murders – could link any of the suspects, in fact. And that was if Violet had witnessed anything from the powder room window, looking as it did over the fountain courtyard, and been seen by the murderer as she did so, then no wonder she was now dead too.

Lady Gorebridge answered Cressida, if not directly, then at least with more information. 'He feared exposure more than anything else. And, of course, as a patient, she'd have proof of all his dealings with her. Dealings that are highly confidential, not just for her, but think of the knock-on effect for all of us ladies? I think she was asking a hefty sum from him to pay for her silence.'

'But why would she reveal anything? It would embarrass her too, would it not?' Cressida asked, but Lady Gorebridge merely shrugged.

'It's what I heard. And Charles is very upset by it. He's done nothing but good for us ladies. He's a saint. And a sinner.' She smiled at Cressida in a way that implied Charles had sinned rather a lot with her specifically, then downed the rest of her champagne and, with one more glance over her shoulder, went back into the games room.

Cressida looked over to Alfred and gestured for him to join

her again. Anyone watching the two of them would wonder what on earth Cressida was telling him to make his eyes so wide and his mouth so gaping, and it was only after she'd all but placed his pipe back into it for him, and picked up a waddling Ruby from the floor that he was able to speak again.

'Well,' Alfred said, taking his pipe out of his mouth. 'Scout's honour and all that. I won't say a word. But let's hope London society doesn't leave tonight thinking I'm a wet blanket, well, under the blankets.'

'Alfred!' Cressida spluttered, and wasn't quite sure where to look. 'I'm sure they won't. You're about half the age of all of their husbands.'

'And twice as handsome.' He winked at her, which Cressida usually found deplorable, as it usually happened at the end of an evening by a man with lascivious intent; but from Alfred, it was fine. In fact, more than fine...

She smiled at him. 'Yes, twice as handsome. And brown-haired and brown-eyed, so even if you were, I could probably get away with a lascivious affair with someone like Clayton Malone, instead of resorting to the blonde doctor.' She cocked an eyebrow at him. Then more seriously said, 'But, of course, Victoria couldn't. If both husband and wife are blue-eyed, you can't risk a brown-eyed baby.'

'Hence Victoria seeking out Dr Hart, who would also be willing to keep things quiet. A professional, so to speak,' Alfred agreed.

'Alfred, do you know what this means?' Cressida rubbed Ruby's head as she thought.

'Go on, spew forth, old thing.' He clenched his pipe back between his molars.

'Dr Hart has a motive for killing Victoria. She was black-mailing him.'

'That never ends well,' Alfred agreed, through pipe-clenched teeth. 'Dotty's books are rife with blackmailers coming to sticky ends.'

'Exactly. And it wasn't just him. Lady G said all the ladies he'd helped – her included and Lydia Puck-Norton and Margaret de Bouvet – well, they'd *all* be exposed. That adds more names to people who'd have a motive to want Victoria silenced.'

'Silenced?' Alfred raised an eyebrow and, once again, Cressida's expression mirrored his.

32

'Cressida Fawcett!' The angry voice belonged to Cordelia Stirling, who came barrelling down the corridor towards them.

Cressida instinctively moved closer to Alfred, even though she couldn't believe Cordelia could do much to hurt her, not here in plain sight of the whole hotel. Not unless she had practice in killing, of course. Cressida shook that thought away. She may not have ever much liked Cordelia Stirling, but having that sort of bias towards her wasn't right.

'Cressida,' Cordelia snapped at her again as she got closer, standing now in front of her, her hands firmly placed on her hips, the long fringe of her short dress catching up with her with a swish-swish.

'Cordelia,' Cressida said, if not timidly, then with a certain precaution. 'What's wrong?'

'What's wrong? What's wrong is Marcus has been hauled over the coals by that policeman chum of yours. Suggested he was planning on killing Victoria to inherit the estate.'

'Oh, that.' Cressida breathed a sigh of relief and then wondered how she could avoid giving away the fact that she'd been sitting in on the interview, hidden from view. 'Andrews told me they'd had a chat. Just part of the investigation. Nothing out of the ordinary, I heard.'

'Out of the ordinary? You're liaising with a Scotland Yard detective behind all of our backs and accusing people of killing Victoria.' She had built up a head of steam and Cressida realised she was the appointed punchbag.

Alfred, however, took a firmer view of the situation. 'Now, look here, Cordelia. Cressy's doing nothing of the sort. She's only doing her best to find Victoria's killer. And I'm afraid it sounded like your Marcus had quite the motive.'

'But,' Cressida squeezed Alfred's arm in thanks, while taking over in order to calm the situation, 'from what I heard, he had an answer that explained the situation. He's an artist and wanted his freedom, not the onerous responsibility an estate such as Beaumont Park would bring.'

'Did he say that? Really?' Cordelia looked miffed. 'That he wouldn't want to inherit Beaumont Park?'

'Yes. But, sadly, for the free spirit that is him, it's looking likely.' Cressida shrugged and Cordelia brightened up.

'Yes, I suppose it is. For the best, I think. He's awfully talented, but, of course, daubing a few canvases in the south of France for wealthy patrons only gets you so far. If it wasn't for his Uncle Peter's money, he'd be as poor as a Hampstead Heath sailor.'

'You mean his uncle is paying his allowance? Lord Beaumont – not his family on his father's side, the Austrians?' Cressida asked, realising that a sailor stuck on the middle of Hampstead Heath would have no job at all, and therefore no income.

'The Austrians are poor as church mice. Or *kirchenmauses*.' Cordelia giggled.

But Cressida didn't think it was funny. Marcus had not only said to Andrews that he wasn't interested in his uncle's estate due to the responsibility of running it, but that he was independently wealthy too. Why did he lie?

'Cordelia, is Marcus nearby? Can I see him?' Cressida asked, stepping closer to Cordelia, who, in response, stepped back, a look on her face as if Cressida had just offered her a three-day old haddock.

'Why? You don't want to interrogate him, do you?' Cordelia crossed her arms.

'Of course not, I want to apologise for getting him into hot water with the police,' Cressida once again crossed her fingers at the little white lie. 'Could you take us to him? Please?'

Cordelia pouted, but nodded, and with a haughty air turned and expected them to follow her as she took them along the corridor to join her beau in the ballroom.

'Marcus! Marc darling!' Cordelia flounced through her little group of friends – fellow debutantes of the season – and collared her sweetheart. 'Cressida here wants to apologise for allowing you to be raked across the coals earlier.' She stood back, tapping her foot as Cressida and Alfred approached.

'Yes, sorry about that. Not really my fault though. Of course DCI Andrews would naturally want to talk to anyone associated with the Beaumonts tonight. I hear he gave you a bit of a going-over?' Cressida found it hard to side against her favourite policeman, but she could see Cordelia softening as she spoke, if not Marcus as yet. But his reply was pleasant enough.

'Understandable in the circumstances, of course,' he agreed. 'But I do think he made quite a thing about my motive for killing "Aunt Victoria", as he kept calling her.' He rolled his eyes and shifted in his seat, which was one of the ballroom chairs, gilt-edged but upholstered in the navy blue of the hotel's livery. The table he'd been sitting at, along with some of his and Cordelia's friends, was now empty, the plates of food cleared away and just a few glasses of champagne and liqueurs on it, reminding Cressida how late the evening was getting.

Cressida was relieved Marcus was so open to talking. And she was pleased with herself for not reacting to the untruth about Andrews. As far as she could remember, but not let on, he'd only referred to Victoria in that way once. Though it was always interesting how different people remembered situations and conversations. And she definitely remembered Marcus saying he was independently wealthy of the Beaumonts.

'I suppose there is a lot to gain by being the owner of Beaumont Park,' she tried her luck, hoping he'd bite.

'But like I said to the copper,' Marcus waved a hand with a certain loucheness in front of him, 'if I wanted to inherit Beaumont Park, wouldn't it be Uncle Pedro that I'd bump off?'

Not if Victoria was pregnant, Cressida thought to herself again. *But how could you know that?*

'Marcus, don't even mention it,' Cordelia snapped at him. 'Cressida here pretends to be one of us, but she's working for the police. A real snake in the grass.'

Cressida was hurt by Cordelia's words, but tried not to show it as she pulled away from Marcus and sat back in the dining chair next to him. She let Ruby down so that the small pup could stretch her legs, but she just sat there, at Cressida's feet, plumply, looking up at her. She looked over to where Marcus was scowling at her, and at Cordelia's sneer that had turned into a look of triumph.

'Now, look here,' Alfred started, but Cressida reached up and tugged on his tailcoat to shush him.

She stood up and faced Cordelia and Marcus. 'No, you're right. I am working for the police. DCI Andrews and I worked on a couple of cases before you met us at your parents' castle, Cordelia. He's a good man and an excellent detective and I'm proud to help him out. To that end, call me a snake if you like, but don't think that means I've got scales over my eyes. If you know of anything – anything that happened at Beaumont Park, or to do with the entailment, or even your former aunt's last will and testament – you will let me know, won't you?'

'Why should we?' Cordelia asked, her arms crossed in indignation, but her voice less cocky than it was before.

'Because I should imagine you'd prefer everyone here tonight, London society in all its gossiping glory, to witness you having a friendly chat with me, rather than a less friendly one with the detective chief inspector.'

Marcus and Cordelia both looked aghast at Cressida, but she was unrepentant. Victoria's killer had to be found, and time was running out to do that. If it meant putting the willies up the suspects, then she would.

That she had found it rather satisfying, she would keep to herself.

That Alfred nudged her in the ribs and grinned at her as they left the ballroom was the icing on the Christmas cake.

33

In reply to Alfred's rib nudge, Cressida slipped an arm into his as they left the ballroom and headed back to where they hoped they'd rendezvous with Dotty, George and DCI Andrews. Cressida knew it would be a little while before any news on the previous Lady Beaumont, Caroline, could be attained by the police, but she wanted to tell Andrews all about the latest titbit gleaned from Marcus Von Drausch. Not to mention their conversation with Dr Hart and the revelation from Lady Gore-bridge over his very special form of treatment. Or, indeed, the rumours of Victoria blackmailing him with threats to go to the press.

'Hart never gave us an alibi,' Cressida mused as they opened the door to the smoking room.

'He never gave us a chance to ask,' agreed Alfred, who held the door open for her.

She was delighted to see Andrews there, with Dotty and George too, folding away the letters lest they get jumbled, or lost.

'What ho, all,' Cressida heralded them. 'We've met Dr Hart.'

'And?' Andrews asked, passing Dotty the last letter. The three of them made a rather festive tableau in front of the fire, Andrews like a wise man or shepherd and Dotty and George kneeling on the floor with the letters as if tending to the manger. Ruby ran in, as much as her growing belly would let her, and nuzzled herself onto Dotty's lap, snuffling as Dotty pulled herself and the enlarged dog onto one of the chairs, letting George finish tidying up the letters.

She filled him in on all she'd learned from the doctor and Lady Gorebridge. It could have been quite awkward explaining Dr Hart's particular treatment, but, luckily, Andrews got the gist straight away. Dotty, however, blushed about seven shades of pink and murmured something about karmic sugar again.

'Victoria may have been blackmailing Dr Hart, Lady G definitely seemed to think so. You see, Ottoline – that's Lord Beaumont's friend – said that he was thinking of divorcing Victoria. But I suppose that wouldn't happen if there was the slightest possibility that she was pregnant with his heir,' Cressida shrugged.

'But if the treatment had worked, why blackmail Hart?' Andrews opened his notebook again.

'I've been pondering this. Say the pregnancy didn't work, or Lord B found out it wasn't his, Victoria would have been divorced and left destitute and her reputation in ruins. I think blackmailing the doctor was her backup plan. Something to feather her nest if she found herself needing some money pronto.'

'That's quite ruthless of her,' Dotty said. 'To be willing to threaten a man's livelihood and risk exposing all those society ladies, while also sleeping with said man in order to get an heir that would ensure her husband wouldn't divorce her, even though he knew she'd had an affair... I'm exhausted just talking about it. And shocked, to be honest.'

George nodded approvingly, but it made Cressida think of

something. 'She always was a bit ruthless, though. I mean, I don't blame her, but there was someone else in the running for Lord B during our deb year, do you remember?'

Dotty shook her head. 'No, but then I wasn't interested in him at all myself.' She glanced up at George. 'At no one really.'

'Hmm,' Cressida narrowed her eyes. A thread had been pulled. A ruthless streak ran among them, they all knew that. Mamas desperate for their daughters to marry well had the sharpest elbows known to man or womankind. And the daughters themselves… there was often a rivalry for the choicest husbands. Perhaps an older man like Lord Beaumont, with his titles and estate – and his money – wasn't such a bad catch after all, if you thought he might not be around too long into the marriage. A thread… it was dangling there…

Andrews' voice brought her back into the room. 'Is it enough to get her killed? Strangled, even? I still don't know how we missed that.'

'Now you know how I feel not noticing the champagne bottle under Victoria's legs,' Cressida shrugged. 'And just like that bottle, the marks were hidden from plain sight. But once I moved her choker, I could see that it must have been something thick and heavy, a real thumper of a rope. Oh, Andrews, it was horrible. Poor Victoria, she looked so peaceful there, but with this red bruising and marking.' Cressida raised a hand to her own throat, then shook the image out of her mind.

'Your discovery of that changes everything, of course,' Andrews noted. 'We're no longer looking for someone with the force to kill with one blow.'

'And it means there was no way this was an accidental death or a spur-of-the-moment act of violence. She was hit over the head, pushed into the fountain and then someone decided that wasn't enough, they had to strangle her. Someone really, really wanted Victoria dead. They must have hated her. And they didn't mind getting close as sardines to do it.'

'That's true,' agreed Andrews. 'So, we have a husband with a clear motive – or two if you count the infidelity with the lover as well as the doctor. Then we have a doctor with a motive, and a lover who was found with the smashed champagne bottle neck in his pocket. And the heir apparent to the estate who will inherit everything if Lord Beaumont has no children—'

'And who I've just found out actually isn't independently wealthy and lied to you when he said he had money from his father's side. Though, admittedly, he seems like he's more interested in the generous allowance coming in rather than taking over the running of the actual estate,' Cressida added.

'I see. We definitely can't rule him out. Back to the list.' He was counting on his fingers and had got to the fourth finger, then touched the pinky on one hand, making it five. 'And there's a supposed friend who was jealous of her relationship with Mr Malone. Though I really don't see Miss Smith-Wallington being so brutal.'

'Though she has lost her evening gloves and did admit to removing the letters from Violet's mouth, which gives her a plausible excuse if you were to find her fingerprints on them. Sorry, I should have told you that earlier,' Cressida said, seeing a frown cross DCI Andrews' brow. Cressida screwed up her forehead too. There was something about those letters, something within them that she hadn't pieced together yet. She sighed and looked at Andrews, carrying on where she left off. 'But Dora says she was stuck in the cubicle behind where the body was found, and heard something said about soap.' Cressida crossed her arms.

'Yes, Miss Smith-Wallington said both of those things to Kirby – finally – when he took her statement. Says she heard no other voice, just the attendant, she thought, saying something about a soap dispenser,' Andrews confirmed.

'Who mentions soap just before they're killed?' Dotty asked, to varying degrees of shrugs from the others in the room.

But Cressida looked at her. 'Say that again, Dotty?'

'I just said, "who mentions soap before they're killed",' replied Dotty, now looking as confused as Cressida. 'Why? Have I said something strange?'

'No, not strange. But I think you might have hit on something, Dot. I just can't work out *why*. Because you're right. No one would kill someone over a disagreement about soap.'

'There was nothing in Miss Smith-Wallington's testimony about it being a disagreement,' Andrews ventured and Cressida nodded, taking that in.

'You're right, Andrews, she didn't say that. They weren't disagreeing.' Cressida was lost in thought. Then she perked up and looked at Dotty. 'I have an idea. All of these clues – the champagne bottle neck, the letters, the gloves and hanky, the funny-sounding words – you remember I mentioned that busboy talking about someone being smelly... no, pongy – and the soap, the missing handbag... it's all knotting together. And you know what my dear friend Maurice from Liberty would say at this point?'

Dotty looked at her watch, then unhelpfully replied, 'That you should have finished choosing your fabric ages ago and he'd like to close the shop now it's almost midnight?'

Cressida rolled her eyes at her friend. 'No. He'd say measure twice and cut once. Like with curtains, or any sort of fabric cutting. Measure twice and cut once. I need to go through all of this again, retrace our steps from the moment we found Victoria—'

'Or indeed the moment we arrived,' added Dotty, much more helpfully this time.

'Yes, in fact from then – you're right. From half past six this evening. It's worked before and it might just make sense of all these things.'

'I do hope so,' said Dot with a certain resignation. 'As I'm certainly losing track.'

'There's a thread, Dot.' Then Cressida turned to face Andrews and Alfred too. 'There's a thread here somewhere among all these confusing clues. We just need to find the right one and once we do, pulling it will unravel all the answers.'

She just hoped they still had enough time.

34

As Cressida and Dotty walked back towards the lobby of the hotel, Ruby in Cressida's arms and what must have been some of the last dances of the night played by the band coming from the ballroom, they chatted. About the murder, of course, but also about other things that had happened that evening, namely, Dotty's almost-proposal.

'It would have been so romantic, wouldn't it? A proposal in the snow on Christmas Eve,' Dotty said wistfully.

'It would have been, yes, chum,' Cressida agreed. 'Has he said anything since? When you were dancing and keeping an eye on everyone for me?'

'Oh, it was just chit-chat by then. Alfred was with us for some of the time, and of course Cordelia and her new chap.'

'Marcus Von Drausch,' Cressida clarified, then squeezed Dotty's arm as she continued. 'I fear Cordelia will hate me even more than when I appeared to poach Alfred from her in Scotland, when she finds out that Andrews still has Marcus clearly in his sights. I'm not entirely convinced she shouldn't be a suspect too. We all know what a temper Cordelia has, how ambitious she is and how much she hates to lose. She seems more interested in him inheriting Beaumont Park than Marcus himself does, I'd say. She gave me both barrels for Marcus being dragged over the coals earlier.' Cressida shifted the weight of Ruby in her arms as they rounded the corner of the corridor and walked the last few yards towards the lobby. 'I was pleased Alf was there to shield me from her, to be honest!'

'He'd never let anyone hurt you, not that I think Cordelia would. You don't really think she might be the murderer?' Dotty looked shocked, as Cressida shrugged. Dotty shook the idea away. 'Speaking of my brother, did I detect a little softening in your aspect towards him?' Dotty nudged Cressida in the ribs.

Cressida would usually retort with some version of her adamance that she would never marry, so how could she possibly be interested in Dotty's brother, but, for once, the protestation just didn't come. Instead, she felt that fluttering in her stomach that she'd become rather acclimatised to whenever a certain chestnut-haired gentleman was mentioned. 'Oh, Dotty...' She stopped walking and turned to her friend, their arms still linked. 'Dotty, we kissed. Properly, romantically, mid-rescuing me from the hamper, kissing. And again by the fireplace just after you and George left to see Dodo. And it was... it was perfect. Both times!'

The squeal from Dotty made Ruby prick her ears up and Cressida laughed too, Dotty's enthusiasm was infectious.

Once Dotty had composed herself, she threw her arms around Cressida's neck, unable to get too close because of the recently enlarged pup in her arms, and then pulled away, but still clasped Cressida's shoulders in her excitement.

One of Cressida's satin evening gloves slipped a little down her arm and Dotty pulled it up for her. This made the hairs on Cressida's arm tingle, and not just because of Dotty's delicate touch. It had pulled another thread in her mind.

'Cressy?' asked Dotty, 'Are you all right? You look like you've just swallowed a bug.'

'Charming,' Cressida replied, then huffed out a breath. 'Sorry, it was just as you touched my glove. Something sparked off in my mind. It's probably nothing, but will you be a dear and remind me of it later?'

'Of course,' laughed Dotty. 'I'm glad it was only that, not you about to tell me that kissing my brother was a huge mistake or something.'

It was Cressida's turn to grin. She couldn't help it. Despite everything else going on and the immense time pressure they were under, she knew that she was unequivocally, absolutely and madly in love with Alfred Chatterton.

The two young women embraced again, and then, Dotty's arm linked through Cressida's, and Ruby once again snuggled into her mistress's arms, they entered the lobby where the grand Christmas tree was standing. Cressida could clearly see – with her decorator's eye – where one of the large glass icicles was missing. She pointed it out to Dotty.

'Grim,' shivered Dotty, squeezing Cressida's arm tighter.

'Agreed. But also, note the height. *Our* height,' Cressida pointed out.

'You mean, someone didn't bother to go and find a footstool in the heat of the moment and take a less obvious one?' Dotty replied.

'Hmm, touché. But it does mean that it didn't have to be a very tall man.'

'That's fair, I suppose. But the bottle to the head and the strangling, that's a man's crime, don't you think? So very violent.'

'I thought so too, when we first saw poor Victoria in the fountain. But I've been thinking about it, and I have to say that I don't like the thought one bit.'

'What do you mean?' Dotty looked quizzically at her friend.

'Well, I think you're right that it's a very violent crime. One filled with malice and a certain amount of forethought—'

'But wouldn't forethought mean the killer would bring a gun? Or a knife? Victoria was hit with a champagne bottle, Violet killed with a tree decoration. Those are impromptu weapons, surely?'

'Yes, but I think the killer was waiting for the right time to do it. And use weapons anyone else here tonight could lay their hands on to throw suspicion on others with a motive.'

'And there were plenty of them here tonight: jealous husbands, argumentative friends, ex-lovers, heirs to her estate—'

'And more than that,' Cressida pulled at the thread and finally found it starting to unwind. 'Whoever the killer is would have had to have known all that about Victoria. Known everything. And hated her for it.'

'Hated her? I suppose, yes, enough to kill her,' mused Dotty.

'Not just kill her. Look her in the eye as they squeezed the very last breath out of her. That's why she was hit over the head to stun, not to kill. So she wouldn't struggle as the killer strangled her? So the killer could – oh I hate to even think this, but so the killer could *enjoy* murdering her.'

'Oh, Cressy, you give me the shivers.' Dotty shook all over. 'But I have to concede, you do paint a picture that makes a lot of sense. But who? Who would do that?'

'Well, the men all have strong motives – a jealous husband, an ex-lover, a blackmailed doctor, an heir to the Beaumont fortune...' Cressida listed off the main suspects again.

Dotty took over. 'But you found ladies' evening gloves spattered in blood. Therefore putting Dodo, Ottoline Spencer and... would you include Cordelia in your suspects?' Dotty asked, fearing she knew the answer.

'Definitely. And Lady Gorebridge and all of Dr Hart's other ladies too. But out of those, only Ottoline has a concrete alibi, and Dodo is the only one who was on the scene when the poor girl in the powder room was killed.'

'Except she wasn't the only one, was she?' Dotty posed. 'Dodo heard Violet talk to someone.'

'Yes, about soap dispensers. All very strange.' Another tingle shot up Cressida's bare upper arms and she shivered it off. These threads were dangling more than a frayed hem, yet she couldn't quite grasp them. 'Back to the beginning, Dot. Here we are at the lobby. Of course, it's been the scene of me talking to Clayton, and someone stealing that icicle, and it was where simply everyone arrived, including us—'

'And the murderer,' added Dotty, releasing Cressida's arm and walking around the great Christmas tree. 'It's the place to start all right. Let's turn our watches, metaphorically at least, back to six thirty this evening.'

'And a warm embrace between two letter-writing lovers.' Cressida nudged her friend, then looked around the lobby. It was late now. Almost midnight. And she could already see disgruntled ball guests arguing with the cloakroom attendant and the policeman on the main door.

Cressida was running out of time. Once one entitled aristocrat got their way and ordered their cab, they all would, and all of Cressida's suspects would be gone. She wanted to measure twice and cut once, but she better hurry up in doing so. Otherwise someone here tonight, as the clock counted down to midnight, would get away with murder. Or indeed, murders.

35

'Cressy, are we retracing our footsteps or Victoria's?'

'Footsteps...' Cressida repeated, and when Dotty looked at her, she shook it off. 'Sorry, Dot, carry on.'

'Well, ours I can remember, what with my joyous reunion with George, I made sure I memorised every moment. Though now it's all been rather shoved aside, as I can't get the image of poor Victoria's body out of my head.' Dotty wrapped her arms around herself, her hands rubbing the tops of her arms not covered by her elbow-length evening gloves.

'I suppose we need to work out Victoria's movements. Though we can only go on what we've heard from others. We know she arrived here, in the lobby, and met her husband and Ottoline and said goodbye to her friends—'

'Who included Dodo, who was seen arguing with Victoria in the ballroom soon after they arrived,' Dotty reminded her.

'A nasty argument at that, according to Ottoline, though not so horrible according to Dodo.'

'Should we go to the ballroom then?' Dotty asked, looking with some distaste now at the large Christmas tree with its deadly ornaments.

'Not yet. You see, Victoria saw someone else here in the lobby, didn't she? Clayton.'

'Not necessarily,' Dotty contradicted her. 'Clayton told us he'd seen Victoria, but not where. Just that they'd met up and agreed to swap the letters over. Victoria was cross as he didn't have them on him there and then, but then neither did she—'

'As she didn't have her handbag on her. Honestly, Dot, this missing handbag of hers, it could be really important and have more evidence in it. We really need to find it.'

'So we better start retracing her steps then. One by one.' Dotty linked her arm through Cressida's again and they hurriedly walked towards the ballroom.

'Victoria was seen arguing with Dodo here.' Cressida stood by the door that led from the ballroom to the piano lobby, then moved aside for another waiter who was balancing yet more empty champagne bottles and used glasses on a tray as he swept past them.

Ottoline noticed them and gave them a little wave from the sofa.

'See what I mean?' Cressida raised an eyebrow as she shifted Ruby's weight in her arms to return the wave. 'And at this point Victoria didn't have her evening bag. And bearing in mind she'd only been in the lobby, and found those seats with her husband and Ottoline before entering the ballroom, it must be in there, with them.'

'Cloakroom?' Dotty asked.

'I didn't notice it when I had a shifty earlier.' Cressida raised an eyebrow. 'I leaned quite far in and could only see furs and overcoats. Nothing on the floor or nothing shot blue with silk like her dress.'

'The piano bar it is then,' Dotty agreed and they crossed between the rooms, finding themselves once more in the pastel decor of the piano bar, the pianist now on a break and the music from the ballroom floating through.

Cressida put a squirming Ruby down and straightened her dress before standing with her hands on her hips. Ruby toddled off towards the piano stool again and Cressida was just heading over to Lord Beaumont and Ottoline when she realised they were now deep in conversation. She paused and turned, as if something had caught her attention, and strained to hear what they were saying.

'... can't leave yet, Peter. The police won't let us...' That was Ottoline speaking, of course.

'But it's midnight, Otty, or thereabouts... time's up, wouldn't you say?' Lord Beaumont answered her.

'If they don't find Victoria's killer... midnight... get away...' It was harder to hear Ottoline this time, as their voices had hushed.

'But it is...'

Cressida felt a nudge at her ankle and turned around. Dotty was the other side of the room, but Cressida looked down and saw Ruby barrel into her once again.

'What are you doing, Rubes? Are you all right?' Cressida's mind suddenly went to the health of her small dog and the even smaller pups within. She had never felt broody before – she was a woman who didn't even fancy getting married, let alone having children – yet she suddenly felt incredibly maternal and protective towards her pet. Ruby, however, did not need coddling. Instead, she trotted off towards the piano stool, and Cressida followed, meeting Dotty beside the glossy white grand piano that had been being played all night.

Ruby waddled forward and Cressida saw that she was wagging her tail as she hopped around a bit in front of the hamper of crackers that was sitting just behind the stool.

'What's she doing?' Dotty asked, cocking her head on one

side. 'It looks like she's trying to Charleston. And, dare I say it, she's doing a better job than me.'

'Ha,' Cressida said, but her mind was clocking back to when she'd seen her pup do something similar before. 'She was doing this earlier. When we were talking to Lord Beaumont and Ottoline. I thought she was just annoying the pianist—'

'He was playing "Deck the Halls" for about the fifth time, so I don't blame her,' Dotty interrupted.

'That's as may be, and yes, those fa-la-la-la-las can get a bit much, but I don't think it was the pianist that Ruby was after. It was what was behind him,' Cressida said, as she took a few of the navy blue and silver crackers out of the hamper, letting them drop to the floor as she delved further in. With the pile of crackers building up behind her as she knelt in front of the wicker hamper, and the depths of the basket itself almost plundered, Cressida wondered if pregnancy had made Ruby's senses go skew-whiff. Until there, under the last two crackers, she saw a pale blue silk evening bag.

36

'It's Victoria's, it has to be!' Dotty exclaimed, but in hushed tones.

Cressida reached in and pulled the elegant bag out of the hamper, then placed all the crackers back into it again. She put the bag carefully on the glossy lacquered top of the piano and then, with a kiss of thanks, lifted Ruby up onto the stool so she could be part of the action.

'Just because one is pregnant doesn't mean one deserves to miss out on all the fun, eh, Rubes,' she said as Dotty picked up the delicate bag, which though slim, had a certain weight to it.

'More letters? Dotty suggested, weighing the bag in her hands.

'And divine silk, too. It matches her dress and shoes. It's not a silk one sees much of, I think. Look at the texture. It's woven with cotton, if I'm not mistaken. Quite unusual.'

While Cressida was rhapsodising about the silk, Dotty had prised open the clasp and was looking in the bag. 'Letters, just as you thought, Cressy.'

Cressida looked over her shoulder and waved to Ottoline, who was watching them carefully. 'Let's take it to our next stop on the retracing Victoria's steps tour. Hopefully somewhere more private.'

Cressida picked up Ruby and Dotty carefully hid the small, silk bag under her arm next to her own evening bag.

Without waving to Lord Beaumont, or Ottoline Spencer, as nonchalantly as possible they walked back towards the ballroom.

The band announced the final tune of the evening, and those who had the energy cheered as they took to the dance floor. Alfred had been right, though, and the ballroom had less activity in it than before. More guests were slumped on the dining chairs and the wisps of smoke from cigars hung heavy across the tables.

The buffet tables were almost depleted, with just bowls of sugared almonds and slices of rich, iced fruit cake left. Cressida tried not to get distracted by the leftover marzipan, though she often wondered why people, whose palates obviously were drawn to the cloying sweetness of icing and the rich fruitiness of cake, got all squeamish at the thought of soft almond paste. Cressida could feel her stomach rumble and she realised that, bar a few canapés, she really hadn't eaten much tonight. She reminded herself that poor Victoria and Violet had had a much worse evening, and she nudged Dotty towards the powder room as the next step on their measure-twice mission.

As they turned the corner, a thought came to Cressida.

'Pongy!' She grasped Dotty's arm as she blurted out the word.

'Excuse me?' Dotty looked affronted. 'I'll have you know I'm smothered in Elizabeth Arden.'

'No, not you, Dot. That.' She pointed to the bag under Dotty's arm.

Dotty removed it carefully and gave it a sniff, then adjusted her spectacles as they'd slipped down her nose. 'Smells fine to me.'

'Smellier. Sommelier.' Cressida shook her head, the realisation slowly coming to her. 'But why pongy here?'

'Are you quite well, Cressy? If they've cleaned up the powder room, I think we should go there and splash some water on your face or something. You're talking gibberish.'

'Not gibberish, Dotty, but phonetics. Or homophones. Or something like that.'

Dotty was about to pat her hand and suggest a hot drink and a cool flannel when Cressida tore off towards the powder room. The policeman was still on the door, and without a word, Cressida thrust the pregnant Ruby back into his arms.

Dotty came along later and mouthed an apology to him, though he looked more than happy with the trade-off, and Dotty closed the door to the powder room behind her, as the constable made pouting faces to Ruby, who took the adulation in her stride.

The powder room was still very much the scene of an appalling crime, and although Violet's body had now been removed, there was a large red stain on the pale pink plush carpet and ribbons taken from the frilly curtains under the basins used as temporary tapes to stop anyone entering the cubicles. This gave it the effect of being a particularly feminine crime scene, but Cressida knew that there was nothing elegant or delicate about murder.

Making sure they avoided the stain on the floor, they stood in the centre of the boudoir-esque powder room and Dotty demanded answers. 'What were you on about, Cressy? Pongy and smelly. I know you're not a normal society heiress, but there's eccentricities and then there's *eccentricities*.'

'Sorry, Dot, but you should know me by now. I was piecing it together. You see, there was a nice young waiter that I chatted to earlier and he said that he'd seen Victoria walking past the kitchens, which are just round the corner from here. Or at least he said he saw a pretty blonde lady dressed in blue. And he and the other busboys and waiters were laughing as they heard her saying the word pongy. They thought it was funny, because, well, they're young men, but also because they find it hard to get their mouths around the French word sommelier, the head wine waiter. They call him the *smellier*. And that made me wonder if pongy was also a word they didn't know, but sounded so much like something else. And it's this,' she pointed at Victoria's evening bag. 'It's pongee. A type of textured and woven silk. It's not often used in decorating, but, of course, we know it from the fact that lots of our evening bags – and shoes – are covered in it.'

'Pongee, to pongy. Oh, I see.' Dotty placed the bag down on the top of the vanity unit.

'And I think that means that Victoria was about to head outside with her killer, and they heard her complaining about—'

'Those lovely shoes!' Dotty exclaimed. 'We saw them ruined, didn't we? The snow outside had made a watermark on the silk.'

'And I think, a drunk Victoria – Dodo said she'd downed a martini after their argument – was being coerced by her killer into going outside, maybe under the guise of helping her to sober up a bit. But she was overheard trying to explain to that person that her pongee shoes would be ruined in the snow.'

'And how did she know it was snowing?' Dotty asked. 'I'm trying to remember, but I think it only started just as George and I went outside.'

'You're right. It wasn't snowing when we arrived. All those coats in the cloakroom were dry when I was talking to Stanley behind the hatch. So she must have looked out of the window...'

Cressida turned to the large window that was swathed in the luxurious curtains. She'd stepped through them before and admired the view, the view right across to the fountain. The fountain in which Victoria had been found dead. *Strangled.*

Cressida moved towards the curtains. 'I thought the attendant had closed them, but maybe...' She peered through the thick interlined fabrics and shivered as once again the chill from the plate-glass window hit her. She saw the courtyard and fountain, now covered in snow, a thick blanket that had fallen in the hours since they'd arrived. Then she saw it.

The final piece in the puzzle as to how Victoria was killed.

Hanging loosely behind one of the curtains was the tieback. A thick strong piece of rope, in beautiful gold and pistachio green threads to match the decor and the curtains, plaited and twisted into an ornate rope with which the curtains could be held back during the day.

Cressida looked towards the other hook, behind the matching curtain.

And it was empty.

37

Dotty could tell there was something amiss by the look on Cressida's face as she reappeared from behind the curtains.

'What is it? What have you found?' Dotty asked, as Cressida pulled her arm from behind her with one of the curtain tiebacks grasped in her gloved hand.

'It's what I haven't found that's the important thing,' Cressida said rather cryptically and Dotty narrowed her eyes at her.

'But you're holding a rope. A rope that could... Oh, I see. You think that a curtain tie was used to strangle Victoria? How awful.'

'Not just a curtain tie. The matching one to this one. There's an empty tieback hook behind the left curtain – well, there's one behind the right curtain now too as I've taken this one.' She held the tieback aloft. 'But there was one missing. The thing is, I can't remember if it was there when I looked before.'

'You've been rummaging around behind the curtains already tonight?' Dotty was starting to get confused.

'Yes, when I was talking to Violet, the attendant. But I... Oh I just don't know. I didn't notice if it was there or not and I pride myself on noticing these things!' Cressida sounded exasperated.

'Well, you have noticed it now, that's something,' Dotty reassured her. 'And I'm sure whoever took the other one banked on no one noticing it at all, not for weeks.'

'They wouldn't need weeks, just until the clock strikes midnight tonight, then all the suspects and most of the evidence will be gone. And it's almost midnight now. Jeepers. We need to be quick, Dotty. We only have a matter of minutes!'

'And what shall we do, Cressy? Quickly read these letters? I wonder if there's anything else in this bag...' She started nosing into Victoria's handbag. Her face changed when she pulled out some more papers that were crammed in next to the bunch of letters from Clayton.

'What's that, Dot?' Cressida asked, moving away from the curtains, the tieback now wrapped around one of her hands.

'It looks like a letter, but it's not handwritten. It's typed and signed... Oh, it's from Dr Hart!'

Cressida moved across and read the letter over Dotty's shoulder. It was a simple letter from the doctor's secretary, but signed by the doctor himself, congratulating Victoria on her pregnancy.

So it was true. Victoria was pregnant.

'Ottoline said they'd been up in London as Victoria had an appointment. Do you think this was the reason she was in town so close to Christmas? I suppose, like tides and taxes, one's monthly cycles wait for no man,' Cressida mused. 'It would explain why she insisted on them coming, and, of course, she wanted to celebrate with her friends and husband and tell him the good news,' Dotty said.

'And put paid to any talk of divorce. With a baby on the way, he couldn't do that. And if the baby was blue-eyed and blonde, as it was bound to be if it was born to two blue-eyed parents, then Lord Beaumont would have no reason to think he was a bastard, born of Dr Hart instead of him,' agreed Cressida.

'And Victoria's place would be ensured as Lady Beaumont, with an heir—'

'Making Marcus no longer set to inherit,' interrupted Cressida. 'This really doesn't look good for the young artist, that is true, but I still don't think...' Cressida left Dotty's side and wandered over to the window again. She swept the two heavy curtains aside and looked out to the courtyard. She looked at the falling snow and the fountain, that still bubbled and sprayed despite the sub-zero temperature. She thought of the footsteps that she'd seen and the mix-up the kitchen boys had had about the silk of the shoes – pongee, not pongy.

Then she glanced at the hook that would have held the murder weapon, assuming that the curtain tieback in her hand matched the marks on Victoria's neck. She would have to get it to Andrews and see what he could analyse from it.

Cressida popped her head back through the curtains, the difference between the chill of the window aperture and the pastel warmth of the powder room so apparent. It was such an innocuous space, a space where ladies felt the most cosseted and comfortable outside of their own home. That it had contained the murder weapon wasn't lost on Cressida.

She left the chill of the window, letting the curtains fall again, and looked around her.

'Did Violet have to die because she witnessed something through this window? But then why leave Victoria's letters with her body?'

'Because Andrews mistook them at first for being from her to Clayton, didn't he? On first glance, they were signed with a V, which—'

'Which it only took a few moments to decipher was wrong when we looked at the content, all about Beaumont Park and the goings-on there. But, by then, some doubt had been cast on Clayton again.'

'And we got to read the letters,' Dotty added. 'Or at least unofficially. Officially, it was meant to be the police who read them. But why leave them for the police to find? They've been so useful to us.'

Cressida tapped a finger against her cheek as she thought. 'You're right. I think there's been quite a bit of framing going on here. Clayton and the champagne bottle neck, and his letters left with Violet. Letters that had been stolen from his coat pocket...'

Cressida scanned the room. She took in the thick cubicle doors that were painted the same pistachio green as the walls and complemented the pink carpet and pink frilly drapes below the basins. Soap dishes sat primly next to each basin... Cressida looked at them, narrowing her eyes.

'Soap dishes not dispensers... but the soap smelt smoky at first...' Cressida paced alongside the basins. 'She might have seen someone from the window or someone might have over-heard us talking through one of these doors. I feel terrible that I asked her to identify possible suspects just before she was killed. But those footprints, the silk, curtains and that soap... Oh.' Cressida looked up at Dotty, then her face looked less enlightened and more confused again. 'But the timing is all wrong. And the saddle.'

'The saddle?' Dotty whispered, evidently wondering if Cressida had gone quite mad this time.

'The pregnancy changed everything, of course.' Cressida ran her hand along the edge of the vanity unit that held the basins. 'No soap dispensers, just dishes with Palmolive bars...'

'I still don't know why Violet would mention a soap dispenser.' Dotty pushed her glasses up her nose and pulled her evening gloves up that had slipped down to below her elbows.

'I don't think she did. I don't think she said anything of the sort. I think, just like the smellier and the pongee, it's actually something completely different.'

'I'm afraid you've lost me, Cressy.' Dotty leaned against one of the cloakroom doors.

'Not your fault, Dot. Someone's been running rings around us and hiding their tracks all night. And I think I know who.'

38

'Miss Fawcett!' The voice reached Cressida and Dotty as they left the powder room before the tall, gangly, young policeman did. 'Lady Dorothy! Wait there please!'

'What is it, Kirby?' Cressida turned around, aware that the curtain tieback was still in her hand, as was Victoria's evening bag including Clayton's letters.

Kirby pelted down the corridor, dodging past a couple of giggling women with half-empty champagne bottles in their hands, in order to reach the two friends in haste. He had one hand holding his helmet on and Cressida could see the panic in his eyes.

'Sergeant Kirby, what's happened?' Cressida asked, stepping forward to meet him as he careered to a stop just inches from them. She looked across to Dotty who had prised Ruby from the indulgent policeman by the door as she'd been worried that Kirby might barrel right into her.

'Miss Fawcett,' Kirby panted, 'the chief wants to see you. There's only been another one.'

'Another what? Oh...' The realisation of what Kirby was saying struck Cressida. *There couldn't be, could there?*

With one glance at Dotty, Cressida followed Kirby back down the corridor, keeping pace as much as she could. She had to know though, she had to be sure.

'Kirby,' she called to him through hurried breaths, 'are you saying what I think you are? Is there... another body?'

'Yes, miss, I'm afraid so.' The young policeman was uncharacteristically succinct. That was all he said as he led Cressida and Dotty at quite some speed towards the lobby. Instead of meeting up with DCI Andrews by the Christmas tree as Cressida supposed he might do, he took them around behind the reception desks and through a service corridor towards the internal depths of the hotel.

The corridor took them past flip-flap doors to the back of the kitchens and then offices and pantries, some in darkness with the lights off and doors closed, a few still with staff in them. A glance through one of the doors showed Cressida the chefs cleaning down the kitchen and the busboys washing the last of the glasses.

Steam billowed out of one of the doors which was propped open, no doubt to give the workers, on this most festive of nights, some respite from the sticky heat of the ovens or washing tubs that were in there with them.

Eventually, Kirby slowed and Cressida could see the familiar tweed-clad sight of DCI Andrews standing next to the hotel manager, Mr Butcher.

'Andrews!' Cressida called out, appearing to him from behind Kirby. 'Andrews, please tell me there's been a mistake... Oh jeepers. Oh dear.'

Dotty, who was just a fraction behind Cressida, running more carefully due to her precious load, caught up and, shocked at what she saw, placed a hand over her mouth. In front of them and framed by the serious faces of Andrews and Mr Butcher was the body of a young housekeeping maid. The way she was laid out on the floor resembled how Violet had looked – the body all tumbled over. There was a similar tangle of limbs and loose hair. And it took only a moment for Cressida to work out why.

The body of the young woman, dressed in the smart navy blue of the hotel's livery, was at the bottom of a laundry chute.

Cressida wondered how the guests in the ballroom would react if they found out that not only had there been a murder here tonight, but that there'd been three.

'Dear heavens, was she pushed down there?' Dotty said, the horror in her voice evident. 'The poor thing!'

'Yes, Lady Dorothy. This is a Miss Susan Potts, employee of the hotel, died by—'

'Being strangled,' Cressida interrupted him.

Andrews looked up at her as she raised the hand that wasn't holding her handbag, and showed him the tieback cord from the powder room. Then, together, along with Dotty, Kirby and Mr Butcher, all eyes glanced down to the body. Around her neck, almost hidden by her loose hair, was the matching tieback from the pair from the powder-room curtains.

'Is that...' Dotty started to ask the question, then nuzzled her face into the chubby dog's warm fur.

'It's the matching pair, yes,' answered Cressida, then she explained it all to Andrews. 'When Kirby found us, Dotty and I were retracing our steps – you know how Maurice from Liberty always recommends: measure twice and cut – or in this case accuse – once. Well, we were in the powder room, wondering how Violet was involved and who might have been in there to overhear me asking her to help me – which I regret so very much – or if she might have seen something from the window, which, of course, looks out to the fountain courtyard, and that's when I found this.' She handed the cord over to the policeman. 'Look at the way it's braided. I would bet anything that it matches the welts on Victoria's neck and, of course, it's identical in colour and size and everything to the one around poor Miss Potts' neck.'

Andrews took the cord and examined it, then passed it over to Kirby, who had a handy evidence bag on him. Kirby dropped it in, before sealing it and removing the cord around the maid's neck and placing it into another, similar bag.

'That's a good find, Miss Fawcett, thank you. In the powder room, you say?'

'Yes, where Violet was murdered. But, of course, the cord was used to kill Victoria and then Miss Potts.' Cressida paused, then repeated the maid's name. 'Miss Susan Potts. Susie Potts! Oh gosh, Violet was waiting for her in the powder room! To relieve her after her shift had ended, but Susie hadn't turned up.'

'When was this?' Andrews asked, as Kirby flicked open his notebook.

'Oh, lordy, I'm not sure. About quarter past ten, perhaps. Violet said she'd been on turn-down duty for the hotel rooms, leaving little presents for the guests on their pillows as she prepared the beds. Violet said she must have been held up.' Cressida raised a hand to her throat, regretting her own choice of words. 'Tell me, how did you find the body?'

'I can answer that,' Mr Butcher chipped in. 'It was one of the overnight staff who was just starting her shift. You see, we have porters and front-of-house staff, chefs and waiters and the like, throughout the day, but the hotel runs on a skeleton staff throughout the night.'

'Even on Christmas Eve?' Cressida asked, aware more than ever that the clock was ticking down to midnight.

'Even tonight, Miss Fawcett. We have several guests staying overnight, so we have staff on hand who will be on call for any emergencies, and to get the kitchen going for breakfast service. But, before that, and when there's no call on them from a guest, they start the jobs the dailies haven't finished. Such as sorting the laundry from the chutes.'

'Oh, I see. And was this chute opened and—'

'That's right. We're close to the laundry room here.' He pointed to the door from which Cressida had noticed steam billowing just a moment ago. 'It's next to the prep kitchen and all the sheets from the room changes throughout the day are deposited in the chute from the floors above. The night staff start the washing and drying so that the sheets are ready for the next day's change-over.'

'When was this door opened?' Cressida looked at the small metal door that was set into the side of the corridor. It was only about waist high to a man, but quite wide – wide enough to easily pull out bundled sheets and, sadly, in this case, a dead body.

'Only a few moments ago. Mrs Benson started at eleven o'clock and claimed she had a cup of tea, then set about her business, with the laundry chute first on her list.'

'So the time of death must have been around then?' Dotty asked and Cressida turned to look at her. Poor Dotty, what a ghastly night she was having. This should have been a Christmas Eve to remember, and it certainly would be, but for all the wrong reasons.

'No, the time of death seems to be much earlier in the evening. I'm no pathologist,' Andrews excused himself, 'but I can tell from the bruising and pallor that she's been dead for a few hours.'

'That makes sense actually,' Cressida said thoughtfully. 'I should imagine Miss Potts was killed very soon after Victoria, using the same murder weapon – the curtain tieback. That's why we never found it. I was wondering where it could be concealed, but it was here all the time.'

'She can't have been killed just to dispose of the murder weapon,' Dotty stated. 'So why was she killed?'

Cressida bit her lip as she thought. She needed more to go on and she knew there was something important about this body. Dotty was right to ask – why was this poor maid killed? What had she seen, or who had she come across?

'Mr Butcher, did Miss Potts always work upstairs?' Cressida asked. 'Only, I wonder if perhaps she saw something happen in the courtyard?'

'She was employed as a chambermaid, yes, but with so few guests upstairs and so many of the ones staying at the ball itself, I'd asked her to help out in the powder room too with Violet. But I do remember seeing her head upstairs just as we were securing the hotel after Lady Beaumont's death. She had the boxes of Fortnum & Mason's chocolates for the guests with her.'

'So she was on the same floor as the entry to the laundry chute?' Andrews posed the question.

Cressida looked at the body. The way it had fallen out of the chute meant that it wasn't just the maid's arms that were now at hideous angles to her body. Her legs were tangled too, yet they were hidden by white bedsheets, which had wrapped themselves around her as she'd fallen down the chute. Cressida bent down and, with a nod from Andrews, started to untangle the sheets around the maid's legs. Andrews joined her and soon they could see the pale and misshapen legs of the dead body. A look passed between them as they both took in what they noticed, but it was Cressida who said it first.

'There's no shoes. Miss Susan Potts has no shoes on.'

'Why would that be?' Andrews quizzed her, standing upright with an audible click from his knee and an accompanying wince on his face.

'She was certainly wearing them when I saw her head up the back stairs to the guest rooms,' Mr Butcher said, scratching his head, and using the toe of his own shoe to move the bed sheets around a bit in case the maid's shoes were merely concealed in the folds of white linen.

Cressida thought for a moment. *The snow, the pongee silk, the footprints...* She turned back to DCI Andrews and gave him an answer. 'Because someone – and by someone, I mean the murderer of Victoria Beaumont – needed this poor girl's shoes.'

39

DCI Andrews, Sergeant Kirby, Mr Butcher and Cressida and Dotty stood in solemn silence for a moment next to the dead body. Cressida was deep in thought.

'I thought I knew who it was, but her shoes weren't wet. And they matched her outfit...'

'What are you thinking, Cressy?' Dotty asked.

'I had a hunch is all, but I've got it all wrong. This proves it couldn't have been her.'

'Who?' Andrews took over the cross-examination.

Cressida seemed to ignore him. 'Of course she had an alibi all the time. She was one of the only ones who did.'

'Ottoline Spencer?' Dotty asked and Cressida finally looked at her and nodded.

'Yes, Ottoline. In the letters, Victoria told Clayton that she didn't like her half so much as Ottoline implied she did. And Ottoline is clearly in love with Lord Beaumont herself. I thought she might have done away with her young rival. The bloodied handkerchief with PB on it, that pointed to her too, as she was using one of his hankies tonight. She probably steals them on visits to Beaumont Park and collects them as souvenirs, sticks them under her pillow or what have you.'

'You really are having romantic thoughts these days, Cressy,' Dotty muttered, but shushed herself as Cressida's brow furrowed. 'And, of course, the massive handbag she carried around. I thought that was the perfect spot for hiding curtain tiebacks, icicles and letters, but you don't need a handbag for an icicle, it can be hidden in plain sight, and as we've just seen, the cord was disposed of in quite another, more hideous, way.'

'What do you mean about the icicle?' Dotty asked, but Cressida's brow was furrowed, deep in thought.

'I know it sounds a little left-field, Mr Butcher, but I think she's on to something,' Andrews reassured the confused-looking hotel manager. He looked even more confused when Cressida suddenly got down on her knees, wincing herself as her beaded tassels on her dress pressed into her flesh, and started rummaging around the sheets.

'Spencer, soap dispenser... ha,' she muttered. 'And that constant smell of smoke. And, of course, gloves, those bloodied gloves. Aha...' Cressida could feel something under one of the sheets and patted the ground around it until she found the edge of the white, starched bedding, then ferreted her hand in and rummaged until she'd found the object she'd felt from above. With one much swifter motion, she pulled out the item. It was a ruined, still wet even, blue silk evening shoe. Cressida held it up and examined it. 'Just as I suspected! Oh, she was clever. Even down to the hanky and the bottle neck. And oh so ruthless with that saddle too...'

'Saddle?' Dotty asked. 'I thought you were talking about the murders tonight?'

'But it's all linked, Dotty. You-know-who isn't who we thought it was. This is... calculated. And cruel. Gosh, oh so cruel.'

'But who is it? Who are you talking about?' Andrews asked,

taking the shoe from Cressida as she pushed herself up from the floor.

Before she could answer, there was a yell from the other end of the corridor.

'Cressy! Dot!'

They turned around and Cressida automatically smiled as she saw Alfred running towards them. But her smile disappeared when she saw the look on his face.

'Alfred, what is it, what's wrong?' Cressida called out to him, and watched as he in turn took in the scene around them and the look of horror grew more distinct on his face.

'There's something happening in the ballroom. A rush to the doors. Everyone wants to leave, and in a hurry.'

Andrews swore under his breath. He looked at his watch. 'It's midnight. I thought we had just a bit more time.'

'I told the door staff to keep everyone here until midnight, I did everything I could,' Mr Butcher shrugged as he replied to Andrews, but from the colourless look on Alfred's face, Cressida could see this was more than just a host of aristos keen to get back to Kensington and Chelsea. Something else had happened.

'Alfred, Alfred, what is it?' she asked as Alfred pulled his eyes away from Cressida and clasped his sister, still carrying Ruby, by the arms.

'What, Alfred? You're scaring me.' Dotty froze to the spot.

Alfred looked back at Cressida, then to his sister again.

'It's George. I can't find him. And there's something happening in the courtyard. The French doors to the terrace are open, the curtains all drawn back. Quick, come quick.'

40

At the mention of George being in trouble, Dotty had passed Ruby back to Cressida, carefully but quickly, and all together they rushed back down the service corridor, through the reception area, past the large Christmas tree and into the ballroom.

'How could I have been so blind,' Cressida muttered under her breath to Ruby. 'I've been such a fool.' She glanced at Dotty, who was holding her brother's hand and pelting down the corridor as fast as she could, fancy dancing shoes and evening dress allowing. *If something happened to George...*

Cressida thought it all through again. She now knew there was only one person who could have killed Victoria. There was only one person who had the time this evening to creep upstairs and steal the shoes of an innocent chambermaid, killing her to quite literally cover their tracks. There was only one person who it could be.

Cressida careered to a stop and carefully placed Ruby down. Dotty, Alfred, Andrews, Kirby and Mr Butcher all came to a near calamitous stop alongside her by the doors to the terrace, which had indeed been opened and were now widened by the force of the blizzarding squall outside.

The curtains, that Mr Butcher had so thoughtfully drawn across all the windows with a view to the courtyard earlier in the evening, all blew around as if possessed by the spirits of the dance floor itself. Cressida knew exactly who she'd see outside, and she braced herself for it.

And that person was indeed now in front of them, standing in the courtyard of the Mayfair Hotel, wrapped in furs, but clearly visible against the blanket of white that coated the ground, the stairs and the stone cherubs and horses of the fountain itself. And she wasn't alone.

Two sets of footsteps, this time deep in the settled snow, led down from the terrace.

One led straight to the crumpled body of George Parish, face down in the snow.

The other set led to the person who Cressida now realised had been on a deadly mission all night. Someone who Cressida realised that, despite her reputation otherwise, was in fact the most cruel, manipulative and dangerous adversary she'd ever encountered.

Dora Smith-Wallington.

'Don't come any closer, or he dies!' she yelled out at the shivering figures, Cressida included, on the terrace.

'George!' screamed Dotty, running to the edge of the terrace and gripping onto the stone ledge before seeing the broken champagne bottle brandished by Dora.

'Stand back, Dorothy!' Dora yelled, holding the shorn-off edge of the bottle close to George's neck. 'I've done this before and I'm not afraid to kill him.'

'But why?' cried Dotty. 'Why him?'

'The silly fool followed me out here, said it was dangerous!' She laughed and kicked up some of the recently settled snow into George's face. 'Asked what I was doing out here in the cold. Insisted that I come back into the warm and wait for you.'

'Why didn't you? You could have left at midnight?' Dotty said through her tears. 'Everyone else is.'

'He said the police – and you, Cressida – were closing in on a murderer. A murderer who could be getting desperate and targeting nice young ladies like me.' She laughed again, brushing settling flakes off the sleeves of her fur coat. 'Despite my best efforts to put you off my scent, I couldn't take that chance. I had to find another way out, where I wouldn't be seen.'

Another sudden gust of wind blew loose snow off the terrace and into the eyes of everyone standing on it. Cressida raised her arm to protect her eyes from the pin-prick sharp flakes, blinking them away as best she could.

'Did he try to stop you? Why hurt him?' Cressida shouted through the storm.

It was hard to see through the blinding flakes, but Cressida was sure that Dora just shrugged. And she definitely heard her answer, almost a cackle through the blizzard.

'Why hurt him? Why not!'

Cressida was stunned by Dora's cruelty. She'd lost any sense of reality. Thank heavens Alfred had called them when he had. And he was right, the upper-class stampede – as Cressida had predicted – to leave the ball had begun. If she'd turned around at that moment and headed back into the warmth and safety of the hotel, she would have seen what must have been over one hundred guests pushing their way out of the ballroom towards the lobby in one mass of black tailcoats, jewel-coloured dresses and white tuxedoes.

But Cressida didn't turn around. She was concentrating on the scene unfolding in the courtyard. No one on the terrace had moved, as Dora had demanded, but Dora was swinging the champagne bottle with its deadly edge dangerously close to George, who hadn't even twitched since they'd all rushed out there and found him.

Found him at the mercy of heartless, vicious Dora Smith-Wallington.

It's always the ones you least suspect, Cressida thought to herself, not letting Dora out of her sight for a moment.

Andrews broke the silence. 'Miss Smith-Wallington, put the bottle down. We can talk about this.' He was standing at the top of the stairs, gradually edging towards the top step, his shoes now caked in compacted snow. Cressida knew how icy it was, and worried not only for Andrews' own sake, but also that if he took a tumble, any sudden move, accidental or not, might trigger Dora into doing the unthinkable.

She wouldn't even regret it, thought Cressida. *That's what makes her so dangerous.*

'Come on now, missy,' Andrews said again, his foot hovering over the top of the terrace steps. A few flakes dropped down from his leather brogue and rolled along the step, gaining a little momentum, before dropping to the next step and disappearing into the inch-deep snow.

'Stay back,' Dora yelled from her position by the fountain.

A groan from George caused relief from all on the terrace, but just elicited another kick from Dora. A kick from a foot wearing a very plain navy blue shoe.

'Dora,' Cressida shouted down to her, as Dotty clasped her arm. Her movement dislodged a drift of snow and ice and they all froze as the deadly sharp, very real icicles hit the ground and smashed to smithereens. Seeing them sparkling there like diamonds affirmed what Cressida has suspected; how Dora had smuggled the glass icicle into the ladies' room. An image flashed back into her mind from earlier in the evening when a gaggle of young ladies, their hair glistening with tiaras and diamanté hairpins, were gathered outside the powder room. 'Dora,' she said, 'I think I know how you've been doing this. And I think I know why, but I want to hear it from you. Why?'

'Of course clever Cressida will have worked it out,' snarled

Dora, still brandishing the broken bottle, waving it in the direction of the steps, where Andrews was still pinned to the top step, not yet daring to go further.

'It's not worth killing another person tonight, miss,' he called. 'You're trapped here in the courtyard, there's no way out.' He pointed to where Mr Butcher was now positioned, accompanied by a burly chef holding a large, shining cleaver, and the policeman who loved pugs by the door that led out from the other side of the courtyard. There was no other exit. Dora *was* trapped. 'Put the bottle down and come quietly, it'll be best for you.'

'*Best for me? Best for me?*' Dora spat the words out. 'Best for me would have been marrying the man I was supposed to marry five years ago. But no, beautiful Victoria with her pushy mama had to take that from me. Do you know my father was already in talks with Lord Beaumont before Victoria did that thing with the feather boa at the Wainwrights' coming-out ball?'

'You wanted to marry Lord Beaumont,' Cressida said. 'You were the "you know who" who was calling on her constantly and giving her the creeps. Not Ottoline, as we thought when we first read the letters.'

'Lord Beaumont didn't let Victoria ban me from the house altogether,' Dora said, as if it was an achievement. She clasped her fur coat tighter around her with the hand that wasn't gripping the broken bottle and added, 'And good thing too as he owed me at least that.'

'But Ottoline...' Dotty asked, more to Cressida than Dora. 'I thought Ottoline was the one who loved Lord Beaumont.'

'Loved? Who said anything about loving that gouty old toad,' Dora almost laughed as she said it. 'I don't love him, yuk.'

Dotty furrowed her brow, her concern for George and her confusion over Dora's motives almost too much for her. 'Then why kill all these people? And why hurt George! If it's not for true love?'

'Cressida understands,' Dora said, all mirth gone from her voice and her glare fixed on Cressida. 'Don't you?'

All eyes now turned to Cressida, who sighed. 'Yes, I understand, Dora. You think marrying Lord Beaumont was the only way you'd be free.'

'Free? Free from what?' Dotty asked, her brow furrowed and her eyes searching for an answer on Cressida's face.

Cressida shivered as a gust of chill wind scattered sharp flakes of snow and ice across the terrace. But she answered Dotty, keeping her voice raised so Dora could hear her too. 'It's the same freedom I'm always talking about. But achieved in a very different way. I pride myself on not wanting to marry, I can't see the point when I have the most wonderful freedoms without the will of a man imposed upon me.' She couldn't help but glance at Alfred, who met her eye with a look she couldn't quite decipher at this moment. She turned back to Dora, who was glaring at her through the blizzard. 'I don't need a man because I have an income, friends, my own flat in Chelsea, my motorcar—'

'You have it all,' Dora interrupted her. 'I have none of those things.'

'Hence spending Christmas here in town with your rich relatives,' Cressida thought out loud. 'Cousin Simon and his friends.'

Dora shrugged. 'Yobs. Just because they got the family money.'

'Let me guess,' Cressida called down to Dora. 'If we asked Simon and his friends about your alibi for Victoria's murder... he might not be as sure as you are that you were with him?'

'He's a fool. I could have made him say anything. I can't tell you the fun I had growing up, pinching his little fleshy arms and then when he cried and pointed his sticky little finger at me, I cried too and "poor, sweet cousin Dora" couldn't possibly have done it.' She made a sort of chuckling sound. 'Stupid Simon. Why should he have all the money?'

'Did you think of killing—'

'Simon? Yes,' Dora conceded. 'But he is flesh and blood. That would be the last resort. I might have to if you don't let me go tonight and swear you saw nothing, heard nothing.' Dora's eyes were crazed, and they scanned all the faces on the terrace.

'You still think you could seduce Lord Beaumont? I assume that was the plan after killing Victoria? Marrying an old, rich man would give you the freedom to live how I do, isn't that right,' Cressida called down to the murderer in the courtyard. 'What would you have done to him? Kill him as soon as you were married?'

Dora laughed. 'That's where Victoria and I weren't so different, you know. She was going to take him skiing and hope it finished him off with a heart attack. I might have tried arsenic, so much quicker.'

Shocked gasps from the terrace only made her laugh again.

Dotty, though, dashed away a mix of hot tears and cold snowflakes from her cheeks. 'But, Dodo,' she protested, 'you've always been so *nice*. The festival queen, the quiet one with a seat next to you at the table. Always so forbearing and... well, nice.'

Dora nudged George again with her plainly shod foot and looked a little displeased when he twitched. Then she looked back up at Dotty. 'Do you know how hard it is keeping that act up? *"Oh Dora's a good egg, Dora will sit sweetly and laugh at your jokes"* – urgh, the things we do to make ourselves amenable to men!'

Dotty gasped, but Cressida kept her focus on Dora. 'I sympathise, Dodo, I really do. Life still isn't fair for us women, not at all. But you can't go around killing people to get what you want. Victoria didn't deserve to die in that fountain tonight. You tussled with her, losing beads from your dress in the process, no doubt. Then you hit her' – she pointed to the smashed bottle in her hand – 'and then you strangled her. You wanted to—'

'I wanted to look her eye as she died,' Dora finished Cressida's sentence for her. 'I could have just hit her or shoved her head underwater, but then she might not have known it was me. Me, killing her to revenge the way she stole my life from me. The life I was supposed to have.' Dora was shouting now and gesturing with the lethally sharp broken bottle as she did so.

Cressida could feel a shudder from Dotty next to her and a muttering from Alfred and Andrews. This was far more dark, more wicked, than any of them had imagined.

Dora didn't stop, though, and Cressida wondered if it was finally having an audience that was feeding her ego, encouraging her to confess all. 'She crossed me, you see. She crossed me when all I wanted was almost mine. She swooped in and stole Lord Beaumont from right there...' She jabbed the air in front of her with the bottle and Cressida could feel Dotty flinch as it was so desperately close to where George was still lying in the snow. Dora continued, her breath as she spoke like that of a dragon as she shouted up to her onlookers on the terrace. 'I'd tried to get her to ride out with me. I thought Lord Beaumont could have another wife die in a tragic riding accident. Ottoline might even get blamed again – Victoria was, with my help, certainly finding all the right clues to suggest that.'

'The letters,' Cressida murmured. 'It's all in the letters. The saddle, the "you-know-whos". Even Lord B saying something about "after what we'd done".'

Dotty, still gripping the balustrade, her satin gloves soaked by the melting snow, was the one to call back down to Dora. 'And it's why you were framing Ottoline. Two birds with one stone. Victoria out of the way and Ottoline, who Lord Beaumont might turn to in his grief, accused of murder.' She paused. 'But why tonight, Dodo? Why Christmas Eve?'

'I think I know,' Cressida said, her voice raised so that Dora, down in the snowy courtyard, could hear too. 'It was Victoria's pregnancy, wasn't it?' Dora nodded. 'You had to act now, before Victoria had time to tell Lord Beaumont.'

'Yes, I couldn't rely on him divorcing her anymore. You know how he found out about her affair with Clayton? Me of course! I told Ottoline, and made sure certain copies of *The Bystander* were left in the drawing room of Beaumont Park for them both to see. I knew then that busybody Mrs Spencer would tell her darling Peter and Victoria would be out on her ear. Then I could have swooped in. Once I'd made Peter suspect that Ottoline had murdered Caroline, of course.'

'So, you framed Ottoline, I understand that, but why then also frame Clayton by putting that champagne bottle neck in his pocket?' Cressida asked, genuinely confused.

Dora laughed again, and nudged George with her foot once more as he groaned on the floor. Dotty yelped in sympathy. But it wasn't George or Dotty that Dora glared at as she next spoke. It was Cressida, and the words stung like an icicle to the heart.

'Oh that – well that's your fault, Cressida. All your fault!'

41

'My fault?' Cressida stammered, looking to Dotty and Alfred for some affirmation that surely Dora must be wrong. She felt the firm, strong and blissfully warm arm of Alfred wrap around her shoulders and it bolstered her just when she needed it. 'How could it be my fault, Dodo?'

'I had to confuse you! You just *had* to be here tonight, didn't you. When you're usually back in Sussex in your lovely wealthy parents' lovely big manor house. Your reputation is getting around, you know – and not the one that involves you drinking martinis and singing all the refrains from *The Pirates of Penzance*. I saw you on that dance floor, and knew I had to sow as much confusion as I could.'

'You were the one who said Clayton might be responsible, and it was you who spun that whole soap dispenser sounding like Mrs Spencer nonsense. You killed Violet in the powder room, didn't you?' Cressida had worked it all out now. 'I knew I could smell smoke and you had that long cigarette holder—'

'I thought I could stab that silly girl with it. I had it in my hand as I was sitting on the lavatory having a puff when you asked her to point out who she'd seen with Victoria that night.

But, of course, you'd trace that back to me in an instant. But it rather handily gave me the idea of using one of the tree decorations—'

'Of course, I saw you, just outside the powder room, though, of course, I didn't realise it was you. The glint of diamond I saw in your hair that reminded me, of all things, of Victoria's wedding, that was the icicle. You carried it in your chignon, so no one would notice it – it would just look like one of the glistening headpieces we all wear.'

Dora nodded and threw her head back with satisfaction. 'It worked a treat! No one noticed at all. But just as I was about to head into the powder room, I saw you hovering by the door of the cellar. I knew Violet could say nothing to you while you were down there, so she could wait while I—'

'Tried to kill me and throw me into the hamper,' Cressida finished her sentence. 'And while I was trapped, you went back upstairs to deal with poor Violet.'

'Not checking that you were actually dead was my biggest mistake tonight,' Dora snapped the words back up to Cressida, who shivered, realising how close she'd come to dying. If that sack had been over her head for one more minute...

'Why kill Violet if you thought Cressy was dead?' Dotty called down, her words rousing Cressida back to the here and now.

'Because she'd talk at some point. Especially as Cressida had put that thought in her mind. I must say, it was a surprise when you walked into that smoking room, right as rain. Asking questions as if you were Sherlock blooming Holmes back from the dead. And with those letters too.'

'It was a good ruse to place the letters in her mouth. And then move them and make sure I knew about it meant your fingerprints were explained away,' Cressida retaliated, still trying not to think about how close she had come to being killed.

'Letters you'd stolen from Clayton's pocket, but how did you know they were there?' Dotty took over.

Dora rolled her eyes. 'Girls do talk, you know. I was with Victoria before the ball tonight. I think Lord B had insisted she was nice to me. He does feel bad that he went back on his promise to me and my family in our debutante year. I think he knew what it meant to us. The Fanshawes were already well off. Victoria could have married the fishmonger and still lived like a countess.' She looked scornfully at the fountain, then laughed. 'But Victoria was such a silly goose and told us all over cocktails at the Savoy that she was pregnant and how she'd done it, with her plan to blackmail the doctor if Peter should ever find out. Then she said – and oh the sanctimony of it – that she and Clayton had had to part ways. But being the star-crossed lovers that they were and oh so devoted to one another, they'd agreed to give each other their letters back, lest anyone ever get their hands on them.' Dora kicked the edge of the fountain and winced. 'That she managed to snag one rich husband was one thing, but to have her choice of lovers and a baby on the way. It was too much! Just too unfair. I do wish I'd got a chance to read them, I'm sure I could have had a lot more fun.'

'You should have done,' Cressida said, determination in her voice. 'They were what gave you away in the end.'

'Go to hell, Cressida Fawcett,' Dora spat out the words, then looked down at George. 'It's time to go, I think. Come on you.' She prodded him with her toe.

George groaned again and rolled over, eliciting a gasp from Dotty as she saw the red welt on his head where he'd obviously been hit by the champagne bottle.

'No, not George, please don't take him!' Dotty shouted over the balustrade.

'It's nothing personal, Dorothy,' Dora shrugged. 'But I need you all to stand back while George and I leave.' She looked at the door to the kitchen corridor and saw that it was still blocked.

'We'll come past you all then. Leave like the very proper guests we are. And look at me, Dora Smith-Wallington, finally with a man on her arm.'

'The hotel is still surrounded by police, Miss Smith-Wallington,' Andrews warned. 'You won't be able to leave.'

'If anyone tries to stop me, he gets this in the neck,' she brandished the razor-sharp cut edge of the bottle again. Then she reached down and, with quite some strength, grabbed George by the collar and hauled him up.

Just at that moment, a rather rotund, and momentum-driven, four-legged ballistic charged through the snow towards Dora, at first surprising her, then confusing her, and finally unbalancing her. As Ruby went straight for her feet, the evening spent in another woman's ill-fitting shoes took its toll on Dora's balance. The weight of a heavily pregnant Ruby and the iciness of the packed snow beneath her made Dora topple straight over into the fountain. The champagne bottle crashed and splintered to the ground, rendering it harmless, or at least, not lethal. And, in an instant, with snow and ice allowing, those on the terrace rushed down to the fountain.

Andrews and Kirby were first on the scene to handcuff Dora as she splashed and screeched in the ice-cold water. Dotty and Alfred rushed to George's side, helping him stand and getting him back into the warmth of the ballroom where he could be thawed out and given essential first aid, by Alfred, and kisses, by Dotty.

And Cressida went straight for her mischievous, if heroic, pooch, aware that those shards of glass could hurt a paw. While Dora Smith-Wallington was being cautioned by the detectives of Scotland Yard, she scooped up Ruby, nuzzled her to her face and told her she was a very, very good girl indeed.

42

The fire in the smoking room had been allowed to dwindle as the final guests had retrieved coats, hats, gloves and mufflers from the busy cloakroom attendant. But now it crackled back into life and warmed the shivering group of friends as they thawed out in front of it.

Sergeant Kirby had taken Dora to Scotland Yard, leaving DCI Andrews to follow on behind once he'd had a restorative whisky in front of the fire. He also wanted to pick Cressida's brain before returning to the station with the evidence and deductions that would see the multiple murder charges for Dora Smith-Wallington stick.

'Miss Fawcett, you thought it was Ottoline Spencer at first, didn't you?' he asked, before taking another well-deserved sip from his glass.

'Quite frankly, yes. While you and Kirby were doing all that sterling work securing the hotel and checking on staff, I headed straight to Mrs Spencer, and of course Lord Beaumont—'

'Who we had suspected from the start, erroneously it seems,' admitted Andrews.

'Within minutes she'd given us an alibi. It seemed too good

to be true, her finding Lord B's lost watch at, what luck, just the time she needed an alibi.'

'You'd never get away with that in one of those books I read,' chortled Dotty, who was curled up on the elegant chintz sofa, with George resting his sore head on her shoulder. 'Far too convenient!'

'I know, and I was suspicious. It did seem too good to be true. But in this case, it was true. They had an alibi, even with Dora's best attempts to frame Ottoline, and of course Ottoline not really helping herself by being so quick to point the finger at Clayton, and ironically, Dora.'

'I wonder if she had an inkling?' Dotty asked. 'I mean, if she was at Beaumont Park so much and obviously saw Dora there, with Victoria, well, maybe that's why she jumped to such a conclusion about it being a nasty argument. Perhaps she'd seen them have humdingers in the past?'

'Good point, Dot,' Cressida agreed. 'We'll have to ask her, though I believe she and Lord B have taken rooms for the night and retired to bed. Seemed all a bit too much for him in the end and he said he felt funny. I hope Victoria wasn't taking Dodo's advice and adding arsenic to his tea as well as threatening him with downhill skiing!'

'Speaking of threats,' Andrews butted in. 'All that black-mailing of the doctor was unconnected to the case after all?'

'Yes, and no. In the end, it was wrong of us to suspect him of her murder, though he had a motive, what with the blackmail-ing, but he did play a part in her death.' She sighed. 'His special treatment had worked and she was pregnant. And she'd told Dora that before the ball tonight. And being in the Beaumonts' inner circle, however much Victoria despised her, meant that Dora knew that now Marcus would no longer inherit. And if you're looking for a time to kill your rival and you want the most amount of suspects in the room with you, and for there to be the perfect reason for at least one of them to strike, tonight's the night. So yes, the doctor had nothing to do with Victoria's death, except that his treatment had worked. I think that's why Dodo stole Victoria's handbag before she hid it in the cracker hamper. She wanted to see if Victoria's boasts about being pregnant and therefore "safe" in her marriage were true. She knew Victoria had come straight from the Harley Street appointment to cocktails, where she'd told them all, so it was a safe bet that that confirmation letter was in there. Once she'd seen that doctor's note, it was as good as a death warrant for Victoria.'

'And it put Marcus Von Drausch, and even Cordelia Stirling, in the frame,' added Andrews, nodding then taking another sip.

'Poor Marcus, he really will have to inherit and run Beaumont Park now,' mused Dotty.

'I shall play my tiniest violin for him Lady Dorothy,' Andrews said, a wry smile on his face.

'Well, let's hope Lord B rallies by the morning. I'm sure Ottoline will look after him.' Cressida rubbed Ruby's belly as the small, if heavy, dog lay on her back in her lap. 'You know, the other reason I thought it could be Ottoline was the fact those footsteps in the snow were just like Victoria's... subconsciously I knew they belonged to a woman. But, of course, Ottoline didn't have wet shoes, so again, it really couldn't have been her. And come to think of it, you know, when we were dancing,' Cressida sat more upright as it came to her and Ruby snorted in displeasure at the movement, 'I remember seeing someone with no shoes on. I thought the dancing must have hurt someone's feet, and I even thought of kicking off these heels, but they're from Liberty, so no thanks.'

'You mean you actually saw Dodo with no shoes on just after she'd killed Victoria, before she killed Susan to get her shoes?'

'I think it might have been. And then when I saw her sitting by herself in the ballroom, she was rubbing her heels. I remember thinking that it was odd as her shoes looked very plain, a sensible heel height, wide, navy blue leather, but that's because they were Susan Potts's shoes and they pinched.'

'Serves her right for stealing a dead woman's shoes,' Dotty huffed.

'More than that, Dot, killing her for the shoes. Can you imagine? She was spinning me all sorts of yarns about men not being worth the effort too. Perhaps she really was thinking that!'

'Just think, if Lord Beaumont had married her instead of Victoria none of this would have happened,' Dotty mused.

It was Andrews who answered, putting his glass down and pushing himself up from the armchair. His knee clicked again and Cressida looked with concern at her favourite policeman. 'Miss Smith-Wallington may have had a motive tonight, but I believe she had a taste for murder too, Lady Dorothy. If Miss Smith-Wallington had married Lord Beaumont, Lady Victoria might not have been found in a fountain tonight, but from her own mouth we had the confession that she would have killed Lord Beaumont, and possibly Mrs Spencer too. All she wanted was the money, estate, land—'

'And the freedom that those all bring,' interrupted Cressida. 'Freedom comes at a cost. Except tonight that cost was just far too high. As you say, Andrews, I fear it wasn't just the freedoms from societal pressures that Dodo craved, but the freedom to be above the law. To act with impunity as she so wished. Thinking back now, there were signs. That guinea pig at school that got stuck in the drainpipe... the tears afterwards, but there was never really a good explanation of how it got there. Poor thing.' She raised a hand to Andrews, who gripped it in a fatherly goodbye. 'I'm sorry your Christmas was ruined, Andrews. A long night ahead for you, I fear?'

Andrews sighed. 'That it will be, Miss Fawcett, that it will be.'

'Well, when you're done, please come to Mydenhurst.

Mama and Papa would love to see you and I should imagine there will be a turkey sandwich or two lurking at least until twelfth night. Bring Mrs Andrews too. Come and stay.'

'I must say, the thought of a turkey sandwich is a welcome one. Thank you, Miss Fawcett.' Andrews straightened his tie and cuffs, the hint of a smile on his tired face.

Cressida gently encouraged Ruby off her lap and stood up. Dotty uncurled herself from her seat by the fire and George, who had had a restorative whisky and was feeling much more chipper, got up to say goodbye, too. Alfred, who had been leaning against the fire, moved towards the Scotland Yard policeman and shook hands with him.

'We'll see you out, Andrews,' Cressida said, as they left the smoking room and its roaring fire and headed back towards the lobby.

The Christmas tree still stood there, innocent to the fact that one of its decorations had been hidden in a chignon and then used to kill. It glistened and glinted in the lights of the lobby's chandeliers; so beautiful yet intrinsic to such a brutal crime. Cressida was surprised to see that some guests were still slowly collecting coats and pushing the heavy revolving doors, braced against the snowstorm outside.

'I hope you can get a cab, Andrews.' Cressida said, looking out at the blustery white blizzard outside. 'Or a sleigh.'

Andrews surprised Cressida by leaning over and giving her a hug. 'Merry Christmas, Miss Fawcett. Pass on my best to your parents when you see them tomorrow and do drive carefully.'

'I will, Andrews.' She looked rather coyly up at Alfred, who was standing next to her, beaming at her, which was quite a feat while his pipe was still firmly clenched in his teeth. 'Though I don't suppose I'll be having a particularly early start.'

At that, Andrews raised his hat to them, held off from wink-ing, much to Cressida's delight, and walked through the revolving door, his back soon lost to the fiercely flying snowflakes out in the street.

Cressida turned to Alfred, but instead of meeting her gaze, he took his pipe out of his mouth and used the stem to point to where his sister and George were now standing, her hands held in his as he slowly lowered himself down on to one knee.

Cressida clamped a hand over her mouth so that no sound of her gasp escaped to break the beautiful moment. With her other arm, she grabbed hold of Alfred, who in turn wrapped an arm around her.

A gentle nod of Dotty's head was followed by a squeal and Cressida allowed herself to exhale.

Her darling friend looked so happy, standing under the last piece of mistletoe that was dangling over them, the man she loved holding her in his arms. Despite the evening's horrors, something beautiful and wonderful had come out of it. Dotty was engaged.

Cressida looked down at the warm, furry body that was leaning against her ankle and two globe-like eyes blinked up at her. Dotty engaged, and Ruby with pups.

Life was moving on for two of the lives that were so entwined with hers. And with Alfred's arm protectively wrapped around her, well, perhaps her life might be about to change, too. And, for once, she wasn't about to fight it.

A LETTER FROM FLISS

Dear reader,

I want to say a huge thank you for choosing to read *Death in the Mayfair Hotel*. If you did enjoy it, and want to keep up to date with all my latest releases, just sign up at the following link. Your email address will never be shared and you can unsubscribe at any time.

www.bookouture.com/fliss-chester

I hope you loved *Death in the Mayfair Hotel* – the sixth in the Hon Cressida Fawcett series. If you did I would be very grateful if you could write a review. I'd love to hear what you think – did you guess who did it? I hope you loved the festive setting – maybe you fancy a mulled wine or piece of Christmas cake now, too? Reviews from readers like you can make such a difference helping new readers discover my books for the first time.

I love hearing from my readers – you can get in touch on social media or my website.

Thanks,

Fliss Chester

KEEP IN TOUCH WITH FLISS

www.flisschester.co.uk

 facebook.com/flisschester

x.com/socialwhirlgirl

AUTHOR'S NOTE

The dedication at the front of this book is a poem by the American poet, Edna St Vincent Millay called 'First Fig'. Written, I'd like to think, though I have no proof, the morning after a night out where one too many cocktails were drunk, tables danced on and eyelashes fluttered. I think Edna and Cressida would have got on like the proverbial house on fire. And it won't surprise many of you that I, too, enjoyed the odd cocktail or two during my years as a single girl about town in my twenties. So, the first thank you must go to all my friends (I hope I don't have foes!) who helped make those years so fun, frivolous and fantastically fabulous.

With martini finished and high heels kicked off, my thanks must also go to my editorial team at Bookouture. I'm so pleased that there's now an official 'credits' list at the end of the book, as each of them does deserve a mention for getting this book out of my head and into your hands. None more so than my editor, Rhianna Louise, who is a joy to work with, while getting the best out of me and onto the page.

My literary agent, Emily Sweet, is also always on stand-by if I need any support – or a good gossip. I ask you, what else could one want in an agent?

Research for this book mostly came from the memories I've made over the years in hotel bars and at Christmas balls. If I had to pick one, it would be to thank my great friend Charlie, who took me as her guest to the staff Christmas ball at The Savoy. Who would have thought, fifteen years or so later, I'd be using those memories to write a murder mystery – or even that I'd remember the night at all after all that champagne!

And, as always, thank you to my crime-writing friends – you're not only an invaluable resource of instant hive-mind knowledge, but I know you'll also always be on hand for a Christmas glass of fizz at The Ritz, too. Pincers high, ladies and gents, pincers high.

Last, but of course, not least, thank you to my family – my mum who always told me to be 'anything but dull, darling', and my husband, Rupert, who took me gin-blending on our second date and hasn't looked back since...

PUBLISHING TEAM

Turning a manuscript into a book requires the efforts of many people. The publishing team at Bookouture would like to acknowledge everyone who contributed to this publication.

Audio
Alba Proko
Melissa Tran
Sinead O'Connor

Commercial
Lauren Morrissette
Hannah Richmond
Imogen Allport

Cover design
Debbie Clement

Data and analysis
Mark Alder
Mohamed Bussuri

Editorial
Rhianna Louise
Lizzie Brien